POLICE PROCEDURALS RESPECTED BY LAW ENFORCEMENT.™

"Carolyn Arnold provides entertainment and accuracy."
—*Michael D. Scott, Patrolman (Ret.) Castroville, Texas, United States*

"For Police procedurals that are painstakingly researched and accurately portrayed look no further than Carolyn Arnold's works. The only way it gets more real than this is to leave the genre completely."
—*Zach Fortier, Police Officer (Ret.) Colorado, United States*

"Usually it's hard for me to read cop books without picking them apart, but I read the entire Madison Knight series and I loved them all! The way Carolyn wrote Madison describes me and the way I work and even my personal life to a t."
—*Deputy Rebecca Hendrix, LeFlore County Sheriff's Department Poteau, Oklahoma, United States*

ALSO BY CAROLYN ARNOLD

Brandon Fisher FBI Series

Eleven
Silent Graves
The Defenseless
Blue Baby
Violated

Detective Madison Knight Series

Ties That Bind
Sacrifice
Found Innocent
Just Cause
Deadly Impulse
In the Line of Duty
Life Sentence

McKinley Mysteries

The Day Job is Murder
Vacation is Murder
Money is Murder
Politics is Murder
Family is Murder
Shopping is Murder
Christmas is Murder
Valentine's Day is Murder
Coffee is Murder
Skiing is Murder

Matthew Connor Adventure Series

City of Gold

Assassination of a Dignitary

CAROLYN ARNOLD

JUSTIFIED

HIBBERT & STILES
PUBLISHING INC.

HIBBERT & STILES
PUBLISHING INC.

Justified (Book 2 in the Detective Madison Knight series)
Copyright © 2011 by Carolyn Arnold

Excerpt from *Sacrifice* (Book 3 in the Detective Madison Knight series) copyright © 2012 by Carolyn Arnold

www.carolynarnold.net

June 2017 Hibbert & Stiles Publishing Inc. Edition

All rights reserved. The scanning, uploading, and electronic sharing of any part of this book without the permission of the author constitutes unlawful piracy and theft of the author's intellectual property. If you would like to use material from the book (other than for review purposes), prior written permission must be obtained by contacting the author.

This is a work of fiction. Names, characters, places, and incidents are the products of the author's imagination or are used fictitiously. Any resemblance to actual events, locales, or persons, living or dead, is entirely coincidental.

ISBN (e-book): 978-1-988064-11-6
ISBN (paperback 4.25 x 7): 978-1-988064-12-3
ISBN (paperback 5 x 8): 978-1-988064-30-7
ISBN (hardcover 6.13 x 9.21): 978-1-988353-07-4

*Dedicated to my grandmother.
A sweet woman who I lost decades ago
but who will never be forgotten.*

"*A smile lights with but the warmth of the soul.*"

Prologue

He had to do it. He had no choice. Pushed into an unpleasant corner, he had no other option. How could he allow himself to be walked all over, manipulated? All that he had sacrificed for her, laid on the line.

It was pitch-black, the wind moaned, and small flakes dared to precipitate. It was a bitter cold, the type he felt through to his bones.

He knocked on the door.

He had chosen the back side of the house for added seclusion. If the cover of the night wasn't enough, surely this approach would diminish the possibility of a curious neighbor trying to play the hero. He didn't need any cops showing up. This was to be a private visit.

He knocked again, harder and more deliberate. A light came on inside followed by one on the back porch. Finally, he was getting some attention.

She opened the door the few inches the chain would allow. "What are you doing here?"

"Trying to reason with you." The chills left his body and a calm, radiant heat overtook him.

The door shut. The chain rattled. The door reopened. "You can't just show up whenever you feel like it." She let him in, more likely for her own comfort given the way she was dressed. Arms crossed in front of her chest, an act of modesty over a lacy piece of lingerie. He had seen it before. Shivers trembled through her, and she gripped her arms tighter. "What is it?"

He disregarded the tone in her voice, the condescending

overture it carried. He ignored the body language that screamed for him to leave. He went to touch a ribbon that served as a strap.

She stepped back. "Please don't—"

"Claire, we're meant to be together." His lack of control surprised him; his voice had risen in volume with each word.

"You should leave."

There was more to her words. And the way she was dressed. "You move on already?" He took steps forward, heading for her bedroom.

She grabbed his arm and pulled him back. She didn't deny his accusation, and she refused to look at him when she did speak. "It was your choice. I gave you the option."

He swore her eyes misted over. "Not really much of one."

"You should go."

He shook his head as if it would bury the jealousy. But the fact there was someone else here, lying in her bed, waiting on her to come back…

He would do what he came to do, regardless. He had too much to lose.

Chapter 1

The coffee came up into the back of her throat, and Madison Knight swallowed hard, forcing the acidic bile back down. This was a messy crime scene, the kind she did her best to avoid. She knew Weir, the first officer on the scene, was speaking, but the words weren't making it through. Despite her revulsion, her eyes were frozen on what was before her.

The victim lay on a crimson blanket of death, wearing nothing but a lacy camisole. The blood pool reached around her body in an approximate two-foot circumference. The blood had coagulated, resulting in a curdled, pudding-like consistency. The kitchen floor was a porous ceramic, and the blood had found its way to the grout lines and seeped through it like veins. Arterial spray had splattered the backsplash like the work of an abstract painter who had fanned a loaded brush against the canvas.

Cynthia Baxter was hunched close to the body taking photos and collecting shards of glass that were in the blood. She was the head of the forensics lab, but her job also required time in the field. She looked up at Madison, nodded a hello, and offered a small smile. Madison knew her well enough as a friend outside of work that the facial expression was sincere, but the scene had dampened it from reaching her eyes.

Weir stood back at the doorway that was between the front living room and the kitchen. "Such a shame, especially on Christmas Eve."

Terry Grant, Madison's partner, braced his hands above his holster and exhaled a jagged deep breath.

"What's her name and background?" Madison asked Weir with

her eyes on the victim.

"The vic is Claire Reeves, forty-three. Lived here alone. No record of restraining orders or anything out of the ordinary. Nothing noted as her place of employment. Her maid, Allison Minard, found her. She's over at the neighbor's. Officer Higgins is over there with her."

Madison managed to break eye contact from the body, glanced at Terry, and settled her gaze on Weir. His words came through as though out of context.

"Detective Knight?" Judging by the softness in his tone of voice, Weir must have read her reaction to the scene. His eyes inquired if she was okay, but the silent probing would have been squashed by the wall she had erected. He continued. "The maid's pretty shaken up."

Madison could understand that. She had experience in processing murder scenes, and she could barely handle this one. She did her best to keep eye contact with the officer, but her fear, her distaste for blood, kept pulling her attention to the dead woman.

Claire Reeves. That was her name before she had been reduced to this. To be killed in this manner pointed toward an emotional assailant. Her lack of clothing was an indication that she likely had an intimate relationship with her killer.

Madison scanned the room. There was no sign of a struggle, no overturned chairs or broken dishes. The only thing standing out was a tea towel bunched on the floor in front of the stove as if it had slipped off the front bar. "Any evidence of forced entry?"

Weir shook his head.

"She let her killer in." Madison's gaze returned to the victim.

She was someone's daughter, someone's best friend, someone's lover. Normally Madison didn't have an issue with separating herself from crime scenes and keeping them impersonal. Maybe it had something to do with all that blood and the fact that Claire had been murdered just before Christmas.

Claire was on her back, albeit slightly twisted, from the fall to the floor. Her legs were crumpled beneath her. A large slash lined

JUSTIFIED 5

her neck, and based on the angle and directionality, her killer had come at her from behind. Logic dictated the killing method as typically belonging to a male, but something about the maid finding the body didn't make sense.

"The maid was scheduled to work on Christmas Eve?" Madison asked.

"Supposedly she got a text message from Claire. She called us right after she—" Weir pointed toward the vomit at the far entrance to the kitchen.

Madison had noticed it on the way through. She took a shallow breath, hoping to cleanse her focus despite the stench of the crime scene having transformed to a coating on her tongue. "Did you see this text message?"

Weir shook his head. "She couldn't produce it. Said she must have accidentally deleted it."

"Anyone think to check Claire's phone?"

"I'll go check on that now." Weir's cheeks flushed. "Anyway, Higgins is with her, and Richards should be here soon." He excused himself with a wave of a hand.

Cole Richards was the medical examiner.

Cynthia rose to her feet, picked up her kit, and addressed Madison. "What are you thinking? Love affair gone wrong?"

"It looks like it could be but rarely are things that straightforward."

"Isn't that the truth? But I know you'll figure it out."

"Hey, I'm here, too," Terry said.

Both women smiled.

"Okay, *both of you* will figure it out."

"Better." Terry smiled.

Cynthia left the kitchen in the direction of a hallway that led to the bedrooms. Based on the vic's attire, it would be a reasonable progression to search there.

Madison moved toward the body. "Wonder where her underwear is."

"Maybe they were of the edible variety." Terry gave her a goofy smile.

"At a time like this, you're going to bring out that horny grin of yours?"

"I'm only a man."

"Uh-huh, that's your excuse for everything." Her gaze drifted to the backsplash and then the floor around the victim. She was looking for any cast-off blood spatters that could have come from the weapon or for any voids. "She was standing in front of the sink taking a drink when her killer came up from behind her. He would have wrapped his arm around her, holding her steady, when he slashed her throat." Madison glanced back at the body. "It looks like the cut went from right to left." She swallowed hard. Periodically, the smell of the blood hit in intensive waves equal in scale to tsunamis.

Terry nodded. "We're looking for a left-handed killer."

"Someone call?" Richards entered the kitchen.

"Are you a left-handed killer?" Terry teased and received a mild glare from the medical examiner.

"Hey." Madison smiled. The man's presence had the ability to make her happy—ironic given his job description. Too bad he was married.

"There's my favorite detective." He returned the smile. His dark skin contrasted with the brightness of his teeth, which were a pure white.

"Nice to see you, too," Terry said.

"I was actually referring to Knight."

"Ouch. She always gets the spotlight."

Madison laughed. "Oh someday, Terry. Someday, when you grow up, you can be a—"

"Ah quiet. You and I are not even talking right now." Terry continued the show with a dramatic crossing of his arms.

"Moody like a female." Richards shook his head.

"Excuse me? Moody…like a female? Are you implying that we're moody? That I am?" Madison challenged him.

"Never." He waved his hand in a gesture of making peace.

"Uh-huh." She laughed, but it faded fast. Small talk was often used to ease the intensity of a scene, but doing so here caused her a few seconds of guilt.

"Hey, I'm with Richards on this. Only thing is, he's afraid of you, Maddy, whereas I'm not. If anyone can attest to the mood swings of a woman—"

"I know you can," Madison began, "and only you can get away with that comment right now."

Terry's wife was two months pregnant, and according to him, she was somewhat temperamental.

"I should be a good husband and dispute what you're implying, but I can't. She's driving me nuts. Drove all around town the other night looking for black cherry ice cream only to come home and be asked what took so long."

"Nice to know they're all the same." Richards's joviality ended abruptly as his focus went to the victim. "It's pretty safe to conclude COD was exsanguination. Based on the amount of blood loss, her carotid artery was severed."

His comment drew Madison's attention to the red expanse on the floor. Her coffee threatened a repeat showing.

Richards continued. "The blood pressure in her brain would have dropped so rapidly that she would have lost consciousness pretty much immediately. She would have bled out in less than a minute. The blood separation testifies to the fact that it had left her body some time ago. She's also coming out of rigor, so it puts time of death over twelve hours ago. But I'd estimate closer to fourteen or sixteen. Somewhere between two and four this morning. Of course, I'll take her temperature and conduct other means before I verify with certainty."

Richards bent down beside the victim, put a rubber-gloved hand on her face, and continued. "The killer was no professional, I can tell you that." He traced a finger along the jagged edges of the slash. "He was hesitant." Richards carefully turned the body over, handling it with care as if it were a priceless china doll. "Lividity shows she was killed here." He pressed fingers to the skin, and even under the touch, it remained a bluish color. "This also confirms that she's been dead for over twelve hours."

Madison had to step back from the body just for a few seconds. She moved to the doorway near the vomit, a normally potent scent, yet all she could smell was blood.

She looked out the window in the back door. The walkway was buried under eight to ten inches of snow, but that wasn't what had her attention. It was the boot prints leading to the door. She knew Weir had said something about which entrance the maid had used, but her focus had been on the blood at the time. "Did Weir say which door the maid came in?"

"The front," Terry answered.

She stepped aside to let Terry see out. "Let's put it this way. Either the maid's lying or we know where our killer came in."

Chapter 2

Sam Thompson and his wife Linda owned the home next to Claire. Although a man of easily six foot four, his height seemed to buckle under the intense glare of his wife. She stood in the doorway of a neighboring room where numerous people went about their evening conversing with light chitchat and laughter.

Madison and Terry were in the dining room with the husband.

"I promised Linda this won't take too long."

Madison could imagine him wiping his forehead, as if sweat formed there, or flexing his fingers on a temple to ease the concentration of his wife's controlling stare. Madison glanced at her again. The scowl, the arch of her brow, and her narrowed eyes, said it all: *Our dinner is ruined.*

The table was set for eight with full place settings. A carved turkey sat in the middle of the space on an antique platter, possibly passed on through generations and only brought out for special occasions. Mashed potatoes, stuffing, and cranberry sauce were set out in three bowls. They had all the fixings of a perfect holiday dinner. Yet despite the spread of food, all Madison could smell was the blood that was lodged in her sinuses.

"Where is she?" Madison was referring to the maid, Allison Minard.

Thompson directed them to another side room and gestured with his head, *In there.*

"I promise we'll be as fast as we can."

"I'd appreciate it."

A woman was on the couch, leaned back, arms crossed, and head shaking. Her long, black ponytail swayed with the movement. She stopped and looked at Madison and Terry.

An officer was in the room with her and sat braced on the edge of a recliner. He quickly rose to his feet when he saw them.

Madison sat where he had been, but Terry hung back and leaned on the doorframe.

Seconds passed in silence, but words weren't always needed. Energy, body language, and facial expressions usually communicated plenty. Allison's chestnut eyes weren't puffy and her cheeks and nose weren't red, so she hadn't been crying. If she did feel bad about her employer's death, it hadn't physically manifested yet. The head shaking could have been in response to several things—recounting her shock of discovering Claire dead or in reaction to something the officer had said.

"Allison Minard," Madison began, breaking the silence.

Allison matched her gaze to Madison's, and while her looks could have pegged her as midtwenties, the wisdom in her eyes spoke to late thirties, maybe even early forties.

Madison went on. "You're the one who found Claire Reeves?"

"Yes." She exhaled, sinking further into the couch and crossing her legs. "I've been through this with the other officers." She twisted a wrist, looked at her watch. "And I've got to go." Her crossed-over leg bobbed up and down, fast, without a set rhythm.

"You have something more important to do?"

"Actually, yes, I do." She offered no further explanation and her posture stiffened.

"I'm sure that whatever your plans were, they can be postponed a little longer—"

"Always whatever Claire wants. Even in death she's a conniving bitch." Allison crossed her arms tighter, adding height to an already well-endowed bosom.

"Why were you working tonight?"

Allison remained silent.

"Claire is dead. She was someone who you knew, Miss Minard, someone with whom you had regular contact. And if you take it from our viewpoint, short of a spouse, the last person to see someone alive or the first person to report the find is the first suspect—"

"I'm not the killer!"

Madison leaned forward like the officer had, yet she was not anxious to leave; rather, she was desperate for answers. She placed two hands on her thighs. "Prove it to us. Help us by reconstructing everything as you found it."

Allison broke eye contact and looked around the room. "I don't see why I have to go through it again. I have a party to get to."

Madison couldn't help but contemplate how selfish and single-minded people could be. If anything came up to interfere with their agenda, the mentality was, *How dare it?*

"I'm sure they'll wait on you to get things started." Madison's disgust over the woman's priorities couldn't be masked. "A woman's dead—"

"Like I said, I had nothing to do with it."

"Miss Minard, Claire Reeves was murdered." Madison placed emphasis on *murdered*. "I would hope that you could find it within yourself to see the bigger picture."

"Maybe you should know the *full* picture. Any number of people would have wanted her dead."

"Were you one of them?"

"I'm not going to answer that."

"I'll take that as a yes."

"I didn't kill her. Why would I? She gave me a job when I had nothing."

Quite the contrast to *she's a conniving bitch...* There was something hidden deep within Allison's eyes, something she was holding back. Guilt perhaps? And if so, on what scale?

"You don't seem really shaken up by her death. Maybe more by what you saw," Madison ventured.

"Do you think you can read everyone?" There was a flash of defensive anger in her eyes. "You can't read me."

"On one hand, you give me the impression you didn't like Claire, and on the other, you seem to have a soft spot for her, saying that she helped you out when you had nothing. What made you resent her despite the fact she helped you?" Madison glanced at Terry.

"Normally I admire those who help me out—"

"Well, she was a very anal-retentive person. Meticulous. She had a way she wanted things done, and you had to do it by the book. She had a list of what she wanted cleaned weekly, monthly, and bimonthly. She'd leave it on the kitchen table and expect that I work through it, checking off the items as I went along. Like I was an idiot."

"So that's why you hated her?"

Silence.

"You said a number of people would have wanted her dead. Who specifically?"

"She made a lot of enemies—" she loosened her crossed arms, then retightened "—but I'd start with Darcy Simms."

"Who was she to Claire?"

"Her best friend."

Madison and Terry shared a look. "Her best friend wanted her dead?"

"Hell, I wouldn't put anything past that woman, but there's more. Claire was very active. Sexually." The last word came out tagged with disgust. "Although, I'm sure your CSI people have already confirmed that. I was always cleaning up used condoms from the wastebaskets."

It was possible Claire was caught in the crossfire of a love triangle…

Allison continued. "Let's just say Darcy wasn't as good a friend as she portrayed herself to be. I know her well enough."

"How do you know Darcy?"

"Claire recommended my services to her, and I ended up cleaning for her once. She made up a reason to fire me after what I saw."

"Which was?"

"She was sleeping with one of Claire's men."

"Do you know his name?"

She shook her head, her ponytail swaying the way it had earlier. "Not going to say. All I know is Darcy will sleep with anything that has a pulse. Male or female."

With the last word from her mouth, Allison had erected a

barrier. The energy was tangible, and they wouldn't be getting any more from her right now. But Allison had already said plenty and brought up the possibility of a love triangle. Darcy could have confronted Claire—or the other way around—and things got out of hand. But that didn't fit with the lack of evidence to indicate a struggle or the kill method typically belonging to a man.

Madison pulled out a notepad and pen for Allison. "Please write your name and phone number here."

"Don't see why I should have to."

Madison kept the notepad and pen extended.

Allison let out a heavy breath, scooped the pen from Madison, and scribbled down the information.

Madison observed which hand she used: her right.

"Now may I go?" Her head tilted to the side.

"One more thing. Where were you between two and four this morning?"

Allison stared blankly. "I was at home."

"Can anyone else verify that?"

She avoided eye contact as she tossed the notepad onto the coffee table in front of her. "Want anything else, talk to my lawyer." Allison rose to her feet and snatched her purse from the couch cushion.

"Why a lawyer? Guilty of something?"

Allison stopped moving and faced Madison. "The smart ones get a lawyer, Detective."

"Thanks for your help," Madison muttered sarcastically to Allison's back as she left the room. Madison picked up the pen and notepad and said to Terry, "Well, I guess she *could* be innocent. She's right-handed, unlike our killer, but she does seem to be holding something back."

Terry nodded.

Sam Thompson came up beside Terry in the doorway. "Detectives, I'd like to talk with you."

"Sure."

The man's hands clasped and unclasped. He twisted his wedding band. "I saw someone at her back door in the wee hours. About two or so."

That was the estimated time of death. He could have seen the killer. "What did they look like?"

"Her light back there is bright enough to illuminate a football stadium. And that's what woke me up." He was dancing around the meat of his discovery.

"You said you saw someone?"

"Well, I didn't see anyone at first. Figured the light was one of those motion-sensor ones and triggered by a cat or something. I just got back into bed only to have the damn light come on again. I threw the sheets off and looked out. That was when I saw someone."

"A man or a woman?" Madison didn't know whether to laugh or scream. She struggled for control. *Please get to the point.*

"Not too sure, but they walked like they were in a hurry. But at the same time, they took deliberate steps."

"So this person was in a hurry but deliberate?" Not intended, but her tone mocked his message. "And you're not sure whether it was a man or a woman?"

"I'm only telling you what I saw."

"At the time you saw this person, didn't you say the light was on?"

"The surrounding area was quite dark, and the glare from the light made it hard to see clearly. The person was more of a hazy silhouette, but they wore a puffy jacket." He mimicked the bulge with cupped hands pulsing from his shoulders.

"Which direction were they going, toward the house or away?"

"Toward."

It could have been the killer, and it would explain the boot prints in the backyard. She wanted to verify the view, and she was also curious how a bright light hindered clarity. "Show us this window."

He directed them to the bedroom, pointed toward the window, but stayed in the hallway.

Madison and Terry looked outside. A CSI worked in Claire's backyard but physical distinction was hard to ascertain. It was only due to their size and mannerisms that she could identify the investigator as Mark Andrews. The light was just as bright as Mr.

Thompson had said. "So we have a witness who could have seen our killer but can't identify them. Still no further ahead." When she turned back to look outside, the CSI was gone.

Chapter 3

Twenty minutes later, Madison's cell rang and she answered without noting the caller's identity. "We'll be right there." She hung up and turned to Terry. "That was Mark. He's found something."

Terry glanced at his watch, disappointment washing over his expression. And for a moment, she was envious of what he had and she didn't. He had someone waiting for him.

Maybe it was the giving spirit of the season, or the fact she couldn't stand it when someone didn't emanate the same enthusiasm as she did on a case, but he should be at home with his wife tonight. "Go. I'll take care of this."

"You sure? I can stay a bit longer—"

"No, get out of here. Go. Tell Annabelle that I'm sorry I answered the call." She had been at Terry's house for a dinner party when the call came in. He waved a hand in the air with his back already to her.

His absence left her with a brief sense of nostalgia and loneliness. She couldn't help but pity her current situation. Instead of being with family and friends tonight, she was working a murder investigation.

Her sister, Chelsea, was probably laughing around a tree, stringing up ropes of popcorn while sipping on eggnog, all while insisting it wasn't laced with liquor. Her family always decorated the tree with this last-minute touch, a tradition. Of course, they would have eaten a meal of her sister's cooking, which Madison didn't envy her nieces or brother-in-law suffering through. Chelsea could do pretty much everything perfectly, but cooking wasn't one of those things. The thought caused her to smile and inflicted another stab of homesickness.

And Madison's mom and dad were likely duking it out over which game show to watch, *Wheel of Fortune* or *Jeopardy*. She'd even gladly exchange this moment for that one.

Then there was Blake, a defense attorney by profession, the man she was currently dating from a personal standpoint. The situation there was becoming too complicated. For the number of times she told herself to back off and take things slow, it was of no consequence. Whenever he entered her mind, she felt warm. But he had left her alone for the holidays and was off on a seven-hour road trip to see his parents and siblings, none of whom she had met yet. In fact, she didn't even know their names. He was an expert at changing the topic whenever his family came up, likely a resultant crossover from his occupation.

"Detective?" It was Mr. Thompson.

He broke her from her thoughts and reminded her that she was still in the Thompsons' house. She turned to him and said, "I'm leaving."

Thompson gave her a nod. "Thank you."

As she moved past him, a moment of weakness battled with her commitment to finding a killer—a moment of wanting a *normal* life consisting of loved ones within reach and a Christmas tree.

SHE STORMED INTO CLAIRE'S HOUSE as if she were a woman who had everything under control—and there was that smell again. It threatened to ground her feet to the floor. Instead, she hurried through the kitchen to the side hallway, then into the master bedroom, but it wasn't enough to prevent a reaction. Recycled coffee burned the back of her throat.

In the bedroom, Cynthia Baxter was rummaging through a trash can and Mark stood near a closet. His cheeks were bright red, likely still kissed by the chill of the winter night. He rubbed his latex-gloved hands together.

Madison addressed him, "Okay, whatcha got for me?"

Cynthia intercepted, speaking over a shoulder. "No Terry?"

Madison pressed her lips. "I took pity on him, sent him home."

"Talk about having the Christmas spirit." Cynthia smiled at her and went back to the contents of the garbage bin.

Madison turned to Mark. "You get around fast."

The statement resulted in Mark lifting his eyebrows. Was it confusion or was he flirting with her? It was hard to tell. Everyone loved Mark, but the circulating rumors were undecided as to whether his sexual preference was for men or women. Not that it really mattered.

Madison jacked a thumb toward the hallway, opting to side with his reaction having to do with confusion. "I just saw you outside."

He stared at her blankly.

"What do you have for me?"

"Maybe it's nothing, but it stuck out to me. Maybe, somehow, it's involved with a motive for the murder."

That was a lot of maybes. Mark was the newest member of the crime lab and always eager to not only please, but to exceed expectations. His confidence hadn't quite grown a thick skin yet. "Show me what you found."

He opened both hands, palms up, gesturing for her to look inside the closet. He stepped back, an unsure smile on his lips.

"A filing cabinet?"

"It's not just any cabinet." He moved toward the two-drawer unit and pulled on the top drawer. Instead of it sliding out, it was a hinged door that opened to the left. Behind it was a safe door that required a key.

Cynthia rose from her haunches, hands to thighs, stretching out. "Not bad work for a newbie, is it?"

Madison looked back at her. "Not bad at—"

"Knight." Weir stood in the doorway. "I found the vic's phone."

"Well, I found it," Cynthia said. She smiled at him.

"There's nothing on it."

"Nothing?"

"Pretty much nothing. There are two contacts. A Darcy Simms and Allison Minard, the maid you've met. No text messages at all, sent or received."

"What about call history?"

"Nothing. It's clean."

Chapter 4

Madison had Mark bag the phone for evidence, and Weir excused himself from the room. Madison looked back to the cabinet. "Interesting that the drawer itself wasn't locked, but the inside compartment is."

Mark pointed to an external locking mechanism, showing it was an option. "And there's no sign it was forced open." He shrugged his shoulders. "But the killer could have had the key for the inside safe and maybe forgot to lock the drawer behind himself."

"I assume you haven't found the key?"

He shook his head.

"It's possible the killer was after something and got what he came for, but kept looking."

"Of course," he stated with the enthusiasm of a motivated child about to set out on an Easter egg hunt, but his feet remained planted.

"Mark?"

"Yes, I'm looking." He pressed his lips and formed a weak smile before he dropped down and worked at prodding the edges of the closet.

Madison knew the chances of him finding the key so close to the safe was unlikely. She would have started with Claire's purse or nightstand, and then moved to the next bedroom, which served as an office. She made the suggestion to Mark and turned to leave.

"Maddy, before you go," Cynthia called out to her. "There's lots of evidence to indicate Claire had company." She held up a used condom, dangling it in the air from tweezers.

"Where's Jenn when you need her?"

"It's Jennifer, remember? How many times—"

"One more apparently." She was in her early thirties but had this fixation that her name could never be abbreviated.

Jennifer Adams's specialty was forensic serology.

"Anyway, she's not here, I am." Cynthia kept the condom held out at a full arm's length from her body. "There's a full trash can of these. I think the girl was a nympho. And I get the lucky job of collecting this? I should have called Jennifer in." Cynthia went back to the garbage.

Madison turned to Mark. "We could always call someone in to open the safe."

"The department does have a contract with Confidential Locksmiths, over on Second Street," Mark began, "but they'll probably be closed 'til Friday with the holidays." His expression revealed a mute wince, his lips pulling back and teeth clenching. "Hopefully they're open again then."

She nodded, trying to calm her raging impatience.

She returned to the kitchen, and Richards was loading up the body with his assistant. Her eyes were pulled to the black bag and the blood on the floor.

She walked closer, her willpower enabling her to overcome her fear. It was then she noticed a white fluff in the void where the body had been lying. "Cyn!"

She came out of the room. "What?"

Madison pointed at the find. "Looks like a feather."

Cynthia moved closer. "Our vic wasn't wearing anything with feathers. She doesn't have a bird."

"Nope, and the fact it's underneath her means it was there before she fell. It might tie us to our killer."

BY THE TIME MADISON WALKED into her apartment, it was well after midnight. Her answering machine flashed two new messages. She pushed the button.

"You have been selected for a one-week Caribbean cruise—"

Delete. Next.

"We wish you a Merry Christmas. We wish you a Merry

Christmas…"

She dropped onto the couch and closed her eyes while she listened to her sister's and nieces' voices fill the apartment with some seasonal cheer.

Picturing their faces made her smile, but the images transformed without warning to the horror she saw tonight. Far too much blood for her liking. Blame it on her childhood and Chelsea's failed attempt to climb an oak tree, which had resulted in a compound fracture. Madison was only ten at the time, her sister four, and the blood seemed to pour out of her younger sister's leg endlessly, rendering Madison helpless. Now every time there was a bloody crime scene, the memory came flooding back.

But more than the sight of Chelsea's leg injury haunted Madison now. Claire Reeves had died alone. She didn't even have anyone on record as the next of kin, and based on Allison's statement had a counterfeit best friend. What Claire did have, though, was a lover. Likely more than one. Had one of them killed her?

Of course, it was too early to tell. Madison would find out, but she'd have to put her melancholy aside to get the job done.

"Yeah…Merry Christ…mas," she said aloud to herself, her words fragmented by a yawn.

Chapter 5

Madison's eyes felt like they had been welded shut by the sandman. She heard a faint banging, which at first she dismissed as a dream, but unfortunately it was persistent.

What time was it anyhow? She managed to read the clock through foggy slits. *7:02.*

The knocking intensified. Her visitor wasn't going to leave. Her initial reaction was to throw something hard at the wall and protest the awakening, but she didn't have enough energy for that.

"What?" she yelled, certain her neighbors would pound on the wall to protest the noise, but not really caring if they did. The walls were paper-thin in this place, and usually it didn't take much for them to get excited, but this morning their apartment seemed quiet. Maybe they had drunk their Christmas cheer and passed out, unconscious to the world. Or maybe they had taken her last warning seriously when at one in the morning she had donned a housecoat, fuzzy slippers, and her Glock and paid them a visit. Not necessarily something a good cop would be proud of, but she was just human after all.

Her visitor wasn't letting up.

"I'm coming. Shut up!" She couldn't help it. Patience was never her strong suit, and at this point, on a limited amount of sleep, she had even less of it.

She swung the door open and faced Terry. He had a couple cloth grocery bags in one hand and a small, decorated tree under his other arm.

"What are you doing—"

"Nice pj's."

She looked down at herself and was thankful for full coverage—a pair of blue track pants and a Stiles PD sweatshirt.

"And here I would have taken you for a white lace woman."

"As if." She stepped back from the door to let him in.

"You don't have one, do you?" He glanced around the apartment.

"Have one what?"

"Didn't think so." He met eyes with her and smiled. "A tree, Maddy. Everyone needs one."

She found herself somewhat touched by the gesture but didn't allow him to see it. "Put it where you like," she said.

Terry set the prelit tree down and plugged it in. It had small white lights tastefully dispersed. She fought a smile so it wouldn't give her away.

"It's early. You do know that," she said.

Terry didn't respond to her but went into her kitchen and made himself at home. He set the bags he'd brought with him on the counter and started pulling items out of them: a Tupperware container filled with what looked like batter, one filled with blueberry sauce, another filled with strawberry sauce, and a bottle of genuine maple syrup. He then folded the bags, signaling the end of their contents.

"What are you doing now?"

"You're going to repeat yourself all day like a parrot?"

A cliché. Terry's vocabulary was poisoned with them. "Until you answer the question."

He laughed.

"Is this some joke?"

"Absolutely not." He swung open the cabinet doors, working his way around the compact space in seconds. "Guess I should have brought it with me—"

"What are you looking for? Terry, it's seven in the morning!"

"A nonstick fry pan. I'm going to cook you up some superb pancakes. With Grant pancakes, the secret's in the batter. We know how to make them light and fluffy—"

"Stop there." The sincere happiness he seemed to be experiencing in this moment was breaking through her grumpy exterior. "Light and fluffy?"

"The best." He took out a flipper.

"But why? And why so early?" She brushed past him, opened the bottom drawer on the stove, and put a frying pan on the burner.

"Because we've got to get to work—"

"It's Christmas day."

"Doesn't mean we don't work."

Okay, so he had a point. The strange part was he was the one pushing work this morning, and she was the one being tempted to take personal time. The lab was shut down until Friday, so no forensic results. Their list of actual suspects was short at this point despite Allison's mention that many people wanted Claire dead. The only name they got was that of the "best friend" Darcy Simms.

Terry wiped the inside of the pan with oil and turned the burner on. "Annabelle's on the way with Hershey."

Hershey. She almost said it aloud. Damn, he wasn't part of a dream—or rather nightmare. Nope, *he*, a chocolate lab puppy, was her cursed Christmas gift from the Grants. What was she supposed to do with a dog? And why did they get one that would grow larger than her apartment? Still, she found herself getting somewhat excited about petting the little guy again.

"She's bringing a kennel for him, too," Terry added.

She nodded as if she knew what all that meant. "I'm not sure…" There was such a look of disappointment on his face. "What is the kennel for?"

He laughed. He must have found her naivety entertaining. "For training purposes mostly. Some people keep them in the crate whenever they're not home. We don't like to do that with Todd and Bailey. We like them to have free rein, but you'll want to make sure he's housebroken first."

Of course, Todd and Bailey were beagles, more than half the size of what Hershey would become.

There was a knock on the door.

"I'll get it." Terry smiled at her and answered the door as if this were his place. It was Annabelle, and she had come with a lot more than just a dog. "Hey, honey." Terry kissed his wife's cheek and took a bag from her hands. He still left her with a folded crate under one arm, a bag of puppy chow under the other, and, of course, a hyperactive puppy pulling on its leash. For the excess that Annabelle toted, one would think a dog came with as much baggage and responsibility as did a baby.

Oh, her simple home life was about to change.

Chapter 6

Madison and Terry were in the car heading to Darcy Simms's house. There wasn't much traffic, because most people were likely at home either sleeping or lounging in their sleepwear.

"So, what did you think of my pancakes?"

"They were good." Madison smiled at him. After two large cups of steaming coffee, one and a half pancakes with fruit syrup, her sleepy haze had lifted. She did observe how alert Hershey was for that time of day, though, and it made her a bit nervous. The dog would have to learn to value sleep as much as she did. Maybe once he realized what a rare commodity it was around there, it would come naturally.

"And what about the tree? No thank-you?" He laughed. "Not that I really expected one I guess—"

"Well, maybe if you hadn't decorated it for me—"

"Oh, here we go—"

"Well, you named my dog." No sense telling him that it was perfect, as she had a chocolate addiction and a preference to Hershey's bars. "I'm mean, why even bother handing my gifts over to me?"

"No pleasing you, Knight."

They were both smiling.

"Anyway, at least one of us knows how to say thank you. Speaking of which, thank you for letting me go last night."

"It's fine." She could tell he truly appreciated it. Showing up at the crack of dawn with food proved that, didn't it?

"I know it's hard for you when there's next of kin to notify. Surprised you let me go before that actually."

She couldn't confess her mind was a conflicted mess at the time, and she hadn't considered notification before letting him go. "There wasn't any to inform."

"None to inform?"

"Nope."

"If there had been, I would have come and got you just for that." They always took turns, as neither of them enjoyed doing it. To bring the news to a family that a loved one was murdered was not an easy aspect of the job. "It was your turn," she added.

"Uh-huh. Nobody, eh? How sad."

"The closest person on record was her aunt Beatrice Reeves, but she died two years ago of cancer."

"Is it ever anything else?"

Madison looked at him from the driver's seat, wondering how long it would take for an answer to sink in.

"Okay, when it's not murder."

"Not too often." And not that she needed to be reminded of cancer's reach. She'd lost her grandmother to the disease. The brain tumor, the treatments, and the final verdict that it was inoperable. She was starting to feel like an emotional mangle inside. She blamed the holiday season, but at the same time cursed herself for letting it have such power over her.

Madison spotted the address noted for Darcy Simms and pulled to the side of road in front of the house. There wasn't a car in the driveway and the front walkway was buried in at least six inches of undisturbed snow. "Okay, it looks like we're here, but it doesn't look like anyone else is or has been in a while. I sure hope you didn't drag my butt out of bed for nothing."

"Nothing? You got fed. Doesn't that count for something?"

"Not really." She chuckled and got out of the car.

Madison trudged through the snow ahead of Terry.

They knocked and rang the doorbell a few times and were met with no response.

"Yeah, she's not home," Terry said.

He always had a way of stating the obvious, and it made her laugh. "You don't even realize you do that, do you?"

"Do what?"

She didn't answer the question, but instead realized that she could have still been in bed. "Okay, well, I'm happy I got up for that and dragged myself out into the cold."

"Do what?" he parroted.

She steamrolled past him. "I could have been spending quality time getting to know Hershey."

"I know you better than that, you sarcastic brat…" He seemed to drift mentally, and his next words confirmed where. "Did Allison ever tell us why she was cleaning on Christmas Eve?"

"Just that Claire asked for her to."

"Well, I for one would like to see that text message to prove her services were required that night."

"We know that's not going to happen. She told Weir she had deleted it, remember? So dead end there." Madison pressed her lips. She recalled how Allison only provided the one name—Darcy Simms—yet referred to a man, one she seemed to keep intentionally nameless. "She wasn't very cooperative."

"I think it's worth paying her a visit."

"Heck, I'm out of bed already, we might as well spread the joy."

"Well, we've got a fifty-fifty chance of finding her home."

"Yes, and you're the genius among us." Madison let out a small laugh.

Terry didn't find quite as much amusement in it as she did, but he'd get over it. She smiled to herself, as if it was some sort of payback for the early wake-up call.

"What are you doing here?" Allison Minard spat out as if Madison and Terry being at her front door was a great intrusion of her privacy. Her arms were crossed. Her hips were tilted to the right. She wore a man's blue-collared shirt and that was all, but she didn't seem shy or self-conscious about the fact.

"We need to speak with you," Madison began.

"I've already told you everything. I don't know what more I could possibly offer." She trembled, likely from a chill. "Fine. Come in." Contempt dripped from her voice; the offer was only extended for her comfort.

Stepping inside, the heat of the house cupped Madison's cheeks. She pulled out on the neck of her sweater that rose above her coat.

Madison heard running water, possibly a shower as it came from upstairs. Allison had company, as if her wardrobe wasn't enough to make one realize that Madison and Terry had disturbed a party for two.

"Just something we're curious about," Madison began. "Why did Claire request your cleaning service last night?"

"Why? Because you don't believe I was supposed to be there?"

"Were you?" Madison felt Terry's eyes on her. He must have thought she was too direct.

"Why would I be there if I wasn't supposed to be?"

Her question hung out there, an awkward silence trailing behind it. Allison fiddled with a button on the collar of the shirt. If she was trying to convey a strong stance, she was failing miserably.

"Can we see the text message she sent you?" Madison pressed.

Allison looked at them, her eyes not quite connecting with either of them. "I deleted it. I told the other cops that."

"Huh."

"Is she for real?" Allison appealed to Terry, who shrugged his shoulders. "Well, I'm telling you the truth." She clenched her teeth.

"There's one hole in your story," Madison said. "Claire's phone had no record of the message being sent—"

"Impossible. It came from her to me. This is what I get for deleting text messages after I read them. Here, I'll—" Allison backed away from the doorway and came back seconds later holding a cell phone. "Here. Look at it." She accessed the menus and showed it to Madison. "There's nothing there. You see that? It wasn't just hers I deleted. Can't you cops pull up the history on my phone and prove I received a text message from Claire?"

"We may be able to prove you received an incoming text message from her cell, but beyond that we can't see what was sent."

"Just great."

"You still haven't answered why she wanted you to clean."

Allison let out a rush of air, flailed an arm. "How should I know?

She was entertaining a man for Christmas? Your guess would be as good as any I could come up with. Did you talk to Darcy?"

Her tagged-on question took Madison off guard for a moment. "No—"

"Let me guess, she wasn't home." Her hips jutted to the right.

The sound of running water stopped. Allison's eyes snapped to the upstairs landing. "Listen, if you could leave—"

"Baby!" It was a man's voice.

Allison avoided eye contact with Madison and Terry and tapped a foot on the floor.

"Baby!" he repeated himself, and footsteps headed toward the railing.

Madison anticipated seeing his face, but he stopped moving when Allison said, "I'll be right there." She connected eyes with Madison. "You've got to go."

He called out again. "Put on some coffee." There was a pause. "Hey, who are you talking to down there?"

"Don't worry about it. Coffee's coming right up."

Madison hoped he would be curious enough to come to the top of the stairs, but the footfalls were headed back to where they came from. It was obviously a more casual relationship where any questions didn't need satisfying answers.

"Please go. I've more than cooperated with you." Allison placed a flattened hand on Terry's shoulder blade, gesturing for them to leave.

Madison said, "Just one more question."

Allison let out a rush of air and rolled her eyes.

"This man, the one you mentioned—"

"Nope, no way." She shook her head rapidly. "Not going to say. Leave."

Allison backed them out onto the step and inched the door shut. Madison put a foot out to stop it. She tried to read Allison's eyes, but they were guarded and revealed nothing.

"Where does she work?"

"Her own business. By Design." Her eyes dropped to Madison's boot, which was lodged in the doorframe.

Footsteps were coming down the staircase now, but the door blocked her view. Was it the man Allison was trying to protect?

Allison looked over a shoulder and a smile that started for her guest quickly dissolved when she turned back to face them. She pushed harder on the door. "Merry Christmas."

"Merry Christmas." Madison chanted as she unlocked her apartment door.

Something about Allison didn't sit well with Madison. She'd discovered the body, the text requiring her to clean had been *deleted*. Madison didn't think she necessarily pulled off the murder but suspected Allison knew who was involved. She avoided solid eye contact and had closed body language.

She wanted to dig more into this case now. So what if it was Christmas Day? Normally Cynthia would forward the evidence list electronically, but she hadn't yet. If Madison wanted to read it, she'd have to go to the department for the handwritten reports.

It was then she heard the noise, the faint squeak—no, it was a whine. It took her a moment to ascertain where it was coming from. Hershey. Her breath paused as she contemplated her new responsibility. She walked across the floor, still in her boots, to the kennel, which sat to the side of her living area. He was laying straight out, his nose pressed between the bars, looking like he'd been confined to a prison cell. His whining turned into barking. He wanted out, and now. His deep cocoa eyes watched her.

What am I supposed to do with a dog?

And what was that smell? She was too tired for this. She was always too tired. He kept barking, the noise holding more of a desperate edge as it went on. The sharp barks ricocheted in her head, and almost immobilized her. But there was definitely a smell… She sniffed deeper and gagged. She knew exactly what it was and a look to the back of the kennel confirmed her suspicion. Hershey had left a *kiss*—if you wanted to call it that.

"Bad dog." She was going to be sick… She held her breath, but that ended up making it worse when she gasped for air. She could taste it. How she hadn't detected the odor the second she entered her apartment, she had no idea.

Hershey's barks transformed back to high-pitched whining that was quickly giving her a headache.

"Quiet!" She bent over to unlatch the kennel, the smell overpowering her as she lowered to her haunches. She swallowed the bile that rose in her throat. Guess there were two things she couldn't handle.

With the door open, Hershey bounded out, taking off in a swirl and making his way around the living room, claws clicking on the wood floor as he struggled to remain on four legs.

Where did he find the energy? She owed Terry for this one.

Hershey came up behind her and pulled on her sweater with his teeth.

She shooed him away. "Stop it."

Maybe she should find amusement in his love for life, but at this moment, she was too terrified of the consequences of her Christmas gift. Guess now was the time to rope him up, load him onto the elevator, and take him outside.

This morning at breakfast, Terry had tried reassuring her that having a dog wouldn't be that bad. She'd adjust and even come to welcome this new addition to her life.

"He'll give you company," he had said.

Somehow, she had managed not to roll her eyes when he said this, but she had wondered how desperate she was coming across. As if reading her mind, Terry had gone on to say that dogs were great for those who just wanted someone to listen and not offer advice. There he had her. That would be a welcome addition. People were always in a hurry to provide input and suggestions.

"You're going to have to learn the house rules." A waft of the ripe air hit her. "And rule number one—" She rose to her feet. He jumped around her, let out a single bark, an *arf*.

She laughed. His love for life was somewhat contagious and even managed to minimalize what he had done.

"Rule number one: no doo-doo in the house." She couldn't believe she was talking like this. If anyone overheard this, she'd have to kill them. "Rule number two: no chewing on my clothes."

She knew there would be a much longer list to follow, but those two would suffice for the time being.

Now, how was she going to clean up Hershey's Christmas gift to her? She looked around the apartment as if it would miraculously provide an answer. Too bad she couldn't just wiggle her nose like Samantha from *Bewitched* and have the whole sordid mess cleaned up, a sparkle shining off the edge of the kennel sounding with a chime.

Maybe if she approached it like a crime scene, focused and methodical. But all the blood from the current investigation came back with clarity. Who was she kidding? She wasn't made for cleanup. She had to think of a different analogy. Hershey was a baby, *her* baby, and she needed to clean it up for him.

Gah! She didn't ask to be anyone's *mommy*.

Eventually, after working out several scenarios and enduring numerous out-of-body experiences, she got it cleaned up. She was thankful that Hershey hadn't rolled in it. The thought made her lips curl. Yes, things could have been worse.

"All right, let's go." She headed over to the coat hooks and grabbed the leash that dangled there. She needed to get this over with so she could get downtown. "Come here, buddy." She bent down, and he ran over, jumping at her and trying to reach her face. "Okay, rule number three: no licking."

It wasn't easy trying to get the collar around his neck. He kept jumping at her in an effort to lick her face.

"Calm down."

He should have come with an operation manual. She just got him latched up and the phone rang. She cursed audibly and let go of the leash.

She picked up the phone. "Hello?"

"Hey, baby." It was Blake Golden.

She was happy to hear his voice. She dropped onto the couch and watched Hershey sniff his cleaned digs, the tether trailing behind him.

"I miss you," she said and regretted doing so immediately. The few seconds of silence on his end weren't helping.

"I'll be back Saturday night."

He stated it so matter-of-factly that she felt needy. And she hated feeling that way. Somehow, she had to retract what she had said or at least move beyond it, change the direction of the conversation and make him forget what she had said. "How's the family? You enjoying things out there?" *Small talk?* Surely, she could do better than that.

"Yeah, it's not bad. Mom's drunk on eggnog, and I know it's only the middle of the—" He was cut short by a loud, animated woman in the background. "That's Mom."

Madison laughed.

Blake went on. "My brother ate way too much turkey last night. We have the family dinner on the Eve. He was sick and didn't make it up the stairs to the bathroom."

All the potent smells of the last twenty-four hours mingled together in her mind. "Yuck."

"Don't tell me that grossed you out. You've probably seen a lot worse." He laughed.

Don't remind me...

And he didn't know that side of her, the one that cringed every time she arrived at a scene and couldn't stand the sight of anything remotely disgusting. In fact, he never would have to know.

"Anyway, I just called to say hi, tell you I was thinking about you on Christmas Day."

She gave him the same reaction as he'd given her when she told him she missed him—silence. Maybe their relationship was advancing too quickly.

"I'll be home Saturday like I said," Blake began, "and I want to treat my girl to dinner at Piccolo Italia."

"Sounds great."

Piccolo Italia—literally translated "Little Italy"—was his favorite restaurant. It was world-renowned for its authentic Italian dishes. Their pasta and sauces were made fresh daily. They only served a dinner menu, and the main entrées started at forty dollars and went up from there. But the meals were a good value. Italians had a love for life, but they also had a love of plenty.

What was she going to do when this relationship ended? His treating her to the relatively greater things in life was becoming ingrained in her. It wasn't hard going up, but it was the coming down part, the crashing, that would be hard to readjust to.

Hershey walked over to the side of the area rug, sniffed, and bent down over the wood floor. She kept her eyes on him.

"I'll make reservations for the second seating." He sounded happy, although he was likely having a better time than she was to start with. She was stuck here in mounds of snow, alone on Christmas. "There's something important I'd like to talk with you about—"

"Shit!" A golden puddle was forming around Hershey's paws. "Sorry, I've got to go." She hung up the phone.

Was this dog just a producer of waste? Whatever went in came out moments later?

"Hershey!"

The hardwood better not stain or the superintendent would have her ass. She could hear him now:

"That will be coming from your security deposit! We'll have to refinish the entire floor."

The dog slinked between an end table and a chair. Her anger must have been obvious enough that he detected his wrongdoing. She worked at soaking up the urine with paper towels. It didn't seem to have marked the floor. She disinfected the area using cleaner, and then donned her coat and boots before grabbing the leash that was still hooked to Hershey's collar. She tugged on it. "Come on."

Hershey just stood there, paws welded to the floor.

"You're kidding me. Right? This has to be a joke or—" she looked heavenward "—is this some cruel punishment for a past wrongdoing?" She pulled on the leash again. He didn't budge. "Hershey. Another rule: when I say *come*, you come."

His body quivered, and she felt somewhat horrible for scaring him to this point, but she didn't move to soothe him. Her mind was stuck on where her conversation with Blake had left off—he had something important to talk to her about. It distracted her to the point that she had almost forgotten about her intentions to go downtown. First the dog, and then she'd take care of business.

She glanced at the small, lit Christmas tree on the way out of the apartment and wondered what it would be like to have a normal life. But then, again, who could define normal?

"What are you doing here?" asked Officer Ranson, who regularly manned the front desk down at the station during the day.

Madison tapped the counter. "Could ask you the same." She passed Ranson a smile but kept moving.

Today Ranson's hair was more traditionally colored, black with blonde highlights, but she had a rainbow of hair colors she chose from. Madison could envision the woman stocking up on dye as it went on sale. Superiors had discussed the matter of her color choices many times, and how a person who sits at the front representing the department should appear professional. But Ranson knew they couldn't fire her based on personal style, so she kept it how she liked.

Files were stacked high in Madison's inbox. She functioned best in what appeared to be disorganized to others.

She opened a desk drawer on the left, pulled out a folder, and opened it. It was a list of evidence collected from the scene. She rifled through the case file and the evidence log, drawing her finger down the page line by line. What she was looking for wasn't there.

She picked up her phone and dialed Cynthia at home.

"What?"

"Nice way to answer your phone."

"Saw it was the department and wasn't thrilled."

Madison looked down. "Am I disturbing you?"

"The nice answer or the honest one?" Cynthia lowered her voice. "I've got company. Be happy that I answered."

"So thankful."

Cynthia had her rash of affairs and somehow never allowed herself to become attached to any of them.

"I need to ask you something," Madison started. "Is the evidence log complete?"

JUSTIFIED

"Absolutely. It's been checked, double-checked, and triple-checked."

"There's no note of a cleaning checklist."

"Ah, there wasn't one, then."

"You're sure?"

"Positive. Now—"

"One more thing. I'll need you to take a closer look at Claire's phone and see if you can confirm if a text message was sent to the maid and whether there's any way we can see it."

"I'll add it to my list of things to do. Now, what have I told you about calling me at home about work?"

"Not to do it."

"Ding, ding, ding. 'Night, Maddy."

"Bitch." Madison hung up, a smile on her lips, but the expression didn't take long to fade.

The first twenty-four hours of a case were crucial to solving it, and they weren't anywhere close. Evidence pointed to a man and just because there wasn't a cleaning checklist, it didn't mean that Allison had been involved. But it also didn't clear her. Her alibi was weak. She had said that she was home at the time of the murder, and there wasn't enough to warrant dragging her in for questioning at this point. She would be worth another visit, though.

Madison slipped the file into the drawer, and her eyes caught the label on another one. It read, *Lexan, Bryan.*

This was the one cold case that she just couldn't let go of. It had been the first to smear her previously untarnished close record. It had been four and a half years ago. The most frustrating thing about this murder investigation was that she knew who had killed Bryan, but the law required proof and that was where she fell short. She didn't have sufficient evidence to establish guilt beyond reasonable doubt.

She pulled out the file, opened it on her desk, and wheeled her chair in.

The file contained the basics, what they had in the way of evidence, and it was scarce. Photographs of the crime scene, including a couple of the bullet fragments that were pulled from the vic. Madison's eyes rested on one of these photos. There hadn't been enough to confirm striation and thereby determine a firearm.

The bullets were .22 hollow points, but Madison knew they had been fired by one of Dimitre Petrov's men. Petrov was a powerful Russian drug czar whose hands were bloodied by those he murdered, yet they may as well have been stained with invisible ink for the good it did in convicting him. It was only a rare twist of fate that he was found guilty of murder in the first degree for a man named Leroy Adams and levied with a life sentence.

Madison knew the Russians favored the Sig Sauer Mosquito, and the ballistic tests had been run. Dummies were sacrificed for the art of science and for the justice of forensics. Yet nothing was conclusive.

McAlexandar, who had been the sergeant at the time, had reminded her, "You can't present the evidence, the evidence must be presented."

Where science failed, logic served as a compass. Bryan Lexan was the defense attorney representing Petrov at the time of his conviction. Due to this, he had garnered the attention of the Russians for failing their leader.

She shuffled the photographs to look at one of the victim slumped in his driveway. One bullet to the chest, one to the forehead.

Based on the estimated TOD, they had just missed the shooter. If she had only figured everything out moments sooner, Bryan Lexan could still be alive. And maybe that's what ate away at her the most.

She slipped the photographs back inside the file, put the folder back in her desk drawer, and exchanged it for a Hershey's bar.

Chapter 7

It was the next morning, and Madison and Terry were getting ready to head over to meet with Darcy Simms.

"No cleaning checklist?" Terry looked at her from the passenger seat.

"No."

"Well, then Allison must be the killer." The smirk started from the center of his lips and spread to the corners.

Madison rolled her eyes. "No need for the sarcasm."

He pulled out on the seat belt and clipped it in. "I learned it from you."

She disregarded his comment. "I'm not saying she is necessarily the one who did it. Her thin frame pretty much tells us she wouldn't possess the strength, but I think she knows more than she's telling us." Her cell phone rang and she picked it up. "Detective Kni—"

"Got a call from Allison Minard." It was the sergeant.

"How nice. What did she have to say? Has she confessed to knowledge of the murder?"

"Stop harassing her, Knight. She says you showed up at her home on Christmas Day pressing her."

"I was asking for things she wasn't willing to provide."

"Well, may I suggest, or actually, tell you not to talk to her again unless you have cause to arrest her. Otherwise, I'll have no choice but to log a formal complaint on your file."

Am I to be thankful for the warning? Her earlobes tingled with the heat of anger.

"Knight? You hear me?"

"Yes." She dragged out the one word.

"Good." He paused briefly. "Where are you with the case anyhow?"

He might as well just come out and say it: it had been over fifty hours since time of death and they didn't have any solid leads.

"I'll keep you informed."

"That's the same vague answer you give me every time, Knight."

Then why do you ask the question every time?

She had to bite down on her tongue—hard. "As soon as we know more, we'll let you know." This sort of blanket response was never usually enough to soothe him, but it's what she had to offer right now.

"You're patronizing me again."

"Fine. Here's the bit I have. At first impression, the method in which she was killed and the type of lifestyle Claire led points toward her murder being personal. For this reason, I'd say we're looking at an isolated incident."

"I'm sure you can understand my hesitancy to accept that."

She made the wrong judgment call one time…

"Keep me updated," he barked.

"Always do—"

The sergeant hung up.

Terry's eyes were on her. "Let me guess, the sarge?"

"And yet, Terry, you're not the lead on the case?" She put the car into gear.

Darcy Simms owned and managed By Design. It was an exterior design firm focused on transforming outdoor living spaces, patios, decks, verandas, and even balconies into oases.

Their suite was on the second floor of a commercial building in an industrial area of town. Exposed ductwork gave the reception area a cool, minimalistic feel, but the room was accented with splashes of color. A sitting area consisted of a matched set of three chairs and a couch that were placed around a coffee table. The pieces gave the space a modern touch with their metal legs and brilliant blue plastic molded seats. Large, framed prints hung on the walls showcasing what Madison assumed to be past projects.

A petite woman behind the counter rose to her feet as she watched them approach. She wore a cordless headset over one ear. "May I help—" She held up a finger and then tapped on her earpiece "Good morning. By Design. How can we make your outdoor living fantasy a reality?"

Madison fought off a smirk. At times like this, she was especially thankful for the field of work she was in. She'd prefer the company of dead bodies to that of living, breathing customers who demanded perfection at the lowest price possible. She knew from her current position the ability to kiss ass wasn't part of her genetic makeup.

"Sorry about that." The receptionist smiled at them. "How may I help you?"

"We'd like to speak with Darcy Simms."

Her eyes fell downward, and her aura communicated a deep sense of loss. "You're detectives, aren't you?"

"We are." Madison proceeded with their introductions.

"She's not in that great of shape today," the receptionist began, "with what happened to her best friend and all."

"But she is here?"

"She is." Her gaze lowered to her desk and her cheeks flushed. Madison sensed sadness emanating from the woman.

"We'd like to speak with her," Madison said firmly.

The woman's chin quivered subtly.

"Do you know why we're here?"

She nodded.

"Did you know Claire Reeves?"

She shook her head. "No. It's just that I tend to care too much about others and what they're going through."

Empathy was too rare a commodity in the modern world and to hear this woman experienced it was refreshing. "That's not a bad thing," Madison assured her.

The woman softly nodded her head. "I'll get her for you."

"Thank you."

"Have a seat." She gestured toward a sitting area. Her earlier friendliness had cooled.

Terry took a seat with a moan. "You'd think with all the advances in design, they could offer comfort with style."

"You ask for too much." Her mind skipped from furniture to footwear—same principal. Women were expected to cram their feet into shoes with three-inch pointed heels, comfort being the last item on the list of importance.

Another petite woman entered the area. Her hair was blond and cut in short, choppy layers. Her face wouldn't be memorable if it weren't for her lips, which were plump and proportionally larger in comparison to the rest of her features. They were painted with a bright red lipstick.

Does everyone want Angelina Jolie's lips?

Madison rose to her feet. "Darcy Simms?"

"Yes." She didn't extend a hand for introductions but led them down the hall to her office.

The design here mimicked the feel of the reception area. The walls were bare except for a few tastefully selected modern art pieces. On a filing cabinet, there were a few diplomas in black frames, but there were no pictures of children or a significant other.

"We're sorry for your loss," Madison said.

Darcy pulled a tissue from a box and dabbed her nose, but Madison sensed an insincerity in the action, as if it had been rehearsed and was ready to perform on cue. "I still can't believe she's gone."

"We won't take up much of your time," Madison began, "but do you know of anyone who would have wanted to hurt Claire?"

"Let me guess, her maid told you to come see me."

"Why assume that?"

"The woman never liked me. But I guess you could say that the feeling was mutual." Darcy picked up a pen with her right hand and proceeded to draw lines on a notepad followed by large swirls.

"How did you know her?" She remembered Allison mentioning she had cleaned for Darcy but asked the question anyhow.

"You mean besides the fact she was my best friend's maid? She cleaned for me once."

"Why only once?"

The swirls got larger, and she was applying more pressure to the

JUSTIFIED

pen as the ink was sinking deeper into the pad. "She didn't live up to my standards."

"But she'd do for Claire?"

"Let's just say, and no disrespect intended toward the dead, but my standards were always higher than Claire's. Allison did a horrible job of cleaning my bathroom. I found some hair at the base of the toilet. There was a smudge on it. I don't call that clean."

"Okay, fair enough." If that was the truth, it was unlikely Darcy would have committed the murder. Blood was too messy for the average person.

"Actually, the only reason Claire probably kept her on was because she owed her."

"Owed her?"

"I don't know why exactly. All I know is what Claire told me. She felt indebted to Allison."

"And you don't know why?" Madison needed to find out their background connection.

Darcy shrugged.

"Do you know how Allison felt about Claire?" Madison remembered Allison's outburst at the neighbor's house: *She's a conniving bitch.*

Darcy stopped moving the pen. She sat there, her gaze going through Madison and Terry for a few seconds before her eyes dropped to her doodles.

Madison glanced at Terry, who silently communicated that she approach things another way. "You know of anyone Claire was seeing?"

Darcy met Madison's eyes. "You mean a man or a woman? Claire would get with both. She preferred men."

That explained all the condoms in her trash can, but she wondered about the mystery man's identity that Allison had brought up. "Anyone specifically?"

"She had a few regulars she'd sleep with. One was married," Darcy said. She held eye contact with Madison, a move often utilized to elicit trust and to add sincerity to one's statements, yet it instilled the opposite for Madison. Too much of it and it indicated the person was a liar. They'd look at you in the eyes so they could see if you were buying the line of bull they were feeding you.

"Names?"

"Nope, not giving that to you." She shook her head.

"One of them could have killed your best friend."

Coolness reflected in those eyes. "They wouldn't have. Men worshiped Claire."

"You sound quite sure of that. Where were you on Wednesday morning between two and four?"

"Are you accusing me of her murder?"

"Should I be?"

Silence.

"Where were you?" Madison repeated the question.

"On a red-eye home from Tahiti."

Madison thought of Darcy's snow-covered walkway. "You haven't been home yet?"

"I stayed with a friend."

Madison cocked her head to the side.

Darcy opened a desk drawer, took out a purse, and retrieved a piece of paper, which she extended to Terry. "Here's the ticket."

"Thanks."

"Uh-huh." Darcy stuffed the purse back into the drawer and addressed Madison. "Anything else?"

In response, Madison rose to her feet and tossed a card on the desk. "When you want to share what you're keeping from us, there's my number."

Darcy sat up straighter. "Excuse me—"

"You've got quite the business here," Terry said, breaking the growing tension.

Darcy pried her eyes from Madison to look at him.

Terry went on. "Something that it keeps you busy. Especially at this time of the year."

Darcy grinned. "We carry on a global business here. A few years back—" She paused, her eyes going contemplative. "Well, I guess it would easily be fifteen years ago now... Anyway, we expanded our reach. See, when we see snow here, the south is still inundated with sunshine and heat, and that is good for business."

Terry nodded. "And good for you."

"Yes." Another smile.

"Speaking of work, Claire's background doesn't show her most recent employment. Do you know what she did for a job? Who she worked for?"

Darcy let out a small laugh. "For herself. She was always working for herself."

"I think we're done here." Madison moved toward the door.

Terry followed her lead, but extended a hand toward Darcy. "Thank you for your time."

Darcy put the pen down to shake his hand and was smiling, but the expression quickly died when she noticed Madison watching her.

Madison turned to leave, and at the doorway glanced over her shoulder at Darcy, who picked up the pen again. And this time, she picked it up with her left hand.

Chapter 8

Madison and Terry were back in the department car, and the driving was becoming somewhat treacherous. Fresh snowfall was making the roads slippery, and to make matters worse, the man in front of them must have been driving with two feet, as the brake lights kept coming on.

"You must love getting calls from the sarge," Terry said.

"Oh shut up, Terry. The woman's hiding something."

"You think everyone's hiding something."

"Most people are," she ground out, glancing over at him.

Terry was looking out the passenger window. "You're just fishing for something because you don't like her."

"I'm offended that you think I'm making this personal."

"What is it about you women?"

"You women," she stated with heat.

"Yeah. You meet someone who is prettier, definitely sexier…"

Is he even thinking before speaking?

Terry continued. "And you immediately hate her. Women are always preaching about not wanting to be judged by their appearance, but you're always the first to pass judgment."

She wanted to snap back with a retort, something especially smart and witty, but had nothing. In a way, it was the truth… sometimes. She'd give him a pass this once, and with that decision, her mind went back to Darcy. "Don't you think it is strange that she came back to work just a day after her friend's body was found?"

"She pours herself into work to cover her grief?" He curled his lips and shrugged. "It's not an unusual response."

She let out a moan of frustration. "You know what? Maybe it's you with the perception problem. If she had been five foot two with buck teeth and extremely obese, and I told you about her picking up the pen with her left hand—" He opened his mouth like he was going to cut her off, but she held up a hand. "Please listen to me. At least ponder the possibility that she's hiding something, not that she's necessarily the killer. I would like to know why she doodled with her right hand when she is obviously left-handed?"

"You *think* you saw that. You're not even certain."

She tapped the brakes. The man in front of them made her nervous, but there was no way around. "I *know*. You are impossible. Don't even try and tell me that I'm stubborn. Mind you, I guess you should recognize your characteristic in others." Her cell vibrated on her hip, and she pulled the car to the side of the road. With the new laws about not driving while on the phone, whether it be talking or texting, as a law enforcement officer, she had to set a good example.

Terry pulled out on his seat belt, adjusting the fit over his winter coat. "The sarge?"

She'd soon find out. She answered without glancing at the caller ID.

As Madison listened to her caller, Terry's eyes were trained on her. By the time she hung up, she was grinning. Finally, they were getting some momentum to this case.

Chapter 9

It was an unfortunate requirement that obtaining answers from Cole Richards, the ME, usually involved going to the morgue. Madison flung the door open, and Terry came in after her.

"So what have you got for us?" she asked.

"Now I'm not even worthy of a greeting? Guess I'll talk to you." Richards flashed one his heart-stalling smiles at Terry, overlooking Madison.

"Let me start again," she said. "How's your day going?" She paused a few seconds. "What have you got for us?"

His eyes softened but quickly hardened as he took on a thoughtful gaze and looked in the direction of a steel gurney. Claire Reeves had been laid out and covered with a thin, white sheet. "COD was exsanguination due to the carotid artery having been severed. The slash was so deep that the knife nicked the spine."

"So the murder weapon was a knife?" Madison asked.

Richards nodded. "Most definitely. And I'd say it was not serrated and approximately seven inches long. The X-ray will be forwarded to Cynthia for analysis. Hopefully, she'll be able to determine the type and make of knife."

Richards traced a finger over the wound. "As you can see, it is choppy—"

"Hesitation marks," Madison added.

"Yes. But how does that coincide with the depth of the wound?"

"The killer could have been inexperienced but fueled by determination and anger," Madison suggested.

"Or they didn't realize how sharp the knife was," Terry presented as an alternate theory.

Richards took a deep breath, seemingly not impressed by their spewing out speculations. "As I was saying, the cut was deep yet there are hesitation marks. Also, the victim was a height of five foot nine. Based on the downward angle of the incision, I would say your killer was at least five foot eleven."

She brought up the mental picture. "He would have reached around her, and because of being slightly taller, he would put the knife in downward, compensating for the height difference."

"Correct. If the killer was shorter, or the exact same height as the victim, it would have been more of a reach and would have resulted in the slash being on an upward angle."

Richards's findings brought some disappointment and cast doubt on underlying suspicions about the two women in Claire's life. "Allison is probably about five nine so it wouldn't take much to elevate her, but it would rule out Darcy Simms. She's probably pushing five five." Madison wasn't going to bring up Darcy's writing hand right now.

"She could have worn six-inch heels," Terry said.

"Hey, good point." Madison rolled her eyes.

Richards continued. "And the killer wouldn't be much taller than five eleven because then the downward angle would have been greater." Richards walked around the gurney. "There is no evidence that she fought back. It was over before she had a chance." He lifted one of Claire's hands. "I scraped under her nails and got some trace soaked in blood."

That poor woman: lying on her kitchen floor, helpless, dying in a pool of her own blood... Madison had to stifle her thoughts there, but it was hard to do with Claire Reeves in front of her. Only thing was that to see Claire like this with the wound cleaned, she looked like a mannequin.

So how does a grown woman manage to be murdered, her neck sliced open, without fighting back? It had to have been quick and the killer must have been someone she trusted to get that close. If only they could get a hold of the man she had been with that night. There might be one way to find out his identity. "Have you swabbed her for semen?"

"Yes, and I found some. The sample has been sent up to the lab," Richards began. "I also heard that Crime Scene pulled a bunch of used condoms from the trash. I'd say the sex she had in the hours before her death was consensual. But she must have been a busy girl in general."

"Let's just hope we get something to go on." Madison's cell rang and she answered. It was hard to keep track of everything her caller was saying given the poor connection and the fact that Richards and Terry were talking. But she did catch the gist of their message. She closed her phone and turned to Terry. "We're leaving."

"For where?"

"Claire's. They've got the safe open."

MADISON STEPPED INSIDE CLAIRE'S HOUSE with Terry and wanted to pinch her nose. "It still smells in here."

"What do you expect? The scene hasn't been released yet so it's not like a cleanup crew's been in."

"I would like to know how they plan on rescuing the house after this." It wasn't completely unheard of for homes to be completely gutted and redone after a murder. The smell of death had the ability to seep into every pore and crevice.

They found Mark Andrews in the bedroom next to the safe. He gestured toward it and walked away. "Have at it."

Terry elbowed her. "Wow, you must have done something to him."

"What are you talking about?"

"Well, I'm not sensing love there anymore."

She made a move toward him, readied to punch him. "Let it go."

He got it into his stubborn skull some time ago that the young investigator had a crush on her. If she acknowledged the truth, she'd have to agree with him, although she'd chosen to ignore it.

What she saw before her wasn't nearly as exciting as she had anticipated. "USB flash drives?" There were five, all neon green.

"Now who's stating the obvious?"

"My, aren't we a quick one today." She looked at him blankly and punched him in the arm.

"At least one of us is compensating for you being behind the eight ball," he jibed while rubbing his arm.

She was about to make a comment on his cliché remark, but she heard Mark laughing behind her. She faced him. "You think he's funny?"

He glanced at Terry, then back to Madison. His face became serious. "No, not at all." He shook his head slowly as she kept her attention on him. "Absolutely not."

"Uh-huh." She narrowed her eyes at the investigator. "Have they been cataloged?"

"Yes."

She put on a pair of latex gloves and picked up the USB sticks. They'd have no way of knowing if there were any missing thumb drives. The killer could have taken what he was after and locked the safe behind him. It was also possible that he had copied information from these USB sticks and left them behind to look like nothing was taken.

"We dusted for prints on the cabinet and lifted a few," Mark started, "before the locksmith people came in. They're at the lab for analyzing."

Madison nodded. "Make sure the drives get back to the lab. And make sure someone extracts the data from these and have them smoked for prints."

"Of course."

Madison turned to her partner. "This case just isn't going anywhere near fast enough for me, Terry."

"I know. Patience isn't your strong suit."

She glared at him. "Oh shut up."

Chapter 10

Madison stopped the department sedan at a red light. "Allison isn't going to like it, but we have to visit her again."

"I hope you're joking about that."

"Think about it. Remember Darcy Simms? She mentioned Claire kept Allison on as a maid because she felt sorry for her, *owed* her for something. We've got to find out what." Madison tightened her grip on the steering wheel. "What if steady employment wasn't enough to compensate?"

"But we know Allison didn't do it. She's right-handed. The killer was left-handed."

"But she's about the right height."

"Not even close."

"She could have worn heels to make her taller."

"I mentioned that before. You never gave the comment any credit. Besides, there no evidence that heels were worn."

"And there isn't evidence against it. Well, maybe it wasn't her directly that did the murder. She could have hired someone to do it."

"A hired gun would have made a nice clean cut," he stated drily.

"What if the killer was forced to do it?"

"Okay, so in the dead of the night, the best method of attack is to have two people sneak up on Claire. One perched behind her, another holding a gun to the killer's head? But Claire is oblivious to all of it. She just stands still, drinking a glass of water in front of the sink."

"It doesn't mean the person manipulating the killer was at Claire's. There are other means of forcing people to do something.

Blackmail, for example."

"Possible but unlikely."

"You're such a skeptic. Maybe the blackmail had something to do with why Claire owed Allison."

He didn't say anything and just looked out the passenger window.

"Why can't you just admit it?" she asked. "Manipulation is a possibility, and right now, we need to run with every one we get. We can't afford to sit on our ass while waiting for, hoping for, some forensic finding that will identify our killer."

He waved her off with a motion of his arm, indicating to just go ahead and do what she felt she needed to do.

The light turned green, and she stomped on the accelerator so hard that the tires spun on the icy surface before they finally bit.

"We've got to figure out exactly where Claire made her money, and since neither woman wants to elaborate on that, we'll have to go about it our own way. Call and get her bank records sent over. We need to know how much money this woman had. Deposits and the regularity of them. If she worked for herself, what did she do?" She was driving like a road warrior. At least there were no two-foot drivers in front of her slowing her down.

"Do you have to drive so fast?" Terry mumbled as he pulled out his phone.

MADISON STOPPED IN FRONT OF Allison's house. Terry slipped his phone into the pocket of his jacket.

"They'll have the records for us within the next hour. Told them the urgency." Terry looked from the house to Madison. "You're seriously going to talk to her again?"

"I'm not." She locked eyes with him.

The message sank in. His head shook. "Nope. I'm not going to do it."

"Terry, she's hiding something."

"And if she is, what makes you think she'll tell me?"

"She might." Madison paused a moment. "Come on, I can't talk to her."

"Yeah, because the sarge will have your ass, but what's to say he won't chew on mine?"

"How did you enjoy Christmas Eve with your family?" She pulled out the favor of letting him go early.

"Hmm, let's see. Maybe if someone never answered the call in the first place, I would have enjoyed all of it."

Okay, that plan backfired. "Fine, I'll do it, but you'll be getting a new partner and maybe end up with someone like—"

"Anyone ever tell you that you're a manipulative woman?"

She didn't even have to say Detective Barkhouse's name. He'd been on the force longer than either of them had been alive and had a catalog of stories to go with the years. And every time he'd tell them, they'd change slightly. Either he made them up as he went along or his mind was going. "Thanks, Terry."

"Hey, I never said I'd do it."

ALLISON LEANED AGAINST THE DOORFRAME, her energy making it clear that she wasn't in the mood to talk. "Why are you harassing me?"

Terry shot Madison a dirty look.

"We just want to know why Claire owed you," Madison blurted out.

Allison's composure slipped momentarily. "If I told you anything further, it would make it look bad for me."

"And why is that?"

"I'm not talking to you anymore. Not without a lawyer."

"What are you hiding? Were you involved or are you hiding who was?" Madison couldn't keep quiet even though it made her guilty of exactly what Allison had accused her of—harassment.

Terry tugged on Madison's elbow to get her to leave. She stood her ground.

"Only the guilty threaten a lawyer, Miss Minard," she said. Terry let go of her arm.

"Only the smart do, Detective. I know how you work. You need someone to pin the blame on. Well, it isn't gonna be me. The bitch isn't taking me down with her. No way." She slammed the door in their faces.

Madison stood there recognizing how that closed door resembled the case so far—one dead end after another.

Out in the car, Terry said, "I can't believe I even went to the door with you. And you talk to her in a manner that screams, 'you did it, so why not admit it?'"

"Whatever."

"Don't whatever me. You want to take me down with you? Is that the plan? I need this job."

"Oh, you found me out." She lifted her hands, waving them in weak surrender. "Don't you worry yourself. I can handle the sarge."

"I'll believe that the day it happens." He paused before continuing. "Let's get something to eat."

"So you go from whining to food?"

He shrugged. "I'm hungry. And I've been meaning to ask you how your first night went with Hershey. How was it?"

One would think her not saying anything about Hershey would provide him with some sort of a clue as to how it was going. Of all the avenues of conversation he could have switched over to, why had he chosen this one? He had no idea the amount of willpower it would take on her part not to bring up the messes he'd made and the cleaning up she was left with. But maybe she should let him have the truth: the fact that she didn't need a dog, want a dog, or know what to do with one. But when she turned to face him, he had a boyish grin on his face. "It was interesting."

MADISON AND TERRY WERE GRABBING a bite to eat at a fast-food restaurant, and Terry no sooner placed his cell phone on the table beside his food tray than it vibrated against the wood.

Madison jerked.

"Wow, you're a jumpy one today." Terry laughed and answered his call.

Jumpy? Yes. After all, wouldn't anyone be a little jumpy given a grand total of three hours of sleep? And it wasn't even like they came consecutively. And her with a dog? Maybe when she got home tonight, she'd realize all of this had just been a long, bad dream.

I don't have a dog. I don't have a dog. Maybe if she repeated it like a chant?

Terry thanked his caller and hung up. "Okay, so they've got Claire's bank records, and her credit history was impeccable. She had a platinum Visa, no limit." His eyes took on the look of a daydreamer. "Can you imagine going into a Mercedes dealership? Yeah, I'll take the SL550 in silver. Just charge it to my card, please. I wonder how many air miles that would be." He was smiling, absorbed in a moment lost on her.

"The point?" She laughed. She couldn't help it. His fantasizing about having money was funny to observe.

"The point is our vic wasn't hurting for dough. She was loaded. She had a diversified portfolio valued in the low millions. Her bank account balance was sitting at two hundred twenty-nine thousand."

"Why have all that money sitting there earning basically nothing in interest?"

"Good question. Don't really know. They said there weren't any recent transfers or deposits for large sum amounts. Just regular withdrawals for bill payments, hydro, gas, credit cards. The large deposits are made sporadically, every two to three years, approximately."

"How large of deposits are we talking about?"

"Anywhere from two hundred and fifty thousand to over one point five million."

"Holy crap, that's a lot of money. We'll need to find out where the funds came from."

"And what I do know is if I had all that money to leave behind, I'd definitely have a will in place and life insurance."

"That means someone could have over a million reasons to want Claire dead."

Chapter 11

"We need to find out who stands to benefit." Her cell phone rang and she answered. The call lasted a few minutes, and then she hung up.

Terry was pressing his brow, indicating impatience. "Who was it? Do we have a lead?"

She dragged out the silence a bit longer, just because.

"Maddy."

A smile overtook her expression. "They've analyzed the flash drives."

"And?"

"And they didn't find any prints other than the vic's. From a forensic standpoint, no one else touched them."

"What about the prints lifted from the cabinet?"

"They came back a match to Claire, too. So either the killer never went in there at all or they wore gloves."

"Did they say what was on the USB sticks?"

"All five of them contained identical data."

"All of them?"

Madison nodded. "But here's some good news. We know how Claire made her money now."

Madison walked into the lab, Terry trailing behind her.

"We're still working on printing one copy of everything," Cynthia said.

"Why are you printing all of it?" Madison asked.

"Trust me. You'll prefer a hard copy." Cynthia walked to a table and supported herself against it. She handed a stack of about an inch thick to Madison. "That is only part of it."

"Holy crap."

"Yeah, holy crap. I'm going to need more reams of paper to get all of this printed." Cynthia adjusted her black frames on her nose and then twisted a strand of her dark hair around a finger. She glanced at the tips before releasing the hair.

Madison fanned through the sheets. "Business contracts? They look like scans of the originals."

"Uh-huh," Cynthia said.

"The paperwork is probably in a secure spot," Madison went on. "A safe-deposit box at a bank, for instance. Terry, could you—"

"I'm on it." He pulled out his cell phone.

"Putting copies on flash drives is a high-tech way of storing data. Less mess, less clutter. And it keeps the information handy," Cynthia said.

Madison's brain was stuck on the number of duplicate files. "You told me all five sticks had the same data. I wonder why she had five copies of the same thing."

"Maybe the victim was eccentric or paranoid," Cynthia offered a guess.

"So she was crazy?"

"I wouldn't jump to that conclusion based solely on this. We all have our idiosyncrasies. My aunt Olivia used to twist the light switches on lamps, on, off, on, off. It was like the light going out wasn't enough to signal her brain that the power was off."

Madison fought the urge to burst out laughing, but she was grinning.

Cynthia pointed a finger at her. "Don't you dare. She wasn't crazy."

"She sure sounds like she was."

"Well, like I said, we all have weird things about us, except for me of course." Cynthia laughed.

Madison's focus went back to the papers in front of her. "The dates on the contracts go back as far as twenty-one years ago."

"Claire Reeves would have been twenty-two at that time."

"College age." Madison flipped more pages.

Cynthia continued. "There are eight companies in there. She bought in as a silent partner and, based on the financials, she sold when the numbers turned around. After looking at these quickly, most of the businesses are still operating even though buying back Claire's share nearly bankrupted all of them at the time she wanted out."

"That leaves us with at least eight people who could have been motivated by revenge."

"Yep. And the last time Claire did this, at least according to the files, was three years ago. The company's name is Proud Yankees, and the owner was listed at the time as Barry Parsons. It's an embroidery company specializing in patriotic symbols. I'll work on getting a list of all the names together for you, but this gives you a place to start."

"You said she bought into these companies as a silent partner, but what exactly was she contributing?"

"Hard to say, but one thing's for sure, their cash flows certainly turned around. She must have had a golden touch. Look at these numbers." Cynthia took the profit and loss statement from Proud Yankees just before Claire bought in and pointed to the net loss. Then she flipped over some pages and showed Madison the numbers from just before Claire was bought out. "They'd improved but not enough to offset the amount of her buyout. It nearly bankrupted Proud Yankees. The liquid assets weren't there yet."

Not that Madison could have identified any of this from the grouping of figures in front of her. She was never good at accounting. She preferred thinking on her feet and running with clues. She'd be bored to death number crunching. What Madison did understand was what Cynthia was telling her. "That would make for good motivation. Maybe we'll be able to prove Barry Parsons was at Claire's the night of her murder. Speaking of proof, have you analyzed the condoms yet or the semen collected from Claire?"

"We're working on it, Maddy. Haven't got all the answers for you yet. But I am confident in saying that based on the quantity of sperm, there should be viable DNA. Jennifer still has to extract, process, and run it through CODIS. She's also got the swab from Claire's wound on the top of her priorities."

CODIS, or the Combined DNA Index System, is a collective database that houses DNA profiles of the United States.

"Let me know as soon as you have that list of business names together," Madison said. She put the pile of paper on the table. Cynthia had been wrong about one thing: Madison didn't need the files printed.

Terry hung up. "Dead end with Claire's main banking institution. She didn't have a safe-deposit box with them."

"Okay, well, she had to keep the original legal paperwork somewhere. We'll have to work our way around the major banks in the city and hope we get lucky. We should also get someone back at the house to look for any hidden safes."

"Do you know how long that will take?" Terry's voice held a definite whine to it.

"I'm sure you can manage it, buddy. Casanova..." She only brought out his nickname at opportune moments. He was tagged with it because his mother was a fan of Cary Grant, but instead of just naming him directly after the famous actor, he got the variation.

"Yeah, yeah."

"Let's go."

"Where now?"

"Where do you think? To see Barry Parsons."

He looked confused and she then realized he had been on with the bank at the time when she and Cynthia had been discussing Parsons. "I'll explain on the way. And I'm sure you can manage multitasking by now."

"Not like I have much of a choice."

"Oh, before you guys go," Cynthia said. "The trace under the fingernails came back as strawberry mixed with blood."

"Strawberry?"

"We had found the green tops from them in her garbage, but toxicology has confirmed that strawberries were in her stomach along with a trace amount of alcohol. Nothing that would knock her out. At most she would have been a little relaxed."

Champagne and strawberries—two bitter memories for Madison, as they brought back being engaged to a cheating loser. Of course, it was easy to say that he was a loser, but the truth was that the recollection made her both angry and hurt, leaving her with an emptiness in the pit of her stomach, the kind that came with heartache. The worst part was the man—Toby Sovereign—still wasn't completely out of her life. He was another detective who worked for the department.

She shook her thoughts and said, "Let's go." She headed for the door, but didn't hear Terry's steps behind her and looked over her shoulder. "Now."

"Coming, *Mother*." Terry laughed. "She's a few years older than I am, and look at the abuse I have to endure."

Cynthia waved him off. "What are you going to do? It's Maddy. She'll never change."

Chapter 12

"Proud Yankees isn't going to be open. You do realize that it's Saturday," Terry mumbled to her, while holding his phone to his ear. He was working on reaching out to the local banks.

Saturday. Sometimes the stark emptiness of her life would hit her. How she had gotten to this point where her life revolved around hunting down killers even on the weekends. She wasn't like other women her age who were carting a van full of kids around to soccer practice. In fact, even the thought of children made her nauseous. Surprisingly, it wasn't so much the childbirth or the resulting responsibility that came with kids, but rather the disappointment she would open herself up to. It would only be a matter of time before the father of her children let her down. Guess men were reliable for one thing.

That thought leapfrogged to Blake and what he needed to discuss with her at dinner. She replayed what he had said a million times, trying to hunt for any trace in his tone that would reveal whether it was good news or bad. And maybe it was that the conversation she'd had with him had been two days ago or her fear of being vulnerable, but the inflection in his voice changed with each playback, and she was starting to spin a negative connotation on his words. After all, there's no way it could be good news. It was too early in their relationship for him to suggest moving in together, and surely, he would know that she'd shoot that proposal down.

Maybe she needed to end the relationship now. That would solve everything before it exploded anyhow, and it would prevent Blake from embarrassing himself. And protect her heart. Toby had worked her over enough, no doubt dooming any future romance because of what he'd done to her. He had broken her heart.

"Are you going to turn?" Terry blurted out.

He tore her from her thoughts, and she realized she had almost missed the parking lot for Proud Yankees. She cranked the steering wheel and pulled into a spot. A few vehicles were in the lot.

Terry ended his call and stuffed the phone into a pocket. "Not getting anywhere with the banks today. Most of them are closed now. On Monday, I'll get started on them again if we haven't caught this bastard yet."

It was two in the afternoon, only six hours from her dinner date with Blake. She had to get it off her mind and focus on the investigation. Claire Reeves deserved as much. Maybe she should cancel the dinner.

"I don't see Parsons's Chevy." She got out of the car and slammed the door shut when her cell rang. She answered formally.

"Oh, I love it when I call your cell." Blake's voice was playful.

It made her smile. *Damn him.* Just the sound of his voice sent her into a downward spiral despite her best intentions of not getting in too deep.

"You sound so professional. It turns me on."

"I sound professional because I am professional, Blake," she fired back.

His end of the line went silent, making her feel like an arse for using the tone she had. He hadn't wronged her—at least not yet. "My mind's on a case. I'm just about to question a suspect."

"My girl's playing cop again." His smile lightened his voice.

"Yeah, that's me. *Playing* cop." She laughed.

"All right, I just wanted to let you know that I'm back in town and looking forward to tonight. We had quite the abrupt ending to our last conversation." He paused, and she sensed he was fishing for an explanation as to why she had hung up on him.

The simple answer: Hershey, the demon dog.

"I'll explain tonight," she said.

"See you at eight. You want to meet there? Or do you want me to pick you up?"

"I'll meet you there. Bye." She ended the call.

Terry was watching her with an interested expression. "That must have been lover boy."

"Oh, shut up." She punched him in the shoulder as she brushed past him. "Hurry up. We have work to do."

"So you've got yourself a hot date." And Terry wasn't going to let this go. "Are you going to wear those diamond earrings he bought you? The dangly ones?"

She wasn't going to give him the satisfaction that she'd even heard him. She kept walking.

They reached the front door of the business, but it was locked. The lights were off inside. She was just about to leave when a couple of car doors slammed shut. She hurried off in their direction to the other side of the building from where she had parked. There was another lot.

Three cars were all running; the people must have exited from a side door.

Madison approached a man in a blue ski jacket who was working at scraping ice off the windshield.

He stopped what he was doing but didn't look at them. "We're closed," he said and resumed chipping away at the ice.

Just the sound of it sent a chill up Madison's back. "Is Barry Parsons here?"

He lifted a wiper, let it slam down, and then pointed toward an old Mazda. Rust was eating away at its body, making it look like it had a rash. The car was idling and someone was behind the wheel.

"Thanks," Madison said.

"Yep."

Madison and Terry made their way to the Mazda, a woman passed them a curious glance as she drove past them and out of the lot.

Closer up, it was clear to see the person in the rusted car was Barry Parsons. She recognized him from his DMV photo. She pegged him as tipping the scales at three hundred pounds judging only from what she could see through the window. He had a head of gray hair, and his face was heavily creased. His brown eyes were beady, the bridge of his nose was very narrow, and he had two chins.

She tapped on the glass. "Stiles PD. We'd like a word with you."

He reached for the door panel and a motor whirred, but it wasn't having any effect on getting the window to lower.

"We need to talk to you," Madison repeated, adding more urgency to her voice.

But Barry still didn't make an effort to open the door. He kept pushing the window button, though.

"It's frozen shut," Terry said.

Madison glanced at him, then back to Barry. "We have questions about Claire Reeves."

Barry stopped moving. He stared straight ahead, and Madison sensed he was scheming something.

"Open your door, Mr. Parsons," she demanded.

He cast her a nervous glance and put the car into gear.

"Stop!" Madison drew her gun, held it level with his head. "Stop there!"

He gunned the gas. Ice and snow projected from under the spinning tires, and the car failed to get any traction. He held up his hand closest to the window, put the vehicle into park, and then held up both his hands.

She put her gun back in her holster. "Turn the car off and get out. Now!"

He nodded and complied. The minute his feet hit the pavement, she spun him around, pushed him against the car, and cuffed his hands behind his back. "You're coming with us."

"I didn't do it. I swear I didn't do it."

Madison rolled her eyes at Terry as they loaded him into the back of the department car. "We've never heard that before."

But, wait a minute… Do what? They hadn't told him that Claire was murdered.

Chapter 13

Barry Parsons was seated across from Madison and Terry in interrogation room one.

"You said you didn't do it," Madison began. "Do what exactly?"

"She's dead, isn't she? I heard about it on the news."

Madison scanned his eyes and that part seemed to be the truth.

Barry tapped his fingers on the table. "She was such a bitch."

Madison tossed crime scene photos across the table. "Is that why you killed her?"

"I didn't do it." He fidgeted in his chair as if he had ants crawling on his rear end.

"Then why did you try and run from us?" Madison glared at him, holding her ground. Maybe she could have this tied up in time for dinner. That would be worthy of a celebration.

"I knew how it would look given all that she had done to me."

"What did she do to you?"

Barry sniffled and wiped his nose with the back of his hand. He avoided all eye contact.

"Never mind, we'll get back to that question." They knew about the business aspect, but Madison wondered if that's all there was to the conflict between Barry and Claire.

Barry swallowed audibly. "I'm talking too much. It's just when I heard about her murder, I figured it was just a matter of time before you came after me. I thought it would take you longer."

"We're not slow, Mr. Parsons," Madison began. "We take our jobs seriously, and finding killers is our main priority."

"And I didn't do it."

"As you've said."

"Then maybe you should believe me."

"The guilty say that, Mr. Parsons. The guilty make that plea repeatedly, trying to convince themselves of their innocence."

"No. That's not the case with me." His chest rose and fell at a faster rate. Sweat glistened on his brow. "Oh God."

"Why don't you tell us where you were on Wednesday morning between two and three?" Madison leaned across the table, her arms extended, hands clasped. Her persistent gaze forced his eyes to hers.

"Sleeping."

"So someone can attest to that?"

Barry got up and started pacing on his side of the room. "No, no one can." He ran a flattened hand over his mouth.

"Sit down," Madison commanded.

Barry looked at her and glanced at Terry, who was next to Madison taking notes.

"Fine." Barry dropped into his chair again.

"You're telling me that sleeping was your alibi, but no one can verify this?"

He shook his head. "I know how this looks. I look guilty. I'd have motive to kill her—" He choked on his words. "But I couldn't kill another human being. Not even Claire." His beady eyes were full of panic.

"Tell us how you knew Claire Reeves." She knew the basics from the file, but she wanted to know more. Something in his eyes and his body language made her suspicious of his innocence. There were the obvious hesitation marks, easily explained by a nervous, inexperienced hand, one that was exacting its own revenge in a fire of emotion. "Mr. Parsons, answer the—"

"Fine." He took a labored breath. "When I met Claire, I thought she was a godsend. She came in, rescued my company, but as the saying goes, when something looks too good to be true, it usually is."

"How did she rescue your company?"

"She was really good with computers. She streamlined all our processes, brought us up to this century. We went from fifty on staff to about half because we upgraded to advanced machinery that could do the same job for less than their salaries."

This just expanded their pool of murder suspects by another twenty-five people. "We're going to need a list of everyone let go."

"Sure, I can get that for you." He made a movement as if he was about to get up again.

Madison motioned with her hand for him to remain seated. "Later. How did the partnership break up?"

"She wanted out."

"She forced you to buy her out?"

"Yes, and it wasn't like the improvements had even affected cash flow yet, at least not enough to cover her buyout. It takes years for automation changes to show on the bottom line."

"How did you feel about her forcing you to buy her out?"

He remained silent.

"Mr. Parsons?"

"I suppose it's best that I disclose everything?"

"Most definitely." Madison crossed her arms. She cast a glance at the clock, and for a moment wondered if she'd have to cancel her plans for the evening.

"We were involved personally, as well."

Barry looked at them. "As I can tell by your faces neither of you believe me." They remained quiet. "I didn't always look like this." His face turned red from anger. "But when your life turns to shit, getting fat tends to happen. The drinking, the eating, the gambling." He paused, locking eyes with Madison. "Again, I can tell you that don't believe me, Detective. Well, here's your proof." He reached into a pocket, pulled out a wallet, took out a photograph, and slid it across to Madison.

It was a picture of him with Claire—at least a portion of his current self. Madison showed it to Terry. Her inclination was to dismiss the authenticity. What you saw in a picture wasn't always the truth, and the fact he carried the picture around only testified to his attachment to Claire.

She put it back on the table and pushed it toward Barry Parsons. She didn't say a word. He picked it up and looked at it. Tears filled his eyes, and he sniffled, seemingly lost in a memory.

"They were good times. She was so beautiful." His voice faltered. "I lost my wife because of her, too." He wiped at his chubby face, trying to make the stains of tears and heartbreak disappear.

"To me, you had every reason to kill Claire. You lost everything because of her. Your wife, your business suffered, your—"

"Health. Just say what you're thinking. I'm one big, fat, ugly bastard now, and I blame her. I've spent the last few years wishing that I could go back in time. I nearly went bankrupt! I was left with only the literal shirt on my back. I had to refinance my home to help scrounge up enough money to buy her out."

"How could she force you to buy her out?"

He let out a rush of air. "It was in the contract. All stipulated in the contract." He shook his head. "Can't believe that I was such an idiot. So naive."

"The contract stipulated that should she wish to leave, you would have to buy her out, no matter when that was?"

"Yes, and pay the current market value for her share of the business." His cheeks reddened. "Which at the time, with all her damned improvements, came to over one point five million."

"One point five million?" That was the size of the one deposit in Claire's account.

"She bought in for half." He stopped talking a moment. "She used her damned charm and pocketbook to get her in the door. My wife warned me, too, but I just wouldn't listen. I was too distracted by her tight dress pants and low-cut blouses."

"We're going to need a sample of your DNA."

He sat straighter. "For what?"

"For comparison to what was found at the crime scene. Were you sleeping with Claire on Tuesday night, Mr. Parsons?"

"Hell no!" He slammed his fists on the table. "Like I told you, I was sleeping alone!"

"We can get a warrant for your DNA." Madison was on the hunt. Barry had one point five million reasons and his pride to want Claire dead. She got up and knocked on the door for an officer to come in.

"No, please," he begged. "There were more she did this to…what she did to me."

The officer looked at Madison, and she dismissed him with a wave of her hand.

"Tell us," she said. He was likely referring to the people whose names Cynthia was compiling from the USB sticks, but it was best to hear him out.

"I-I don't have names."

"You're going to have to tell me something more convincing, Mr. Parsons. We're aware there are more people she did this to."

"But do you know about the one after me?"

"How do you know about this other company?" Based on the information from the USB sticks, Barry Parsons was the most recent business partner.

"That part doesn't matter, does it?"

She hitched her shoulders. "It might."

"I followed her and confronted her with what she had done to me, how she ruined my life. She laughed." He snorted. "Can you believe that? My entire life had become a pile of shit, and she found amusement in it. Anyway, she wasn't too happy to see me. She pretty much forced me out of her house—"

"You were in her house?"

"Within the last year, yes. But, anyway, I noticed legal paperwork on her coffee table. I recognized it from before. It was the same contract as ours. I confronted her about it and asked how she could go and do what she'd done to me to someone else. My expressed concern for others was met with another arrogant laugh. I didn't even know the woman I had slept with behind my wife's back." His eyes glazed over. "My wife, she was a good woman. She didn't deserve all I put her through."

Madison's patience level was quickly reaching its limit. "And the contract…from the table?"

"I'm getting there. Now, I just caught a glimpse of a first name."

"One name? A glimpse? That's all?" She was irritated that he had dragged this ordeal out as if he had some rare jewel to offer.

Barry crossed his arms. "I would think one would be better than none?" He looked at Terry, who nodded. "Aaron."

Chapter 14

"I can't believe that idiot thinks that one name is earth-shattering news. One name, that's all?" Madison was complaining to Terry after Barry was shuffled off to have his DNA taken. "What is one name going to do for us? He doesn't even have a company name."

"It might make a difference."

"Guess we'll just run around Stiles calling out all Aarons."

"You can be very pessimistic. Has anyone told you that?"

"My mother, all the time."

"I see it made a difference."

Madison narrowed her eyes at him, and she checked her phone. There was a message. "I'm just going to check my voice mail." She dialed in; it was Cynthia. She erased it. "Time to go to the lab. Cynthia's got the names from the USB sticks ready for us."

Minutes later, they were in the lab.

"I got your message, Cyn," Madison began. "Where are they?"

"The names?"

Madison angled her head. "Yes, the names."

"She has no patience, does she?" Cynthia made the comment, looking at Terry for him to back her up.

"No ganging up on me here. List?" Madison held out her hand, flexing her fingers.

"Fine." Cynthia put the printout on the table in front of Madison. "It's compiled from newest to oldest."

Madison read it from the top down.

1. Barry Parsons
2. Simon Angle

3. Neil Bench
4. Andy Morgan
5. Laverne Tourville
6. Adrian Unger
7. Anita Smith
8. Elizabeth Windsor

"No Aaron and no Allison." Madison looked at Terry, who shrugged his shoulders.

"You'll also be happy to know that Jennifer finished extracting the samples from the condoms," Cynthia said. "I'll be running Parsons's before I leave tonight. Jennifer's backed up."

"Good."

"And if you're happy with that, then you'll be happy with what I have to say next. I have analyzed the swab from Claire's vaginal cavity." She paused, as if trying to build up the anticipation in her small audience.

"And?"

"There was viable DNA evidence there, but—" she held up a finger, licked her lips, and smiled again "—it didn't match DNA from any of the condoms."

"Claire was with two men the night she…"

"According to forensic evidence."

"So there were two men—one she had sex with using a condom and another she hadn't." Madison gnawed on that. "She wasn't raped…or at least Richards concluded sex was consensual. What would make her do that?"

"She trusted the one more than the other," Cynthia suggested. "And it was *condoms*, not *a* condom."

"All the ones from her wastebasket were from one guy?"

Cynthia nodded slowly. "I'd like to think for a period of time. Not one night."

Madison paused, giving more thought to how Claire used protection with one partner and not with the other. "The one encounter could have been spontaneous."

"So, Mr. Condom," Terry said, warranting a look from both women, "woke up to find Claire grinding on some other man, got pissed off, and killed her?"

"Possible, I suppose. But why not kill the man, too?"

Terry's head snapped in Madison's direction. "Don't you have a date to get to?"

"We're working here."

"A date?" A smirk tugged the corners of Cynthia's mouth. "Is it with Blake again?"

Madison wanted to tune them both out, hum and bounce like a child refusing to heed a parent's direction.

"Oh, it's getting serious," Cynthia said. "Look at her. Is she blushing?"

"It's not getting serious."

"You sound cranky enough to indicate that it is."

"I can't leave in the middle of the investigation, not at a time like this."

"Parsons has volunteered his DNA. It's a waiting game there," Terry offered.

Madison tried to catch a look at the time on the wall, hoping that neither Terry nor Cynthia would notice.

"She wants to go." Cynthia laughed.

"You guys are like children on the school ground."

"You just hate the fact that we're right," Terry said.

"You're not—"

"Yes, we are." Cynthia clipped right to the point. "It's getting more serious, and you're frightened about it."

She felt like she was being backed into a corner with both of them intent on bullying the answer out of her. It wasn't going to happen, not today and not like this. She looked at the clock again. "I'm only going because one should honor their commitments."

Terry and Cynthia were both smiling. They looked like they had won, whatever it was they could win with this. Nonetheless, they accomplished something, and Madison didn't like that realization. They were getting too close to the truth—and to her real feelings.

She pushed between the two of them and left the lab. She called out over her shoulder, "Call as soon as you get the DNA results back on Parsons!"

Chapter 15

Madison was still fuming when she walked into Piccolo Italia. She was an adult and had the right to have feelings for someone. It didn't mean she was going to marry Blake and bear his children.

"Right this way." A dark-haired maître d' in a tuxedo suggested she follow him.

The restaurant, as always, smelled delicious and successfully roused her underlying hunger. Garlic, onion, basil, and oregano filled the air along with freshly baked bread, pasta dishes, and steaming seafood.

The tables were set apart to provide privacy, and the dimly lit space created an intimate ambiance. The drapes and walls were a rich burgundy and a candle centerpiece burned on each table. Dean Martin crooned in Italian over speakers set at a low volume.

Blake was tucked into their regular corner. They had eaten here more than she dared to count, and every time they were, they sat at this table. She didn't know if she admired this regular pattern, viewing it as a reliable trait or as evidence of a predictable personality. If she continued in this relationship, would there be any surprises in store for her? Or would they be here years down the road, still huddled into this familiar corner of Piccolo Italia?

Years down the road? That thought scared her. Her heart was being pulled away from her, and she had to put an end to it before she ended up heartbroken.

Blake rose to greet her with a hug and a kiss on the cheek.

The maître d' pulled the chair out for her. "Miss, may I pour you a glass of wine?" He referred to the bottle of red on the table. Blake already had some in his glass.

She nodded, and the maître d' poured her a glass and backed away from the table. The potent aroma of the wine found its way over the smells of food.

"Hope you don't mind that I started without you." He pinched two fingers around the stem of his glass. "You were running a little late."

Of course he'd point that out. He was a stickler for punctuality. She was surprised that he hadn't just greeted her with, *About time you got here.*

She could tell him all about the hellish week she'd been having, how she had a long list of suspects and should be chasing them instead of being here. She could have told him about what she'd found when she went home to change: a big mess in Hershey's kennel. But somehow all of that would come across as if she had a need to defend herself.

Blake reached out a hand for hers, careful not to upset the burning candle. A corner of his lips curved upward. "You must have put in extra effort tonight. You're absolutely beautiful."

"But not to imply that I'm not other times?"

"Of course not."

"Thank you, then." She smiled modestly. There was something in his eyes—a subtle vulnerability? But instead of being pushed back, she found herself drawn closer. *How was it he had the power to alter her mood?* She could have her mind set to do something and then, just the way he'd say something or the way he'd study her face, her commitment to a thought was lost. Maybe his ability to manipulate her was a skill that crossed over from his profession as a defense lawyer.

"You're always beautiful, my girl."

He had this way of calling her "my girl" that made her gush. She wished she could stop it. How infuriating for a woman like her—a professional, independent woman who didn't need a man to complete her life. "I have a dog now." The words burst out, catching her off guard.

"A dog?" He rubbed his thumb mindlessly along the side of her hand. "Why?" He took a draw on his wine.

She smiled. "It was a gift."

He laughed. "Let me guess. Terry's responsible?"

"You got it." She ran her fingers along the base of her glass. "He thought I needed more in my life. Don't really know what he was thinking…if he was thinking." She shook her head. "Let's just say the whole thing is sort of a nightmare right now."

He pointed at her ears. "My gift came out ahead?"

Her hands instinctively went to both ears, and she squeezed on the diamond, dangling earrings that adorned them. "Definitely." She took a large mouthful of wine. "Think I'll have a bit of this tonight, if you don't mind." She held her glass, lightly rocking it side to side.

He grinned with boyish allure. "Not a problem at all. We can continue at your place."

"Uh-huh. You just want to have your way with me." She laughed. The little bit of wine she'd had already seemed to be affecting her stance, her earlier decision to have space. God, she was all over the place. She just needed to make a clean break… Oddly, her mind skipped back to Hershey. "You might not like what you find at my place."

"Really? I've always liked it in the past."

"Oh shut up." She was far too comfortable with him. It was as if she had known him forever. She talked to him like a close friend, the same way she talked to Terry. It made her nervous. Was she crazy to consider breaking up with him?

"Are you ready to order?" The waiter came to the table, a long cloth draped over an arm, a black notepad in his left hand, a pen ready in his right.

"The usual," she said to Blake.

Blake placed their orders, and as she listened to him rhyme off her desire, her gut clenched. She had thought about Blake being predictable, but here she was having the same meal again. Was she becoming that way because of him? Were they getting settled already? And was she losing her identity? She'd apparently lost the ability to place her own order.

JUSTIFIED

After the waiter left, Blake reached for her hand again, and she felt a ball of nausea tighten in her stomach when he touched her.

"As I mentioned on the phone, I have something important that I want to discuss with you—"

"Blake, you know I'm not into all that."

His eyes darkened and she guessed he didn't like that she'd interrupted him, but she didn't regret doing so. She was the other half of this relationship, and she had the right to speak, too. She continued. "I just have so much going on, and with this new case—" She fell silent, knowing she was prolonging the inevitable. Everything good had to come to an end, right? And it might as well be on her terms. "I don't think we should—"

"What? Get married," he blurted out.

She was thankful she hadn't chosen that moment to sip her wine. She nearly choked on her own saliva from the depth of the swallow.

Blake laughed heartily. His eyes looked past her, over her shoulders, before resetting to her gaze. "I'm not ready for marriage, either, crazy girl."

His reaction made her feel foolish. She hadn't said married, he had. Either way, she needed to end things before there wasn't any redemption left for her. Her last desire was for her emotions to occupy all her thoughts and dictate her next step. She had to be strong, but she just didn't care for the way he was coming across. Maybe he was thinking the same thing as her. "You think we should end this?" she asked.

"Have you fallen down and hit your head?" He was still smiling. At least he seemed to find amusement in her wild guesses.

Maybe he's the crazy one.

"It must have been a long, hard week without me," he cooed. He squeezed her hand, and she became painfully aware that despite her brave thoughts of independence, she hadn't pulled her hand away. He kept his eyes on hers. "I think we should take this relationship to the next level—" He stopped abruptly, holding up a hand to silence her. "Not marriage, but I think we should be committed to each other. I think they're calling it *exclusive* these days."

Committed to each other... Exclusive... Commitment hadn't worked out so well for her in the past. She swallowed roughly.

"Maddy?" he prompted.

Her heart wanted to jump right in, but her logic reined her back. "No."

"No?"

"No." She shook her head, pulled her hand back, and glanced over at another couple. The man must have just proposed, because the woman was holding up her left hand and admiring a diamond ring on her finger. Madison looked back at Blake.

"I thought that's what you'd want." His tone was bitter.

"You suggested a committed relationship because you thought that was what *I'd* want? How does that work exactly? I commit to you. You give your promise to me. Then what?" Blake didn't know about Toby, about the broken engagement, about her shattered belief in happily ever after. And she refused to get into that right now.

"This isn't how I saw tonight going." He pressed the wine glass to his lips. If he took a draw, it was small. "Listen to me, Maddy—"

"No." He was trying to manipulate things again, maneuver them in such a way that he'd have a sure thing. He didn't want to commit to her; he felt like she wanted him to. What the hell was that?

He exhaled loudly. "Let me start over."

She waved for him to continue.

"It came out wrong from the start, but maybe if you hadn't interrupted me…"

She felt a surge of rage, of defense, flash through her, but she remained silent.

"Sorry," he said, obviously having sensed her emotion. "Maybe I'm rushing things."

The dejection that radiated off him stabbed her with some regret. He had intended to take their relationship to the next level, and maybe most women would dream of this, but she was afraid to be one of them again. Blake in particular was a successful defense attorney, had money, had good looks, and could easily have a harem of women. So why was he willing to make a commitment to her?

A small twitch was pulsing in his cheeks. He was angry now, and she didn't want the night to end like this.

"I'm happy you're back." She feigned a smile and attempted to redirect the conversation. Maybe this would be a good test. If he was committed to her in his heart, he would fight for her. He wouldn't let one argument or disagreement stand in his way.

It seemed like minutes passed before his shoulders relaxed. "Yeah, I missed you, too." He smiled at her, but it didn't touch his eyes, and she knew that something had changed.

Chapter 16

Blake snored beside Madison. They had gone back to her apartment after dinner. Blame it on the wine.

Hershey had welcomed the newcomer with jumping and barking and a gift in the kennel. She was going to have to send him for obedience training and to be housebroken.

Blake hadn't seemed to mind joining Madison and Hershey outside as Hershey sniffed and did his business again. It was funny because she never took Blake for an animal person, but he and Hershey seemed to have a connection. Blake had even picked up Hershey's mess and disposed of it in the garbage can in front of the building.

"That was above and beyond," she had said, the wine making her easygoing and carefree.

"That's just the kind of man I am." He had kissed her then.

She had pulled back and said, "I bet you say that to all the women."

That hadn't gone over well, but thankfully, by the time they'd gotten back upstairs and started making out; any ugliness from the evening had disappeared. They'd had sex on her couch, and nearly passed out from both exhaustion and alcohol but managed to drag themselves to her bedroom. It was a choppy night of sleep, though, because whenever their bare legs touched, they went at it again.

The memories of last night made her gut wrench in longing and made her take a deep breath, but she had an investigation to get back to. Not that she'd had much private time since she'd met Blake for dinner, but she had managed to squeeze a call in to Terry and Cynthia. Unfortunately, she'd been funneled to both their voice mails.

Blake stirred beside her and rolled to face her. "Good morning, my girl."

Somehow hearing him say "my girl" this morning struck her differently. Maybe more possessively. "Morning."

He reached over and brushed a hand along her cheek. "So beautiful." He moved closer, put an arm around her, and kissed her nose.

She heard a strangely familiar sound, but the morning-after haze that came with drinking too much and a late night wasn't helping her figure out what the noise was. It took a while for it to register that it was Hershey whining. But he sounded closer than the kennel, which was in the living area.

"Hershey?" She felt something at the side of the bed. It scared the shit out of her, and her heart was beating rapidly. She looked down to see Hershey pawing at the bed frame.

"See? Even he wants in bed with you." Blake smiled like a devil that got his way and would again and again.

"Uh-huh." Madison slapped his exposed shoulder. Then she realized something. "He wasn't put in his kennel last night." Panic struck her at the mess he would have likely made. She bolted upright.

"What is it?" he asked.

"Oh, I can't believe we didn't put him in there." She bounded from the bed.

"Nice view."

She was naked and turned to face him. "Don't even think about it."

"Too late."

She threw a pillow at him, and felt a pang of guilt. She didn't have time to fool around. It was time to go. She had suspects to run down, questions to ask, and answers to get.

She stopped moving, the thought of a mess no longer on the top of her priority list. Screw it. If Hershey had stained the hardwood, she'd find a way to cover it up. She rifled through her drawers and pulled out a pair of jeans and a sweater.

"What are you doing? Come back to bed." Blake splayed a hand on her side of the bed.

"Nope. I'm having a shower."

"That sounds like fun."

She turned, pointing a finger at Blake. "You stay there."

He bounded up from the bed and came over to her. "Come on, one more time." He took her mouth.

His lips tasted delicious, like an Italian entrée themselves. She pulled back and looked into his eyes. "You of all people should understand that the job comes first."

"It's Sunday. What can you do today?"

"Catch a killer."

He laughed. "Catch a killer? You know how you sound sometimes?"

"Like a committed cop?"

"Or one that should be—"

"Funny." She tossed another pillow at him.

Blake caught it and flung it onto the bed, and then saluted her. "Dum da dum. Here comes the caped crusader, out to save the world."

"Shut up." She was smiling.

"Fine. Get going." He dropped back onto the bed, rolled over, and mumbled something into the pillow. He dragged himself up again. "Guess I've gotta go, too?"

"Don't worry about it. When you're ready to leave, just lock the door on the way out."

"I'll take care of Hershey."

"Really?" Had she heard him right?

"I'll take him out as long as I can come back up and get more sleep."

"Sure." Since he liked taking care of a dog more than she did, maybe he could take Hershey with him.

"I'll need a key, though. You know if I'm back up before you're finished in that shower…all alone."

"Cut it out." She smacked his arm. "And fine, I'll give you a spare, but don't get any ideas."

"You can't control those." He pulled her to him again.

TERRY JOINED MADISON IN THE department sedan. He was holding a file folder.

Madison turned the key in the ignition. "Was your cell phone off?"

"I didn't answer it." Terry fastened his seat belt.

"The department issued you a phone for a reason, Terry."

"Yes, and they also provided it with a caller identity service." The hint of a smile loomed in the corners of his mouth.

"Do we have the DNA results from comparing Barry Parsons's to the crime scene profiles?"

"You're just all work, aren't you? How was the date with lover boy?"

"Terry. The case," she ground out.

"You have something against small talk?"

"Are we married?" Madison let out a giggle, but he wasn't laughing.

"You've pointed it out to me before that we're partners and that we should talk openly."

"All right, if you want me to be completely honest with you…"

"I do."

"Hershey—"

"Not the dog. Blake! How did it go?"

"It's not open for discussion."

"You love him, don't—"

She glared at him. "I'm warning you."

Terry chuckled. "I'm talking about Hershey now, but we can talk about Blake if you want. You love him—"

"The dog is fine."

Terry's laugh transformed into a knowing smile.

"What?"

"Nothing." A few seconds passed, and Terry said, "I knew he'd grow on you. I'm not talking about Blake before you hit me. Hershey."

"I'm glad you clarified, as you seem to be bouncing back and forth between the two."

"It's fun and exciting having a dog around, isn't it? They make a difference."

They make a difference, all right. She was going home and cleaning up feces and urine every day and taking him out in the bitter night air.

Terry was looking at her with enlarged eyes and a goofy grin. If he only knew the truth about how she felt about Hershey, that smile would fade. Maybe she'd adjust to having a dog… Maybe.

"Yeah, he's good." She pulled out on her seat belt and turned the key. She hoped that would be enough to cast Terry's interest back to the case and away from his other curiosity, which kept gravitating to her relationship with Blake. "I've answered your questions. What about the DNA results?"

"Parsons was not a match."

"It's never that easy."

"He wasn't with Claire the night she died. At least not sexually. His DNA wasn't a match to either the condoms or the vaginal swab. We have nothing to put him at her house, either."

She pointed to the folder on his lap. "What's that?"

"Oh, it's just the list of Claire's former business partners."

"The one before Parsons was Simon Angle, I believe." She had memorized the list from studying it the one time in the lab, but she leaned over to visually confirm it.

Terry didn't move to open the folder. "Yeah, and I got all the addresses last night after you left. The rest of us didn't have the luxury of taking off with lover boy."

"You jealous, Grant? Blake's the man you see yourself with?" She smirked.

"Shut up, Knight."

"Oh, original comeback."

"Actually there's something you should know about Simon." Terry had gone back to business.

"And what's that?"

"According to his file, his wife reported him missing since Wednesday."

Her eyes shot to his, but her foot remained pressed down on the gas pedal. Someone's horn blared at her, but she didn't care. "That's the morning Claire was killed."

The neighborhood was full of neglected two-story houses dating back nearly a century. Porches were dilapidated, making one even leery of stepping a toe on them due to the possibility of breaking through. But the address on file for Simon Angle took them to a street that was a blend of run-down houses and those in the process of renovation. Angle's house fell into the latter category.

The home was brick with a front porch that seemed to have recently been redone, if the fresh coat of paint was any indication. But its brick foundation was chipped and discolored, begging for attention.

Madison and Terry went to the front door and rang the bell. It was one of those wireless kinds that were powered by batteries.

Footfalls behind the door were getting louder, and the door opened to a woman of average height, average weight, average looks. If one had to grasp for a single unique feature, it could possibly be her piercing hazel eyes.

"Regina Angle?" Madison curled her lips. Saying the woman's name almost sounded dirty, like a James Bond girl or something, not that she resembled any Bond girl who'd ever graced the screen.

The woman eyed them suspiciously, the way one would eye a bill collector for a utility service provider. One of her hands stayed braced on the door, ready to slam it. "Who's asking?"

"Detective Knight with Stiles PD."

Regina slid her jaw back and forth a couple times, keeping her eyes on them. "Yeah, I'm Regina. Are you here about Simon?" She didn't sound too worried about what they might have to tell her.

"Yes. We'd like to come in."

"Whatever." Regina motioned them inside the house.

The house smelled of cheap cigarettes and a cat's litter box that was in desperate need of cleaning. As they moved further into the house, Madison had to work at blocking out the stench. It was potent enough to sustain hang time.

"Do you have someplace we could sit?" Madison asked hesitantly. Regina obviously wasn't Martha Stewart, and Madison could picture soiled furniture with crumbs in every crevice.

Regina nodded and led them through French doors to the right of the entry and into a living area. The floors were wood laminate, yet the space still held the original charm that came with an older home. The room had wide baseboards and a ceiling that was at least nine feet high with wood beams that ran the width of the room.

Regina directed Madison and Terry to sit on a faded, pastel floral couch. Balls of matted cat hair sat on top of the cushions. Madison was sorry that she had asked Regina if there was a place to sit. Maybe she'd just remain standing.

"Sorry, it's not Martha Stewart's house here." The sincerity of the apology fell short, but Regina must have read Madison's mind. Regina sat on a couch chair, stretched her neck to the side, and skewed her jaw. "Did you find his body?"

Why would she assume her husband was dead? "Is there one to find?"

Silence.

Madison looked at the couch, considered sitting down, but cringed as she plucked some hair clusters and released them over the floor. Nope, she'd remain standing. "We're not here with news of your husband's whereabouts or wellbeing, but we're hoping you can help us."

Regina grabbed a cigarette pack from a table next to her, pulled one out, and lit up. She crossed her legs. "That's too damn bad, because when I find him, his ass is gonna be wishin' it was dead. That dirty motherf—"

"We're not here to upset you, Mrs. Angle," Terry interjected, saving himself from Regina's foul mouth.

"I prefer Miss Melor, thank you. Maiden name." She sucked in on the stick again, her lips pursing around it with a strong suction. "What are you, religious or something? You don't like swearing. That much is obvious."

"Let's just say I don't like it," Terry grunted.

Regina tapped the ash from her cigarette onto a plate that was on the table. "Why are you here if it's not to tell me you found him?"

"You reported him missing since Wednesday of last—"

"I'm well aware."

Madison clenched her teeth, hating to be interrupted. "When was the last time you saw him?"

Regina clucked her tongue. "Not for a month, and the bastard—oh, sorry—" Regina glanced at Terry "—He owes me alimony."

"Alimony? You're divorced?"

"We're separated. But there's still certain expenses that are left in want when there's no second income."

There was just something in Regina's tone that told Madison kids might be involved. "Do you two have children?"

"Yes. Dee. She's fifteen and thinks she's knows damn everything. If I gave my momma half the grief she gives me, I would've been cuffed on the side of the head." She paused a moment and wiped her mouth slowly with the back of her hand. "She's over at a girlfriend's right now, thank goodness. Cops show up and she flips."

Madison was curious what Dee was involved in and just how often the cops came around. But that was something she could look up later if she wanted to know. "So, if you hadn't seen him in a month, why report him missing last week?"

Regina extended an arm, stretched out her fingers, and looked at the back of her hand. An avoidance tactic.

"You needed your check," Madison concluded.

Regina snubbed out the cigarette butt, twisting it in the ashtray until it crumbled to ash. "I tried reaching him for a week before that but nothin'. His roommate hadn't heard from him, either—"

"What's his roommate's name, and do you know when he last saw him?"

"Jim. He said Simon was picking up some skank, but I don't remember if he mentioned when." Regina tapped more ash on the plate. "I'm supposed to be quitting"—she held up the cigarette perched between her fingers—"but when I think about that guy… It's amazing I don't gravitate to something much stronger."

"Have you ever heard of a Claire Reeves?" Terry asked.

Regina stopped in the middle of taking a drag; her thin cheeks were left concave and her eyes snapped to Madison's. "Yes, I know her. She was murdered recently." She let the smoke filter out of her nose. "But if you're thinking Simon is behind it, there is no way— Wait, a minute, that's why you're really here. You think he's guilty. You think—"

"We know that your husband had a company, Razor Industries, and that Claire—"

"That bitch destroyed everything," Regina interrupted again. "Wiped us out."

"So you'd both have motive," Madison said matter-of-factly.

"No way! I didn't do it. I can't go to jail! Fuck, I'll lose my job, my house, my daughter."

Madison liked how she left the daughter until last.

Regina continued. "Why the hell would I throw my life away over that trash? Please tell me." The volume and strength in her voice diluted as she spoke. Her energy got a strange edge to it, as if she was withholding something.

"You just told us that she destroyed everything." Madison hoped to provoke a reaction that would tell them more.

Regina took a long drag, her hand trembling.

"If you know something, you need to tell us."

Regina let out a puff of smoke. "He said that if he ever saw her again, she was a dead woman."

"Let me get this right: your husband, who has a solid motive, spoke threatening words about Claire's well-being and goes missing around the same time as her murder," Madison began. "We're going to need to know where he was staying. You said his roommate was Jim? We'll also need his last name and address."

Chapter 17

Madison pulled the department car to the curb in front of another two-story century home, but this one had been converted into a duplex that was split down the middle so that each rental unit had two floors. The eaves troughs were worn with age and the wood fascia was in disrepair. They were probably a heavy snowfall away from coming down. Even from this vantage point, the porch boards appeared to be rotted. They were likely one heavyweight away from caving in.

"Is this the place?" Madison looked over at Terry, who held a jagged piece of paper on which Regina had eagerly scribbled down the information.

"This is it. Unit B."

"Okay, here we go again." Madison reached for the door handle.

"Wish we could do this another time."

"Why?"

"Because it's Sunday evening." Terry tapped the dash where the display read 5:15. It was already dark out. One had to love winter. "Is there something else you'd rather be doing?"

"We have a job to do, Terry, and Claire deserves justice."

"The roommate likely hasn't seen Simon since he went missing, either," he griped.

Madison steadied her eye contact. "If you're serious, then go home. I can handle this without you." She didn't make any movement to put the car into gear.

"I can see you're really sincere in your offering."

"Come on, Terry, this Simon guy could be the killer. Maybe something this Jim guy says will lead us to him."

Terry put his elbow on the window ledge and rested his head in his hand.

"Or Aaron?" She pulled out the name of Claire's last alleged business partner. "I know that name excites you."

"Going to steal a line from your speech: oh shut up."

She played the power of silence.

He let out a deep breath. "Okay, let's get this over with."

"That's the attitude, buddy." She got out of the car.

"You could be home with Hershey right now."

She laughed and tucked her head inside the vehicle. "You're going to need to get out of the car."

"Fine."

"Okay, here goes," she said, taking one cautious step onto the porch.

They reached the door and her cell rang. "Why does it ring when I don't want it to?"

"You never want it to ring."

"That's not true." She glanced at the caller's identity—it was Cynthia. She answered. "What are you doing at the lab today?"

"Trying to find a killer."

One thing that attracted her to Cynthia as a friend was her dedication to the job.

Cynthia continued. "No doubt you're on the street working, dragging Terry along behind you."

Madison glanced over at her partner and snickered.

What? he mouthed.

"Yeah, we're working. Terry's happy to be making a difference." She tossed him a cheesy grin. "Must be something good for you to call."

"The murder weapon used to kill Claire was a hunting knife," Cynthia began. "Specifically, a Bowie. I'll send a photo of what they look like to your phone."

A vibration ran through the porch's floorboards, and then the doorknob started turning.

"Thanks, Cyn. I've gotta go."

"Why doesn't that surprise me?"

Madison ended the call even though Cynthia had started to say something, but the door was open now, and a man, who appeared to be in his midfifties, was standing there. He was wearing plaid boxers with a plain white T-shirt. The entry was dimly lit, obscuring his facial features.

Madison clipped her phone to her waist.

"Whatcha want?" He put his arm against the door, displaying a muscled arm with a rash of darkened tattoos.

"Are you Jim Sears?" Terry asked.

"What's it to ya?" He moved closer toward them, as if trying to intimidate them with his size.

"Simon Angle." Madison stepped forward, asserting a strong stance.

"What about him?"

"Let us in, and we'll tell you," Madison responded.

"Fine." Jim let Madison and Terry inside and directed them to a spotless living room.

Each of them took a seat.

"What is it?" Jim had less patience than her.

"We think that your roommate, Simon—" Madison added his name in case Jim had more than one "—may be involved in the murder of a woman."

"There's no way that guy would have killed anyone." Jim stifled a laugh. "It's Regina that told you that, isn't it? The lady's crazy."

"What makes you so certain Simon wouldn't kill someone?" Terry asked.

Jim glanced at Terry and then gestured toward a cat that was curled up on a pillow in the corner of the room. "The guy would go out of his way to help strays, for goodness sake."

Unlike Regina, this bachelor placed importance on cleanliness. Madison wouldn't even have guessed a cat lived here. In her experience, most cat people's homes—even if it was subtle—smelled like a litter box. Then the thought occurred to her: was the same true for those who owned dogs? Wonderful…

"As you can see," Jim began, "I'm kind of stuck with it now."

"Did Mr. Angle hunt?" Unlikely given his soft spot for animals, but she had to ask.

Jim waved off her question.

"That's a no?" *Just to verify…*

"That's a no. At least when it came to animals. But women? That's another story. He basically hunts them. He has a way with them. Maybe it's those puppy eyes of his, I dunno. I'm not a woman. The last time I saw him he was picking someone up."

"And when was that?"

"Over two weeks ago now. I still can't believe that Regina actually reported him missing. She came here flipping out, telling me that I had to let her know where he was." He shook his head. "Stupid, jealous woman."

Jealousy was an all-too-common motive for murder. Maybe Regina had killed Claire over her ruined marriage and fall in economic status. She could have hired someone to do it, knowing the evidence would lean toward a man. "I take it that you don't agree with the missing persons report?"

He let out a puff of air. "Well, the guy owes me money, owes the bitch."

Terry's body stiffened beside Madison.

Jim noticed. "Excuse my language. Anyway, she said he owed her alimony. Why, I have no idea, because they're not divorced. I'd make her take me to court. But the fact that Simon would give her money is just another display of how nice the guy could be."

Could be? Up until that minute slip, Jim seemed to be singing Simon's praises. "He wasn't always a pleasant person to be around?"

Silence.

"Did he have a temper?" Madison pressed.

"He'd been handed a shitty life." He glanced at Terry "Again, I apologize for the language. But Simon would just get real down some days. He'd throw things. He broke a vase that had been in my family for years." He rubbed his jaw and dropped his hand. "In answer to your question, yes, he could have a temper."

"So it is possible that he could have killed someone—"

Jim was shaking his head. "I ain't no friend with a killer. I'd know."

"You could be surprised," she stated somberly. "Do you have any idea how we can reach him?"

"His cell is no longer in service." Jim shared looks with each of them. "I know where he is, though. And I'll tell you if you promise not to tell that wife of his."

MADISON AND TERRY STEPPED OUT of Jim Sears's house and were greeted with cold air and a blanket of white. Snow was falling in large flakes at a fast rate.

"Great. It's a winter wonderland out here." Sarcasm drenched Terry's words.

"Do you have to complain about everything?"

He glowered at her.

She shrugged it off. "So Jim knows where Simon is, but still lets the wife report him missing?"

Terry opened his door. "You can't control everyone."

"He could have told her where to go."

"He probably did." Terry smirked.

She got in the car and twisted the key in the ignition. The engine grinded its protest that it was cold but ended up turning over. She put the wipers on to clear the snow. It worked, for the most part, but it was too deep. One of them—Terry—was going to have to wipe the windshield.

Madison faced her partner and batted her eyelashes.

"Fine." Terry got out of the car, obviously getting her implication.

About a minute later, he was back in the car yawning.

"Hang in there," she said, putting the car into gear.

"What do you mean by that?"

"We're going to the address Jim Sears just gave us for Simon." The trick was in presenting it as a statement and not like their next step was up for discussion.

"Urgh! I thought we'd be calling it a night."

"Are you being serious? We're possibly *this* close to catching the killer." She pictured herself pinching her fingers together and silently cursed her mother for the basketful of clichés she apparently inherited against her will, which included both phrases and mannerisms. "We have no choice, Terry."

"We always have a choice, Maddy, and I choose to let it rest 'til morning."

"You would."

"What the heck is that supposed to mean?"

Her eyes were trained on the road. It was getting slicker as time passed, and people were driving like old women on a Sunday. At this rate, they'd be a while getting to their destination.

"Never mind," she said. "I'll drop you off, and I'll take care of it myself. Like I always do."

"Where did that come from?"

She avoided eye contact.

"You're the one who sent me home on Christmas Eve. You told me to spend it with Annabelle. If I knew you were going to hold it over my—"

"This isn't about that." Okay, maybe a little, but she sometimes felt like solving cases meant more to her.

"Oh, really? What's this about, then?"

"Don't worry about it."

"Nice." Terry let out a rush of air.

If he thought she was going to smooth things over with him, he'd be waiting a while. What made him think she enjoyed driving on the slippery streets through the city on the hunt for some guy that might not even be there?

"Come on, Madison. Go home to Hershey. I can hear him whining from here."

"Kind of hard to hear his whining over yours."

"Hardy har."

It might have come out as a snappy comeback but she'd meant it… "We need to make this one last stop. It's our job, and we owe that much to Claire."

Terry muttered something as he turned to peer out the passenger window.

The rest of the drive was slow and quiet. When she eyed the house number she was looking for, though, she said, "We're here."

Terry got out of the car without saying anything.

"You don't like the job anymore?" she asked.

"It's not that I don't like the—"

"Most days you try and dodge work. There's always something more important going on."

"I'm not getting into it."

"What? The fact that you're married and I'm not?"

"Let's just see if Simon's here."

"Fine." She trudged through the fresh snow on the front walkway, which was a good three inches. Flakes were sticking to her eyelashes.

An inside light came on and a woman wrapped in a wool sweater opened the door. "Officers?" Her frame was thin, her facial features sharp, and she had a turned-up nose.

"We're looking for Simon Angle," Madison said.

Her eyes narrowed, and she wrapped her arms around herself. "Who?"

"We were told he was staying here for a bit."

"Simon? I don't know anyone by that name. I did have a guy staying here recently, but he's gone now."

Had Jim provided this address to mislead them? But that wouldn't make sense, as he'd have to know they would be headed right back to him. Madison ran with a gut feeling and brought up Simon's DMV photograph on her phone. She held it out so the woman could see the screen.

She screwed up her face. "That's the guy who was here, but I know him as Bob."

Simon was using an alias; what was that about?

"When did he stay with you?" Terry asked.

"A couple weeks ago, for about a week."

Madison put her phone back in her coat pocket. "Do you know where he went?"

"Think he was sniffing after some slut with blond hair. Beyond that, I can't help you."

Chapter 18

By the time Madison dropped Terry off at the police station, the roads had become hazardous. Warnings were aired over the radio cautioning people to stay in unless they had to go out.

Madison pressed the brake at a four-way stop and skidded a bit into the intersection. She turned right and was thankful to see that a plow was in front of her. At least it had cleared the street and laid down sand in its wake, but its blinking lights were hypnotizing, and her mind went to Simon Angle.

It was quite possible that Simon wasn't even the killer. As his roommate had said, Simon liked animals and rescued strays. Was it possible for a person like that to escalate to murdering another person? But then again, Simon did have a temper and a shitty life. Had that on top of Claire destroying him been enough to serve as motivation?

Her phone rang, and the screen lit up the interior of the car, nearly blinding her. She didn't pull over but pressed the button to answer on speaker.

"Hey. Where are you?" It was her sister Chelsea. "Are you okay? I've been having a hard time reaching you."

"You're calling my work cell." She preferred it be kept for business purposes only. For a moment, she felt the hypocrisy, as that thought never entered her mind when it came to Blake.

"Like I said, I've been trying to reach you. I left a message at your apartment last night. And I tried it just now, figuring you'd be home on a Sunday—"

"I didn't check my messages, and I'm working a case," she blurted out.

"You're always working on one, M. You need a break." Her younger sister's voice didn't condemn or judge her lifestyle, it only conveyed honest concern.

"Seems to me you say that a lot."

"Seems to me you don't listen."

"I'm driving in a snowstorm right now. I'll call you once I get in."

"Sure you will. I can sense a brush-off. Besides, you have company waiting for you."

"Company?" Blake should have left hours ago.

"A man answered when I called just before now. He's the one who told me to try your cell."

Crap! It was Blake. What was he still doing there?

Chelsea continued, "He said you guys have been seeing each other for months. I think he bought the act I put on about having heard of him. Why haven't you mentioned him to me? He sounded pretty decent."

Madison preferred her personal life to be just that. "I've got to go." She snapped her cell shut before her sister could say another word.

Her mind was a whirlwind of the personal and professional. She couldn't do her job properly if her mind wasn't entirely focused on it. But how could she balance them? The truth was, her relationship with Blake was out of hand and taking up too much of her energy. Just the thought of going to her apartment and finding Blake made her temperature rise—and not in a good way. And what was it that bothered her so much about it? She couldn't even narrow it down. All she knew was her first reaction was one of anger.

Twenty minutes later, she was riding the elevator up to her floor. Five stories to calm herself down. It dinged its arrival and she unloaded, taking a deep breath. The moment of truth. She walked down the hall to her door and turned the knob. It was locked. Okay, maybe this was a good sign. Maybe after taking Chelsea's call, he'd made a run for it. Why answer her phone in the first place, though? Wasn't that kind of rude?

She unlocked the door and entered her apartment. Her place was open concept. Once through the door, a small dining table was to the right. Her L-shaped kitchen was on the left; a counter with stools served to separate that space from her living room.

Her table had a single candle lit in front of a place setting complete with a wineglass. A smell hit her nose… Tuna casserole?

She looked toward Blake, who was sitting on her couch drinking a beer and watching a football game.

"Hey, beautiful. Welcome home." He toasted her with the bottle. His other hand held a twisted rope which Hershey was busy trying to pull away from him.

Blake was awfully comfortable on *her* couch, in *her* apartment…

Had she fallen into an alternate reality like characters often did in science fiction? She looked around her apartment. This was her place, right? Framed photographs on the walls and the wilting potted plants testified to that. Hershey, too, not that he seemed to notice she was home.

She unwound her scarf and put it on a hook.

"Hope you don't mind that I ate without you. Left yours in the oven on low up until an hour ago when I turned it off. It's still sitting in there, but it might need to be warmed up." His gaze went back to the TV.

He had obviously gone to a lot of trouble, but why? She turned her back on him to hang up her coat and stared at the wall hoping to derive some sort of miraculous insight on how she should handle this situation. She spun around. "What are you do—"

"I thought you'd be hungry when you got in." He rose from the couch and tossed the rope for Hershey, who bounded after it.

"It's eight thirty at night. What are you doing here?" She could hear the strain in her own voice.

He put his arms around her…not letting go of the beer, of course. The chilled bottle touched her wrist, and it jarred her memory. She didn't have beer when she'd left this morning. In fact, she never bought the stuff because she didn't care for the flavor.

She stepped back from him. "Where did you get the beer?"

Blake kissed her on the cheek and moved toward the oven.

Inside her head, she was screaming. "You're going to ignore me?"

"I think the answer is obvious," he stated matter-of-factly. He turned to face her and added, "I'm guessing you're not happy to see me here." He didn't sound disappointed or apologetic.

"I didn't expect—"

"I can leave if you like." Still no show of emotion.

She couldn't look at him anymore. Her gaze went to the living area and settled on the coffee table. It was the one tangible item that remained of her grandmother. She feared the worst as she thought of condensation. She hurried toward the table.

"Don't worry, I used a coaster," he said, as if reading her mind. "I'm not a barbarian. I'm actually rather domesticated."

Yeah, in my *place!*

If she faced him, her glare would shoot daggers and pierce him on sight.

The hinges on the oven door squeaked.

"Hopefully you like this," Blake began. "It's nothing too exciting, just tuna casserole."

Just like she had thought. She was speechless.

"I know you like fish."

She turned the television off.

"Ooh, why? It's the second quarter, and the Patriots are already slamming the Giants." His words died on his tongue under her glare.

She kept her gaze on him as she took a seat on a stool at the counter.

"You like fish, don't you?"

"I do," she said through gritted teeth.

"Good." He dished up a plate, not even acknowledging her displeasure. "It still looks hot." He took her dish over to the place setting and sat at the head of the table.

Son of a bitch! Her rumbling stomach had her getting up and going to the table.

"Your sister called," he said as she sat down.

She was already here; she might as well eat. Rather, she'd dig in. The faster she ate, maybe the sooner he'd leave. But it was *so* good…

"I take it you like it." He smiled at her.

Despite her intentions to keep her opinion of the meal to herself, a small moan escaped.

He took a swig of his beer, finishing it off, and set the empty bottle on the table. "Your sister reached you and told you I was here? Is that why you're acting strange?"

"Is that why—" She put her fork down and took a deep breath. "If I'm acting strange, it's because you stayed here all day. And you answered my phone." She flailed her arm toward the kitchen. "You even went shopping and did some cooking."

He sat there with a dazed look in his eyes, but oddly, she sensed that he was feeling smothered. How did that work exactly? Like a switch in the guy's personality apparently. But then she recalled what her sister had told her about making a big deal of their relationship. His bringing up the phone call must have brought that back to him. She loaded her fork again, but before placing it into her mouth, she stopped. "I'm just really busy with my current case." Why those exact words, and how did they even tie in right now? Urgh, sometimes the mind worked in strange ways…but maybe it would distract him from how her sister had exaggerated things.

He got up and headed to the fridge where he pulled out another beer. "Hershey and I went for a walk. Dropped in and got a six-pack. Hope you don't mind." He filled the wine glass in front of her with red without asking if she wanted any and took a seat again.

She stuffed a forkful into her mouth. It would serve two purposes: stop her from lashing out at him and feed her starving stomach. On second thought, it was finally starting to feel like she was filling up. She set her fork down.

"Anyway, you were saying, you're busy with your case."

She sat back in her chair and took the first sip of her wine. "Yeah." With that single-worded confession, all the evidence and facts of the case streamed through her mind. "There's just so much to consider." She glanced at him, and he seemed to be listening, even ready for her next words. "Normally there's not much to go on. At least that's what I'm used to. I mean, you also have the extreme cases where there's so much evidence that you've got your guy in the first seventy-two, no problem. But then there are cases like this one—" she pinched her fingers around the stem of the glass "— where there are so many people who would have a motive."

"So you're complaining about too much evidence?" He took a swig of the beer.

It sounded stupid put in plain English. "Well, it's not so much the evidence, but the growing list of suspects. I mean we've identified the weapon now and some other key things." She stopped talking unsure whether she should divulge any more to him.

"Other key things?" He leaned across the table.

"I probably shouldn't talk to you about this. You're a lawyer." She smiled at him. "And lawyers can't be trusted."

He bobbed his head and grinned at her. "Some of them, but I can be."

Blake had never given her reason to doubt him, but there was still that niggling feeling in her gut, the one that told her every man was hiding something. But when it came to business matters, she was pretty certain he'd stick to a professional code of ethics.

"We've come across a bunch of legal paperwork," she said.

He rested a forearm on the table. "All right. Go on."

"Business contracts. The victim apparently screwed a lot of people over—"

"That's where all the suspects are coming from?"

"Yep. I'm kind of losing count of how many people had motive, actually."

"I doubt that."

He had her; she knew exactly how many. There were seven former business partners, including the missing Simon, the twenty-five let go from Proud Yankees, and this Aaron guy. "Thirty-two, possibly thirty-three."

He pointed a finger at her. "See?"

"Anyway, there's just a lot to go on. But I'd also like to hunt down any life insurance policies she might have had or a will." She paused when she saw a flicker in his eyes. "What is it?"

"What was the name of the lawyer on the business contracts?"

She tried to think back but could only conjure a vague image—a swirly first letter and the rest was a scribble. "I can't remember."

"Stick with me," he began. "If you can't remember the name, what about the signature?"

"I can see it in my head, but it's not clear."

Blake leaned forward, putting his elbow on the table. "Was the same signature on all the contracts?"

She flipped through the papers in her mind, and then she remembered. "Yes, I think it was. Why? Where does this get me?"

"Contact the lawyer, and I bet if he's not the one who drafted her will, he may know who did. Most lawyers get their work from referrals."

He should know. And it made sense. If Claire had gone to a lawyer for one thing, it was plausible she'd get guidance from him in other areas. "I love you!"

Madison got up, wrapped her arms around Blake, and planted a big kiss on his lips, but he wasn't participating. She pulled back. Oh, he thought that she— "I didn't mean anything by it. I just meant that I was happy for your help. It's an expression."

An expression, all right…

He probed her eyes for a few seconds and then consulted his watch. "I better go. I have an early morning." He placed his beer bottle, which he had hardly touched, on the table and stood.

She felt so awkward; she didn't know what to say, what to do. She hadn't meant anything by those words.

He hurried out of her apartment like she had the plague.

"Ah!" She picked up her wine and gulped it back until the glass was empty. As the glass came down, she noticed Hershey. He didn't look too happy that his new best friend had left. He stretched out with a large exhale. "I have another rule for you, so listen up! No interfering with my love life."

Chapter 19

Madison sat behind her desk at the station, her one leg bouncing as she sifted through the legal contracts that had been on the USB drives. She took the last bite of her Hershey's bar and saw Terry coming toward her. She swallowed the mouthful hard and quickly tossed the wrapper in the garbage can hoping to avoid a lecture on her breakfast choice. She was already miserable from a night of tossing and turning. Blurting out "I love you" to Blake wasn't exactly conducive to sleeping. But it wasn't just the words haunting her, it was the possibility that they'd meant more than she'd intended. Compounded on top of that, Hershey had whined most of the night. And it wasn't until one o'clock in the morning that she'd remembered her promise to call Chelsea.

Terry flashed a smile, but this morning it felt like too much work to return it.

"The lawyer's name is David Morris," she began. "And nice of you to show up by the way."

"Someone woke up on the wrong side of the bed."

She shot him a glare. "That would imply *someone* went to sleep in the first place."

Terry draped his jacket over the back of his chair. "Great. It's going to be one of those days."

"One of those days?"

"Yeah." He looked her straight in the eyes and sat down. "One of those days when you're relentless and won't stop riding my ass until—"

"One more word." She narrowed her eyes.

"One more word and what? What are you going to do to me?"

All sorts of images and ideas ran through her head. Of course, they were vague, lacking any clear lines of distinction, but they met with the same result: Terry in pain. She glowered at him.

"Watch it or your face will stay that way." He gestured toward two empty Starbucks cups on her desk. "At least you're taking in caffeine."

And he hadn't even seen the third cup in the garbage can under her desk...

"How long have you been here?" he asked.

"Longer than you want to know."

"So it's safe to say you didn't have a good night."

"Geez, Terry, and you didn't graduate at the top of the academy?"

"Oh, someone's very snarky." He took a draw on his coffee. "You said something about a lawyer named Davis Morris?"

"Uh-huh." She fanned the edges of the paper in front of her. "He's the lawyer who is on all the contracts."

His eyes went blank. "Okay?"

"If Claire used him for all her business endeavors, he might be able to point us in the direction of her will and life insurance policy."

No response, hardly a sign he'd even heard a word she said.

"Terry?" she prompted.

"I just thought of something."

"What?"

"If she trusted him with all her business transactions, then maybe he knows who she was in business with before she was murdered." His eyes lit when they met hers.

Crap, why hadn't she thought it through to that? Her focus was off these days. Just another reason why being in a relationship wasn't a good thing. Relationships were distracting and consumed too much energy and occupied too much mental space. Maybe she could recover and convince him she had thought of that... "That's right," she began. "I just hadn't gotten around to telling you that yet."

"Uh-huh. I know you too well to let you pull that off, Maddy. Besides, you would have led with that."

She rolled her eyes and shrugged her shoulders. "I have to let you feel the spotlight sometimes." She smirked at him, got up, put her coat on, and stood next to him. "Let's go."

Terry looked up at her. "What about Simon Angle? Last night you were ready to drive around in a blizzard."

"Just a minor detour." She still had every intention of pursuing that lead.

"Maybe this lawyer will tell us about Aaron."

Madison laughed. "You're obsessed with Aaron."

"You just see. That little clue, the one you are paying no attention to, will be what breaks the case."

"Whatev—"

"Before we go, though, you might want to wipe that chocolate from the corner of your mouth."

She traced her fingers around her mouth and walked away, a smirk on her lips, her partner's footfalls trailing her.

Chapter 20

Madison leaned on the front counter of the law firm. "We'd like to speak with David Morris."

"Do you have a—" The strawberry-blond receptionist held up an index finger and sneezed. "'Cuse me." She pulled a tissue from a box and dabbed her nose. It looked so raw; its tip was a brilliant red and dry skin lined her nostrils. "Sorry about—" Her eyes squinted and her nose wrinkled up as if she were about to sneeze again. "Do you have an appointment with Mr. Morris?" She consulted the appointment book. "There's nothing on the books."

"That's because he isn't expecting us, but we're detectives Knight—" Madison gestured toward Terry "—and Grant."

Her face scrunched up and then took on the look of panic. "I'll page his office." She went to pick up the receiver but was stopped by a violent coughing fit that shook her body.

Madison stepped back from the counter. Not that she was a germaphobe, but the air would be carrying the plague and the last thing she needed was to get sick.

The receptionist blew her nose and bunched the used tissue in her hand. "I'm so sorry about that. I'll call now." She made the call and hung up not long after. "He'll be right up." She went back to sniffling and dabbing.

Terry tapped the counter. "And when he gets here, you should tell him to let you have the day off."

"I wish, but this place doesn't run itself."

He tucked in toward Madison and said in a low voice, "Hey, someone as stubborn as you, Maddy."

Madison narrowed her eyes at him but turned her attention

behind her when she heard someone approaching.

A man in his midsixties in a tailored suit was walking toward them. He had a head full of silver hair and a mustache and beard to match. "Are you the detectives here to see me?"

There was no one else in the waiting room.

"Are you David Morris?" she countered.

"That's me." David had a pleasant face, but his weary eyes and wrinkles told of someone who worked too hard.

She nodded and introduced herself and Terry to him. "Is there somewhere we can speak in private?"

"Yes, of course. This way." David led them down a short hallway to his office where he sat behind his desk. "Sit, please," he added, offering up two mismatched chairs across from him.

From a first take of the premises, either business wasn't that good or he didn't put a lot back into it. Based on David's expensive suit, Madison sided with the latter.

"We're here about Claire Reeves," she said.

David's shoulders tensed, inching their way upward to his ears. He let out a jagged breath. "Tragedy."

He was the first person to see it that way.

"You were close to her?" Madison asked.

"Professionally."

"We've come across some legal files, business contracts," Madison started. "And you're listed on all of them as the lawyer of contact."

"Claire and I go way back. I can't even remember how we came to be in business together, but it was a good fit."

"How many business contracts did you draft for her?"

"I can't say off the top, but just give me a minute here." He pressed some keys on a laptop that was on his desk.

His typing didn't drown out the faint sound of soft rock, though. Madison looked around the room and found a small alarm clock radio that must have been playing it.

"Here we go. It says here that we've billed for eight."

Madison glanced over at Terry before addressing David, no doubt that disappointment was broadcasted on her features.

"That's the information that we had. We were hoping that you would be able to tell us about a newer contract, one within the last three years."

He looked at the computer and shook his head. "Can't help you there. Last one was just over that. The name of Barry Parsons."

"What about a life insurance policy or a will? Do you know anything about those?" Terry asked.

"Now *that* I can't help you with directly. I did advise that she set those things up from the beginning. But it wasn't until she was bought out of the second company that she took my advice seriously. At least she seemed to." David's gaze traveled over the two of them. "She had a lot of money for a college student."

A college student? Right, the oldest contract on file had dated back that far.

"You said 'she seemed to' take your advice," Terry said. "But you don't know if she did for sure?"

"All I can tell you is that I recommended a colleague, who is an accountant, to help manage her money."

"His name?" Madison asked.

"Alex Knott."

"We'd like his information, please," she requested. "A number and address?"

"Of course." David opened a desk drawer, pulled out a business card, and extended it to Madison. "In this business, it's all about referrals. Without them, well, let's just say we'd be eating tuna instead of caviar. He returns the favor when his clients need legal business advice."

David's words propelled her back to last night and how Blake had mentioned referrals, as well. Her thoughts then skipped ahead to the dreaded words she'd said to him…

"Mr. Knott may have helped her with setting up investments, but do you know who managed her last will and testament?" she asked.

"I recommended someone." David's gaze drifted to some place behind their shoulders.

"Who was that?" Madison asked, but David seemed hesitant to

answer. "Mr. Morris, if you know, we need you to tell us."

"Truth is, I know she didn't go to the person I recommended." He rubbed his jaw, and then met her gaze. "A friend of hers talked her into doing her will online."

"Online?" Terry queried.

"Yes." David glanced at Terry. "You don't need a lawyer to draft a will. Of course, I recommend that you do."

Well, of course, you do.

"This friend of Claire's," Madison began, "do you remember anything about them?"

He squinted his eyes as if deep in thought. "I met her once. If I remember right, she had blond hair and big lips."

Why does everyone want Angelina Jolie's lips? "Was her name Darcy Simms?"

David's eyes met Madison's, and he nodded. "Yes, that's it."

Allison's caution about Darcy was clear in Madison's mind, and if Darcy Simms wasn't the good friend she made herself out to be, maybe she'd even weaseled her way into Claire's will. She obviously had some power of sway to get Claire to handle the legal documentation online.

None of this changed the fact, though, that Darcy wasn't tall enough to have pulled off Claire's murder. But it was the flicker in Darcy's eyes that had told Madison the woman was withholding something. If she was a beneficiary, that alone could give her motive. Had she hired someone to kill Claire? If she had, though, it would need to be someone who could get close to Claire. They needed to get their hands on Claire's will and find out who would benefit from her death.

"Do you know what website she would have used?" Madison asked.

"Legalities.com," he said.

Madison glanced at Terry, and he wrote it down in a notepad. "You remembered the name of the company easily."

"Yes, because I don't believe there's a shortcut for a proper will. The fact that I remember them isn't a good thing." David cleared his throat. "You mentioned another business partner who came after Barry Parsons?"

"That's right."

"She could have prepared that contract through that site, as well. Heck, she'd already been down that road eight times with me. She'd know what the contract would need to contain."

Madison and Terry had to move.

She stood up. "We appreciate all your help, Mr. Morris."

He smiled, the expression reaching his eyes. "Glad I could."

Madison and Terry made it to the door when David called out to them. "Actually, Detectives, one more thing. How's her husband handling all—"

"Her husband?" There was no record of Claire being married.

"Yeah." David's gaze went to Terry, then back to Madison. "Why do I get the feeling you didn't know about him?"

"Because we don't. Her records don't show that she's married or ever was," Madison said.

"It was easily twenty years ago, but I know I didn't imagine him."

"Do you remember his name?"

"Absolutely. He came in a few times, and he was a great guy, very memorable. His name was Darren Taylor."

Chapter 21

Madison's and Terry's strides were long as they left the lawyer's office, and they both loaded into the department car.

"How the hell could we not know about a husband?" She glanced over at Terry. "We need to find him."

She logged on to the laptop in the car and did a name search in the city of Stiles. It garnered fifteen hits, but one of them was the same age as Claire. "We might have him." She pulled out her phone and called, but it rang to voice mail and she left a message. She hung up. "Now we wait."

"Not one of your strengths." Terry smirked.

"Hey."

He shrugged. "It's true."

She pursed her lips and put the car into drive, her mind on hitting the first Starbucks they came across. "How are you coming along with finding a safe-deposit box in her name, by the way?"

"Nowhere yet. I've checked the major banks in Stiles and none of them have any record of Claire Reeves."

Ten minutes later, she parked the car in front of a downtown Starbucks and turned to face him. "I'll take my regular." She flashed him a cheesy grin.

"Oh, so I'm going in?"

"I can't very well just leave the car idling here."

"You could turn it off."

She shook her head. "Nope. You get the caffeine, and I'll call Legalities.com."

Terry locked his gaze with hers for a few seconds. "All right. Deal."

He got out and she watched after him until he'd entered the coffee shop. She pulled up the browser on her phone, found a contact number for the company, and called them.

"Legalities.com, where we make your legal matters an ease." The receptionist sounded robotic, and it wasn't until some silence passed and she said, "Hello?" that Madison realized she was on with a live person and not connected to an automated service.

Madison introduced herself as a Stiles PD detective. "I'd like to speak with a manager."

"One moment pl—" The woman had clipped herself off and transferred Madison's call.

"Hello, this is Lucy, ID number six-five-three-two."

"Lucy, this is Detective Madison Knight with Stiles PD. A client of yours has died, and as an officer looking into her death, I'd like you to send a copy of the documents she'd purchased from you."

"Let's start with their name," Lucy said without missing a beat, the death of a stranger not affecting her at all.

"Claire Reeves. She's from Stiles."

Lucy clicked keys and paused. "I see her file. I will just need you to verify the credit card information she has on file with us."

"I don't have that."

"You said you're a detective." Lucy's voice was riddled with skepticism.

"I am." Madison didn't have time for this woman on a power trip.

"Then you should have the number," Lucy said pleasantly.

Madison rolled her eyes. "As I said, I don't have that information to give you."

"Then I'm sorry, but I can't help you."

You're not sorry at all.

"By denying me access to her files, you are interfering with a police investigation." Madison's earlobes were heating with anger.

"How would I even know that you are who you're saying? I'm sorry, but—"

"Please put your supervisor on the line," Madison ground out.

"I am a manager."

"Fine, get who you report to on the line. Now."

"One minute." Lucy's tone was fiery but that wasn't Madison's concern.

"Hello?" No name or ID this time, and it was a man. "What seems to be the problem?"

"The problem is that your company isn't cooperating with an active police investigation."

"Police investigation? One moment, please."

"No, I—" Too late. She was back on hold.

Madison tapped her fingers on the steering wheel and watched pedestrians strolling along the sidewalk, their breaths fogging in the cool air.

"Detective?" The man was back on the line.

"Yes?"

"I would be glad to help you."

The only thing that could account for the change of heart would be a quick Google search; he'd confirmed Claire Reeves had been murdered.

The man continued. "We keep records of not only the document types purchased but also the final document."

Madison's heart sped up. "Can you tell me over the phone what types of documents she purchased?"

"Certainly. It looks like a will and a business contract."

She'd be able to see beneficiaries. "Send the information to…" She rattled off her e-mail address.

"I'll get it right over. Is there anything else I can do for you today?"

"That's all." She hung up at the same time that Terry opened his door.

"Here you go." He extended a cappuccino toward her and she took it from him. "What are you smiling about?" he asked.

"Legalities.com is probably forwarding Claire's documents as we speak."

"Wow, you got them to cooperate? And without a warrant?"

"Seems so."

"They had a copy of her will, then?"

"Yes, and another partnership contract."

Terry lifted his Starbucks cup as if about to make a toast.

Madison pulled out of the parking spot and merged with traffic, wanting to get back to the station to look at the paperwork.

The first traffic light she came to turned red.

The second one turned red.

And the third one turned red.

"Oh lord, can't we just catch a break? I should put the lights on."

"And abuse the system?"

"It wouldn't be abusing it. We are on a case." She glanced over at him. By the time she turned back to the light, it was green. She gunned the gas.

"Help me."

She looked at him again. One hand hugged his Starbucks and the other gripped the front dash. He lifted it to point out the windshield.

"Eyes on the road, please. You don't want you to hit someone."

"Hey, I've never hit anyone—"

"You've come close before."

How she wished she could slam back a rebuttal, but it was the truth. She had blamed the situation on being a good detective, too focused on the direction of the case to focus on the road. Deflection was the perfect response in this scenario. She lifted her hands off the wheel. "Look, Terry, no hands."

Sheer panic washed over his face and Madison laughed.

"You're such a girl."

Madison settled behind her desk at the station and Terry at his. She was bringing up her e-mail program when she heard someone approaching. But she didn't want to look up. New messages were coming in. Were any from—

"Do you remember the fluff from the kitchen floor?"

Madison pried her eyes from her monitor and looked up to see Cynthia next to her desk. "Of course. I found it."

"Well, I traced its composition. It's a type of down found in top-end skiwear, and Claire didn't own any."

"Were you able to determine which manufacturer?" Madison asked, unable to shake the feeling that a coat had already been mentioned in regards to the investigation.

Cynthia shook her head. "Unfortunately, no. But once you find the jacket, you'll be closer to solving this case."

"Oh, that's all," Terry pitched in drily.

Cynthia shot him a glare. "Yes, *that's all*. I can't do everything for you."

"Hardy har."

"Anyway, moving on," Cynthia began. "The boot prints from the backyard? They were going toward the house, and the stride indicates a person of about six feet."

"Richards told us the killer would be about five eleven," Terry began. "That's close enough to six foot for me."

Madison recalled how a jacket tied into the investigation now. My, her mind was messed up because of her relationship with Blake. Terry must have forgotten, too. "Claire's neighbor—" Madison glanced at her partner "—saw a person walking toward the house in a puffy jacket the night she was murdered."

Cynthia opened her hands, palm out, and addressed Terry. "There you go. You're halfway there."

"We're not halfway there. Not even close," Madison responded and softened her tone when she continued. "But we are ahead."

"That's right." Cynthia sauntered off, having delivered her news.

Madison's attention went back to her inbox and there was one from Legalities.com. She clicked to open the e-mail.

"Life would be so boring if we solved cases right away," Terry rambled.

"Really? I think I could handle a straightforward case once in a while."

He laughed. "I know you better than that. Heck, you would complicate the easy ones."

"Oh—" Her focus was on the body of the email.

"Maddy, aren't you going to tell me to shut up, walk over here, and punch my shoulder?"

"You've got to be kidding me."

"All right, that's it. I'm coming over."

She looked up at him. "The e-mail says that they have a record of her purchasing a detailed partnership agreement from them but that the server containing that data was corrupted and they weren't able to retrieve the information."

"Kidding me."

"I wish. Not that it makes a difference, but they apologized for the inconvenience." She clicked on the attachment that they had included, though. "They sent the will." She scrolled down the screen and felt chilled when she saw the two names staring back at her: Darcy Simms and Darren Taylor.

Chapter 22

Madison and Terry entered By Design. "We'd like to speak with Darcy Simms," Madison said to the receptionist.

"She's in a meeting," the woman replied.

"We'll need you to—"

Darcy walked into the front area and did a double take. "What are you doing here?"

"We could ask you the same." Madison glanced at the receptionist "We were told you were in a meeting."

Darcy jutted out her chin. "I was. What do you want, Detective? I've told you all I know."

What do I want? A good friend would be helpful to the cops investigating her friend's death. Allison had been right about the woman.

Madison took a step toward Darcy. "If you'd like, we could discuss Claire's will out here." Madison looked over at the waiting area where a man was sitting cross-legged. "It doesn't matter to—"

"Sarah, hold my calls." Darcy swaggered down the corridor to her office, parked behind her desk, and leaned back against her chair. "I don't know what more I could possibly tell you. As far as I'm concerned, this is getting old."

"Getting old? Your supposed best friend was murdered less than a week ago. You don't seem upset by it. Of course, if I stood to inherit one million dollars…" Madison tossed out the bait.

"I didn't kill her." Darcy bit whether she realized she had or not.

"So you know you are a beneficiary of Claire's will?"

"Of course, I do."

Madison gestured her hand between herself and Terry. "To us, that looks like possible motive to get her out of the picture."

Darcy's face flushed. "She was my best friend."

"Was she?" Madison countered, not taking her eyes off the woman for a second. "People have killed for a lot less than a million. There's no way you were close to Claire."

"What the hell would you know?" Darcy's cheeks were almost crimson now.

"You seem more upset that we're suspecting your involvement in her murder than you were in the news that she had been killed." Madison's accusation sank in the air like a stone. "Her death made you rich. Why hide that from us if you're innocent?"

Darcy took a deep breath. "It's not like I intended to hide it. I—" she swallowed deeply "—I just didn't think it would matter."

"You didn't think it would matter that you stood to benefit from her death?" Madison asked, unable to mask the skepticism.

Darcy ran a hand through her hair. "I don't know what to tell you."

"You helped Claire set up her will, manipulated her to include you?" *Manipulated* might have been too strong a word, but it was out there now.

Darcy was shaking her head. "I didn't make her do anything. As I've said, we were best friends. Do you know what it's like to have one?"

Madison's mind went straight to Cynthia. "I do."

"Then you should understand that the first thing on my mind when I heard she was murdered wasn't the money."

Madison's temper was ebbing. "All right, fair enough. But if there's anything else you have to tell us, now's the time."

"You have nothing on me."

Quite a defensive response, and it piqued Madison's interest. "You would be the right height for the killer." Out of her peripheral, Madison saw Terry's head turn to her. "If you were elevated somehow, had a good pair of boots." She was reaching, of course, but sometimes you had to push to get people to talk. Madison continued. "And maybe you didn't do it yourself. You could have hired someone. As her *best* friend, you'd have had access to her house."

"Sure, I had access. So what?" Darcy Simms picked up her pen and doodled wide, wild loops. She was using her right hand again. Had she just happened to pick up the pen with her left before? Or was she aware the killer was left-handed and was keeping up a charade? Darcy paused doodling and looked up at Madison. "I should probably get a lawyer here."

A threat with no teeth, as Darcy didn't make a move for her phone or to get up. "Only the guilty have a lawyer," Madison responded.

"Or the smart."

Why did that statement sound familiar?

Darcy solidified eye contact with Madison and continued, only proving her mention of retaining a lawyer was an empty threat. "Claire taught me a lesson early on." She glanced at Terry, blinking deliberately, the rise and fall of her eyelashes almost seductive. "It's not going to look good for me, so I'm trusting you to do the right thing,"

Madison wanted to cuff the woman. She was trying to use her femininity and sexual appeal to distract them from justice. Terry wasn't having anything to do with it, though. In fact, it was strongly the opposite reaction. His jaw was rigid and a pulse tapped in his cheek.

"Of course, Miss Simms. You have our word," Terry said politely.

"All right, then." Darcy clasped her hands on her lap. "What I'm about to tell you happened a long time ago. And I have moved on." There was a strain to her voice which belied her claim. "By now you probably know what she did for a living?"

"You refer to screwing people." Madison put it this way to see what sort of a response she'd get from Darcy.

"She didn't *screw* people as you so delicately put it, but she was a shrewd business woman."

So Darcy felt some loyalty toward Claire.

Darcy went on. "If she had been a man, she would have been revered and respected for her business sense. She kept business as business. She always said that people take their work too seriously, too personally."

"It's kind of hard not to when facing bankruptcy or failed marriages," Madison said.

Darcy glanced at Madison, but put her eye back on Terry. "Anyway, as I was trying to say, she taught me a lesson early on. I had a business."

Darcy Simms wasn't listed as one of the business owners on the USB drives, but Madison ran with it as if Darcy had been had worked over by Claire. "Did she ruin your business?"

"I learned valuable life lessons early on." Darcy didn't take her gaze off Terry.

Did she keep saying that because she was trying to convince herself that being taken was for her own good?

"I'll take that as a yes, then. As you said, this doesn't look good for you. She screwed you over?" Madison deliberately used the word Darcy disliked, and the woman's eyes narrowed to slits. "I find it hard to believe you were okay with it."

"It's a good thing it doesn't matter what you believe."

"It does, actually," Madison stated drily.

"Whatever. I was thankful for her, at least eventually. Of course I hated her initially, but Claire would have none of it. She took me under her wing and explained how business worked."

"And that made you okay with taking her side in a fight against yourself?" Madison asked incredulously.

"It wasn't like that. Anyway, I was honest with you. The past has no bearing on the present or the future."

"There's more than one thing that's not adding up for me in regards to your story," Madison began, "but the glaring obvious is that your name wasn't included among the business contracts Claire had in her home safe."

"You're not as smart as you think you are." Darcy held eye contact with Madison. "Claire did a number on me, and my credit was ruined, what I figured at the time, for life. I wanted the entire thing behind me as fast as possible, so I changed my name."

"And yet you became friends with the very person who caused your trouble. That doesn't make sense to me," Madison said.

Darcy rose to her feet and gestured to the door. "If that will be all."

In the parking lot, Madison turned to Terry. "We've got to figure out what her name was before she became Darcy Simms. I still believe there's a whole lot she's not telling us."

"I'm leaning that way, too."

"Finally, you're coming around to see my point of view."

Terry slid her a sour look.

"Hey, sometimes I think you just disagree with me for the sake of disagreeing."

"You got me." Terry rolled his eyes.

They got into the car and she conducted a quick search on Darcy Simms, and there was the answer as to her former identity staring at her from the screen: Anita Smith.

That name had been in front of them since they'd found the list of business owners. Anita Smith was the owner of the second business on Claire's hit list.

Chapter 23

Madison and Terry had returned to the station after finding out Darcy's former identity. He'd decided to call it a day and had walked off, mumbling something about murder not being solved in a day. If only it could be, maybe she'd have time to sleep.

Even though there were loose ends, she'd conceded to breaking for the day, too. Stepping inside her apartment didn't exactly bring the feeling of satisfaction that came with a job well done, but rather one of unfinished business. They still hadn't heard back from Darren Taylor, Claire's supposed husband twenty years ago, and Simon Angle hadn't been found yet.

Hershey ran to the door and barked as he jumped around her feet. Her heart sank. She must have forgotten to put him in his kennel when she left that morning. She walked around her place, letting her nose lead her, and thankfully, he'd only left a couple messes.

Madison took Hershey outside and when she returned she noticed that the message light on her machine was flashing. Her heart sped up, anticipating that it might be Blake. Maybe he had forgotten about her blurting out *I love you* and wanted to meet. At least she hoped so.

She pressed the "play" button.

"I knew you wouldn't call me back." It was Chelsea, and she didn't sound happy. "Call me," she added before an abrupt click and disconnect.

Madison's heart cinched from disappointment. Somehow her caller being her sister and not Blake stamped home a sense of rejection, as if by Chelsea calling and Blake not that things were over between them. Even that passing thought brought mixed emotions. What would be over exactly? They were just dating. It was casual and something people do all the time. Then when someone decided to move on, there shouldn't be any explanation necessary. And that's all it was between her and Blake…at least she tried to convince herself their relationship was nothing more.

In truth, though, they had been dating for the better part of four months, and she hoped that their time together had meant *something* to him, that his proposal to be exclusive was at least in part motivated by his own feelings for her and not just to appease her. But he was being so cold given what had slipped from her lips. Maybe it hadn't been an accident, though. Maybe life was as some people believed. Maybe things happen for a reason. Her blurting out "I love you" just might be what saved her from getting further involved with a man incapable of reciprocating that feeling.

The phone rang and her heart thumped in her chest. Maybe this was Blake?

Hershey bounded around her feet. She picked up the toy closest to her, which happened to be the twisted rope that Blake and Hershey had played with, and answered the phone. Her breath stalled as she waited for a response from her caller.

"Finally." It was Chelsea. "Do you have a moment to talk?"

"You're like my stalker these days, Chels." Madison laughed, but it was shallow and her insides ached. What felt like needle points laced with acid pricked at her heart. She could bury what she had said and move forward… Why couldn't Blake?

"It would be nice if you returned my calls."

"What is it?" She didn't want her annoyance to come across, but a hint of it touched her voice.

The line fell quiet between them for a few seconds and then Chelsea said, "Mom and Dad are coming to town, and—"

"What?" The last thing she needed was to face her parents, especially her mother.

"I wanted to give you more notice, but I didn't get much. They felt bad they couldn't make it in to spend Christmas with the girls. Anyway, they're coming this weekend, and they'll be staying with us."

"Nice." She sounded so cold and distant to her own ears, but she couldn't help it. Her parents lived in Florida and only took the trip up to Stiles once, maybe twice a year. It was never to come and stay with her, but always the grandkids. It wasn't that she was estranged from her parents, but she might as well have been. They rarely communicated. Birthdays used to warrant a phone call, but in the last few years, it had been downgraded to a mailed greeting card with a fifty-dollar gift card.

"Nice?" Chelsea sniggered. "I know you better than that, Maddy. *Nice* for you means it's fine as long as it doesn't involve you."

Her sister did know her too well, because that's exactly what she was thinking.

"Anyway, I wanted you to know."

"Thanks."

"You're coming, aren't you?"

Did I miss something?

"Coming?"

"Yeah, to a family dinner on Sunday."

Family didn't exactly encompass the relationship she had with her mother, at least beyond the biological. "I don't know."

"Seriously? These are your parents. You only get two. How long has it been since you spoke with them?"

"I couriered them Christmas gifts, sent a card—"

"Spoke with them," Chelsea ground out.

I can't remember.

"I can tell by your silence that it's been too long. You've got to come, Maddy. No choice. Our house at three."

"Three?"

"Yes. Three."

"Thought it was dinner."

"Would be nice to have a bit of a visit in there beforehand, too, don't you think?"

Do you want my honest answer?

"It's really not going to be that bad," Chelsea continued.

"Fine, I'll be there."

"Oh, and you can bring that boyfriend of yours. I'd love to meet him."

"'Night, Chels."

"'Night."

Madison detected the smile in her sister's voice. Either it was there because of her childish curiosity about Blake or because she felt she had arranged a good deed by getting Madison to agree to a family dinner. The latter wasn't because she had been left with much choice. Otherwise, she typically avoided coming face-to-face with her mother.

Their relationship was complicated and the rift between them had grown into a chasm over the years. Nothing Madison did was right for the woman, but their differences got worse when her grandmother, her mom's mom, had died and left all her money to Madison. Even though her mother had tried to dismiss the importance of it, Madison knew that it had cut her deeply.

Madison had offered the money to her mother several times, but she'd refused to accept it and the conversations would end with her mother's protest that nothing had changed between them. But it had.

The fact that Madison had chosen a life opposite marriage and babies became a bigger deal, and Madison's career in law enforcement became a bitter source of contention. In regards to the latter, Madison could somewhat understand her mother's side.

Madison's grandfather, Thomas Wright, had started off as a patrol officer and worked his way up to lieutenant. To mark their thirtieth wedding anniversary and his approaching retirement, he treated his wife to a meal out. But a young man named Jimmy Bates came into the restaurant, armed and holding his gun on her grandfather. Before he pulled the trigger, he had said, "You took my father away from me."

Thomas Wright was shot right there and bled to death on the tiled floor of The Laguna with his wife leaning over him, praying for him to pull through. But it wasn't meant to be.

Bates was the son of a man her grandfather had arrested and who had been convicted of fraud and put away for a life sentence.

He had been motivated by the loss of not only a father but also of a lifestyle that he would have become accustomed to.

But the incident had left Madison's mother without a dad at the age of twelve.

Right when a girl needs a father the most.

Since becoming a sworn officer, Madison had become the recipient of warnings that came as fired missiles in a war zone—repeatedly and without letup. Not that Madison's mother had ever put it in so many words, but her mother didn't want to bury her daughter. Madison turned away from her mother's fear, though, and drew strength from her grandmother, who understood her need to be a cop.

Her grandmother, Rose, had pushed Madison when she felt she couldn't go any further. She helped her to find the strength within to push through the physical pain of training.

"We're made for birthin' babies. Always remember that we've got it over men in three ways: endurance, mental focus, and we've got the looks. We're a triple threat."

The memory caused Madison to smile. Sadly, she'd lost her grandmother two years ago to a cancerous brain tumor. At least she'd been able to celebrate her advancement to detective with her grandmother, and often when Madison needed encouragement to keep going, she'd think of Rose. She'd been so proud of her granddaughter's accomplishments. If only her own mother could be.

Chapter 24

"Hey, about time you got in," Madison teased Terry as he took a seat at his desk across from her.

"Since when do you beat me in?"

"You mean besides the last time?" She smiled at him, referring to the day when she'd downed three cappuccinos in the hope of waking up. Today, she was in a wonderful mood. She had gotten some sleep. Last night, she'd put Hershey in his kennel, a dark blanket draped over it to encourage him to settle down in the same manner someone would do with a bird. The imagery had made her laugh at the time, but whatever worked. And when her head had hit the pillow last night, all her thoughts about family disappeared along with any worry about her relationship with Blake.

Her cell rang and she answered, "Knight." She listened to her caller, and after he identified himself, she was pointing at her phone for Terry's benefit. "We'll be here," she said into her phone and hung up shortly after.

"What is it?" Terry asked.

She was grinning. "That was Darren Taylor, and he's on his way in. Apparently, he was in Tahiti."

"Tahiti? That's where Darcy had been."

"Uh-huh. He said when he got my message, he boarded a flight home, and he should be here any minute. But that's not even the best part." She paused to build anticipation, and it had Terry rolling his hand. "Darren was at Claire's the night she was murdered."

"Really?"

"That what he said," Madison began. "And if he knew about the will and what he stood to gain, he'd have good motive."

The phone on her desk rang, and it was Ranson from the front desk. Madison leaned to her right to get a line of sight to the front counter. A man was standing there, a carry-on bag strapped over one shoulder and a wheeled suitcase on the floor next to him. He must have come straight from the airport. "We'll be right there." Madison hung up and said to Terry, "He's here."

Terry turned around. "That's him?"

"He's the only one at the front counter."

"Oh, this is going to be fun."

"Why do I sense sarcasm?"

"Um, I wonder."

"So what? The man is strikingly handsome."

"Don't let it hinder you from doing your job."

Madison narrowed her eyes at her partner. "You're one to talk. You were lenient with Darcy Simms, and it's not because of her winning personality." She smiled at him with a look of pure adolescence. But the truth was, it didn't matter how good-looking Darren was, because he could be a killer.

She led the way to the front and extended her hand. "Mr. Taylor?" When their eyes met, she felt a catch in her breath. His eyes were the color of steel and carried a mischievousness allure.

"That's me."

Darren's jaw was sharp and angular. His hair reached the top of his shoulders and he had it tucked behind his ears, tufts of it poking out. He carried the unshaven look like a model, and while he wasn't necessarily *GQ* material, he was undeniably handsome.

Madison drew her arm back and resisted wiping her sweaty hand on her pants. She pressed on a smile. "Thank you for coming in so quickly."

"Hey, no prob. When I found out what happened to Claire, I had to." His voice brought with it a hint of déjà vu, as if she had heard it before.

Madison directed him to interrogation room three, where she had him go inside while she excused herself and Terry.

She turned to her partner. "Let me handle—"

"You're kidding, right? You're like a gushing teenager."

Her eyes instinctively narrowed to slits. "Fine, I admit it. He's good-looking."

Terry laughed. "What is it with you women? You go on about how you like your man's hair trimmed and his facial hair groomed. He probably hasn't had a cut in months or shaved in days."

Madison hitched her shoulders. "Stubble suits some men."

"Uh-huh."

"No, it's true. And besides, he's been away, and he just found out about Claire."

"You believe that?"

"Why wouldn't I?"

Terry shook his head and paced around her. "He admitted to being there the night of the murder."

"You just don't like him 'cause he's good-looking."

"That is the furthest thing from the truth."

"Now you know how it feels," she snapped back. He'd know that she was referring to Darcy and his accusations that Madison treated her differently because of her looks.

"Fine. Point taken." He gestured for her to take the lead into the room, and she'd taken one step when the sergeant came up to them.

They had almost made it. She had her hand on the doorknob.

"The husband's in there?" Sergeant Winston exuded the confidence of a man in charge, but the image fractured at the bald head and rounded paunch. "Heard he's got every reason to want her dead." He drew his gaze from Terry to Madison. "Not that I heard it from you. Why is that, Knight?"

And here she had been impressed that he hadn't been hounding her as much with this case, but it wasn't because the sergeant had changed his micro-managerial style. She passed a skeptical look to Terry.

"That's right," Winston said. "At least your partner speaks to me. What's a quick e-mail take, anyway? A minute? Two?"

Either way, it was more time than she had for rehashing leads of a case. Heck, she didn't even have much of a social life. It drove her mad how the sarge always whined about how she needed to communicate better.

"Guess you can't complain that you're not being kept current." She attempted a smile to soften her words, but they were confrontational in tone.

His arms crossed and came to rest on his stomach. "As I've said before, I would like my *lead* detective to keep me informed." The way he'd added emphasis to the word *lead* came out almost as a threat to her job.

"Sit in if you wish," Madison offered.

"Not for me. I'll watch from behind the glass." Winston left and headed toward the observation room where he would be secure behind his two-way mirror.

"And that's why I'm the *lead* detective," Madison mumbled. "I'm not a chicken shit."

"Shh," Terry cooed.

"What?" She turned around and saw the cuff of the sergeant's pant leg disappear into the room next door. "He's gone."

Madison opened the door to the interrogation room. "Mr. Taylor—"

Darren looked up at her, his eyes wet. They were more hypnotizing than before, and he appeared younger than his forty-three years. He wiped his cheeks with the heels of his palms.

She choked back an offering of sympathy. *Stay strong, he could be the murderer.* "You were married to Claire, but there's no legal record of that."

"Long story. Must we start with that?"

Madison would give him a momentary pass. "You told me that you were at Claire's house the night she was murdered. Is that true?"

"Yes."

"Do you care to elaborate?"

"I'll be keeping my answers brief, Detective, if you'll afford me that courtesy. I trust that I've already presented a show of good faith just by being here without a lawyer." The bite to his words eliminated any charm his looks conveyed, and this was enough to help her see things objectively again.

Brief or left unanswered, apparently.

"Mr. Taylor, let me assure you that if you did this"—she tossed a photo of Claire from her kitchen floor and then one of her on a gurney in the morgue on top of it—"all that I will afford you is a cell in a maximum-security prison where you'll dream of daylight and the warmth of the sun on your face." Her words and pictures hadn't elicited any reaction. In fact, the tears had dried up and his expression was blank. It was either shock or his earlier display of grief had been an act. "What do you think when you see her like this?" Madison nudged him.

He glared at her, fire licking his eyes.

"Listen, I'm going to lay it out. You were there the night of the murder, but then you run off to—"

"I didn't *run* anywhere." He sniffled and pinched his nose.

Now he's bringing on the waterworks again.

Madison settled back against her chair and knotted her arms. "It looks that way from here."

He let go of his nose and looked at his hand. "Do you have a tissue?"

Madison spotted Darren's red fingertips and gestured for Terry to get some.

Terry left the room and came back less than a minute later with a box, which he tossed on the table in front of Darren. He pulled out a couple, balled them up, and pressed them against his one nostril.

"Do you get nosebleeds a lot?" People could get them for various reasons, ranging from dry air to medical issues, but Madison also knew they could be brought on by intense stress.

"You're treating me like a suspect." He avoided eye contact.

That wasn't exactly an answer to her question, but it told her that stress was the trigger for his nosebleeds. At least this particular one. She pressed him further, though. "Why shouldn't we think of you as a suspect?"

"Because—" he exchanged the tissues for fresh ones "—I couldn't have done it."

It wasn't me? That's his defense? She'd heard this too many times to count, and it even came from the mouths of killers. "You're going to have to do better than that."

Darren locked eyes with her and she sensed that if she kept prodding him, he'd clam up and demand a lawyer.

She'd let his protest go for now, play diplomat, and see where that attribute would take her, but he still hadn't told them why he was in Tahiti. She'd veer the conversation back to that. "Why were you in Tahiti?"

"I had a job there."

Darren was the second person in Claire's circle who had recently been to Tahiti. Was that significant or coincidental? Intuition told Madison to ask something. "Where did you meet Claire?"

His eyes pulled from the photos to Madison, and he must have swallowed his saliva the wrong way because he started coughing. He dabbed the tissue to his nose one more time before putting his arm down. "We met in Bora Bora. Twenty-some years ago," he added. "And before you assume that I hit her up because of her money, I had no idea what she worth at the time."

"Can you prove that?"

"Can you prove I did?" he fired back. "Anyway, we hit it off. We were both in university and had businesses of our own. We had a lot in common, so we got married. Blame it on too many mojitos."

"Mojitos?" Madison parroted.

"Yeah, awesome drink. It's—"

"I know what it is," Madison said drily.

Darren continued. "Do you know how much the ceremony cost? Over three grand. And, as it turned out, the marriage wasn't even legally recognized." Anger flickered in his eyes.

"She knew that it was a sham wedding, didn't she?"

He rubbed the stubble on his face.

"You found out she was playing you," Madison said and let that sink in. Why had Claire set this all up? She met Darren's gaze. "You had something that she wanted, and she was willing to use you to get it."

"You'd have to ask Claire."

"But she's not around to ask, is she? Is that because you silenced her?" Madison leaned across the table.

"What is it with you law enforcement types? You preach about people being innocent until proven guilty but you work the other way around. Thank God we're not in nineteenth-century England with you suspecting me of treason or you'd already have me drawn and quartered."

Madison ignored his rant. "What did you have that Claire would want?" Madison wasn't going to let this aspect go.

"That sounds a little condescending."

Terry leaned over the table and tapped his finger on Claire's crime scene photo. "Then start talking."

"Can we put those pictures away?"

"It bothers you to see her like this," Terry said.

"We cared about each other."

"*Cared* about each other, but you got married?" Madison took the interrogation back.

"Like I said, too many mojitos."

Knowing what she did of Claire, that her interest in people usually included their businesses and running them into the ground for a personal pay day, she'd run with an assumption. "So she never drove you to bankruptcy or broke your heart when she revealed the marriage was a scam?"

He laughed. "Drove me to bankruptcy? Not exactly. It took a while to get back on my feet, but she didn't have the power to break my heart. You see, Claire and I are of the same mind. We're out for ourselves in this world, not for other people, and we both got what we wanted out of our quote, unquote marriage. We didn't— I didn't, and still don't, believe in love. I wouldn't be stupid enough to let any relationship get to that point."

That sounds like someone I know.

She dismissed her personal feelings and picked up on what Darren had said. He had admitted that it took him a while to get back on his feet, but he hadn't told them exactly what he'd offered Claire. "I'm going to ask *again*. Tell us how Claire would have benefited from the relationship."

"Okay, fine, I'll tell you," Darren said. "I developed a software that streamlines manufacturing processes."

"How?" Terry asked.

Darren glanced at Terry and then back to Madison. "It's basically a database, and it guides the administrator through every step of the manufacturing process from the purchasing of raw materials to fabrication to the sales funnels. It even includes accounting functions, accounts payable and receivable, tracking costs of goods. The business owner would be interviewed in depth, and the acquired information would then be keyed into the program in *detail*. That was the important part. If the details were off in any way, the result wouldn't be as effective. The software would then assimilate the data and suggest modifications to make things more efficient and cost-effective."

"How could that work exactly?" Madison asked.

"Well, think of it this way: there are main functions of any business, but by analyzing every step and every person's position within a company, it can reveal overlaps in responsibilities."

Barry Parsons had to let twenty-five employees go because he'd said Claire streamlined the processes at Proud Yankees. "We have spoken with some of Claire's past business partners. Quite a few have lost their jobs because of this program."

Darren smiled, which Madison found inappropriate given the context of people losing income due to his invention. "It's an expected result and part of the appeal to struggling companies wanting to cut their overhead."

"Huh."

Darren continued with pride, his shoulders straighter than before, his chin slightly upward. "There were even preset results that suited most manufacturing environments. It was up to the administrator to determine which would be best suited to a particular client. Although the system would evaluate which scenarios would have the highest payoffs, the administrator needed to have a background in business to put it into effect. They also needed to know what key info to enter to get the desired results."

The first thing that came to Madison's mind was Darcy Simms, formerly Anita Smith, and the framed diploma on her wall for a

MBA, or master of business administration. Was Darcy involved somehow? Madison shook this reoccurring thought aside and went back to focusing on Claire. "Did Claire steal the program?" she asked.

"I didn't have the money to patent it." His eyes glazed over. "So, yes, she took it from me. I could be really rich off it by now."

He sounded bitter and Madison didn't blame him, but his mention of money lent itself to the fact he probably didn't know about being a beneficiary of Claire's will. Madison wasn't going to bring it up just yet, though. "What was the name of your program?"

"I wanted to call it Globacon, but she didn't think it sounded professional enough. Once she got ahold of it, she ended up calling it Capital Quest. Anyway, like I said, too many mojitos. She came up to me on the beach and—"

"She targeted you," Madison spat.

"Targeted me?"

"Somehow she knew what you had before you met."

"I don't see how." But there was something in the flicker of his eyes, the subtle strain in his voice… He wasn't being forthcoming. "I don't see how," he repeated.

"Claire got the program, but what did you get?"

"Are you sure you want to know?"

"Why not?"

He smirked. "Amazing sex."

"You expect me to believe that you exchanged a lay for millions of dollars?"

He opened his arms, palms upward. He pressed his lips and directed his gaze toward the ceiling briefly.

"Is that why you were at her house the night she died?" Madison held her composure outwardly even though flashbacks to her last night with Blake streamed through her mind.

He leaned in. "You'd like to know?" Based on the light in his eyes and the sexual energy coming from him, he was flirting with her.

"I am investigating the murder of Claire Reeves—" Madison clasped her hands on the table "—and you said you were there the night she died. I'd like to know why."

Darren bobbed his eyebrows. "I was there for sex."

"After all these years and after she screwed you over. Excuse the pun."

Darren winced. "First off, I understand why she did what she had. It was to advance herself. It wasn't personal. I was the idiot for rambling on about my program with a stranger. Besides, love is a fabrication. Something we tell ourselves we're in to excuse our vulnerability. It's a weakness."

"A weakness?" Madison gulped.

"Definitely. I'm sure you've heard it a million times."

Not recently. Oh, she'd be so much better off without Blake in her life. Who needed all this drama?

"I take it by your dazed expression that no one's said it to you recently."

How can you read my eyes so easily?

"I find that hard to believe," Darren added.

Is he coming on to me?

"Then again, you're probably too smart for all the love crap. Men speak words of love as a manipulation tactic. If a woman can be manipulated, she is weak."

The conversation was quickly steering away from the investigation and into the personal arena—*her* personal arena—and she didn't like it. "When did you leave Claire's?"

"Around three in the morning Wednesday."

"That is within the estimated time of death."

His eyes hardened over. "Do I need a lawyer?"

If Madison could play things less aggressive, maybe she could keep him speaking. She thought of Claire's bedroom and all the used condoms found in the trash. "Did you go over to see her often?"

He rubbed at his jaw. "I was wondering when you'd get around to that question. And the answer is, fairly often. Not often enough."

"That's not really an answer."

"Guess it depends on the viewpoint. I had forgiven Claire for what she had done to me years before. It was in the past."

"At what point did you become friends again?"

"I'm confused by your question."

"What's confusing about it? Given what she'd done to you, I'm sure there was a time you didn't speak."

"Actually—" Darren's face scrunched up "—Claire came back to me. Guess she liked the sex, too." He winked at Madison.

"Really? I find that hard to believe," Madison treaded cautiously. "A woman like Claire could have had sex from anyone she wanted. Maybe you hunted her down, manipulated your way back into her world, and struck when you had the opportunity."

"If you had any proof of that, we wouldn't be passing the time talking about my sex life."

Madison cleared her throat. "We are *not* discussing your sex life."

"What would you call this, then? You're curious about me. I could tell the second I looked at you"—Darren splayed his hands on his chest—"but I am hard for a woman to resist." His lingering gaze emphasized the enclosed double entendre.

"I wouldn't have guessed that," she stated nonchalantly, resisting the urge to allow this man any control over her feminine instincts. "As I was saying, we aren't interested in your sex life, but we are in your relationship with Claire Reeves. What made you leave at three in the morning?"

"You know what?" He paused. "I've changed my mind. I want a lawyer." Darren stood up, scrunched up the bloody tissues, and put them in his pocket. "I'm not that stupid. But if you'd like a DNA sample, Detective, I'd be more than willing to provide one for you personally." He winked at her again before leaving the room.

"Urgh." She slammed her fist on the table and lifted her wounded hand, cradling it to her chest. "How dare that asshole come in here and speak to me like that? He's hiding something, and I'm going to find out what."

Terry looked at her and calmly said, "I have no doubt you will."

Chapter 25

Madison opened the door to the hallway and Winston was blocking her path.

"What the hell was that?" he asked. "Why did you let him leave?"

"We didn't have enough to hold him."

"Bullshit, Knight! You've held people for a lot less." His face reddened all the way up and over his brow, to the top of his bald head. "You didn't get to the vital questions, Knight. You skirted around them, flirting with him like a teen at her prom."

Terry tensed up beside her as if anticipating a full-blown confrontation. The sergeant was staring at her, expecting a response, challenging her to say something smart aleck, but she was in shock. A part of her was strongly offended and another part of her felt the sting because his accusation held some truth. Her focus was off. But instead of lashing out with a bitter and fiery mouthful, she hurried past the two men, going after Darren Taylor.

"Mr. Taylor," she called out, hoping he'd stop.

He turned around and flashed her a cocky smile. "You want the sample here and now?"

She envisioned her fist connecting with his nose. "I never said we were finished in there."

"You didn't have to. I called for a lawyer."

"You're a suspect in a murder investigation. You will await your representation here."

"You're putting me under arrest?"

"I am holding you for question—"

"This is bullshit," he exclaimed, cutting her off. He dropped the bag from his shoulder to the floor.

"We are fully within our rights to detain you for twenty-four hours without a formal charge. Seeing as you're a potential murder suspect, I could apply to hold you longer than that." Madison motioned for a nearby officer to escort him to holding.

Darren's face had fallen sober. "Are you really doing this?"

Madison smiled briefly and held up an index finger. "You get one call." She nodded to the officer.

"Come with me, please," the officer said to Darren.

"So this is the way it's going to be between us?" Darren called out over his shoulder. She didn't give any indication she heard him.

Winston and Terry came over to her.

"Much better," Winston said before walking away.

Another vision of a fist connecting with a nose flashed in her mind. He had no right to say what he had earlier. She took her job seriously and always had at the expense of everything else, including a social life. Her heart ached at the memory of Darren speaking about love and brought with it the misery caused by Blake.

He still hadn't called her, and it was Tuesday afternoon. She'd slipped up on Sunday. Based on his history, even if his workload had intensified, he would have at least e-mailed by this point. She had refreshed her inbox a few times in the hope of seeing his name filter in.

"Maddy?" Terry broke her sulking thoughts.

"Uh, yeah?"

"You okay?"

"Of course. Why wouldn't I be?" Her response didn't sound convincing to her own ears, but he seemed to accept them at face value, or maybe he was biding his time to delve into the matter at a future time. Either way, fresh air might do her some good. "I'm just going to step out for a bit."

"Sure." He forced a smile and it confirmed her suspicions. He didn't believe she was fine, and he'd bring up the matter at some point—probably when she was least expecting it and her guard would be down.

Madison stepped out the back doors of the station, assuming

she'd head to the parking lot, get in her car, and pass some time at her apartment, but she opted for a walk instead. She must have been crazy because the snow was falling in flakes the size of cotton balls, and with the wind chill it was easily fourteen degrees Fahrenheit.

But she needed to step back from the case and mull over her personal issues. It wasn't just Blake affecting her focus. The thought of the upcoming visit from her parents made her uneasy. She couldn't be herself around them. They weren't interested in hearing about her work. They didn't care how many closed-by-arrests she had on her record. Chelsea and the grandchildren were all that mattered.

Madison walked along the sidewalk and a shiver laced up her spine. She hugged her coat tighter with one hand and pulled out a pair of gloves from her pockets with the other. At least she had gloves thanks to Cynthia. They'd gotten together and celebrated the holidays early. Cynthia had bought her a scarf and glove set, and she had bought Cynthia a pack of toe warmers, as her feet were always cold, and scented candles for her apartment.

The buildings weren't doing much for abating the gusts of wind and blowing snow, and she wished she had her scarf with her. After a couple blocks, she sought refuge and a break at her favorite place—Starbucks.

Blake thought it was a yuppie place to go, something that people got in the habit of to impress others with their fancy coffees. She'd laugh at him for saying stuff like that. Really, who was putting on the show, the person who had distinguished taste in their caffeine or those who paid forty bucks for an entree at Piccolo Italia? She shrugged her shoulders in response to her thinking process.

Madison opened the door and warmth blanketed her face in a welcoming embrace. Her cheeks tingled at the temperature variance.

Baked goods teased her nose. There was only one thing better and that was when a Starbucks was in a bookstore. She found the irony in her opinion, as she never picked up a book. When did she have the time? But the smell of paperbacks, the paper, the glue, the binding, whatever it was, combined with the smells she experienced now, made her feel safe and at home.

"What can I get started for you today?" asked a girl of about eighteen from behind the counter. She hadn't come into her own yet and was stuck wearing braces into her young adulthood.

"I'll take a venti skinny caramel cap." Madison took her gloves off and unzipped her coat.

"That will be five twenty-eight." There was a pause. "Actually, are you a cop?" The girl pointed to Madison's waist.

Madison looked down and saw her badge. "Detective."

The girl smiled, revealing a mouthful of metal. "Then it's on the house."

"Okay? Why is that?"

Madison had heard of cops being extended favors, discounted meals, free coffee and donuts, but thought the rumors circulated from small country towns. She'd never heard of free Starbucks. "How long has that been the case?"

"At least a few years. The owner of this location and two others in the city made that policy. You sound surprised? But you must have been in here before. You knew exactly what you wanted when you came in."

Maybe her badge hadn't been obvious before. "Oh, that little snake."

"Excuse me, ma'am?"

Madison dismissed the girl with a wave.

"Your cappuccino will be ready down there." She pointed down the counter, and then spoke over Madison's shoulder. "Can I help who's next?"

Madison moved out of the way.

"What can I get started for you today?" the girl asked the next person in line.

Madison couldn't help but smirk. She had to hand it to Terry. He'd been taking five bucks from her every trip he made. There was no doubt in her mind that he knew about the freebies to police officers. He better run for cover, because the next time she saw him, she was going to beat on his shoulder until it lost all feeling.

All these bets they make on cases... When he lost, he probably paid her with her own money.

The barista put a cup on the counter in haste, already moving back to the machine to fill the next order. "Venti skinny caramel cap."

Madison grabbed a lid.

Another cup hit the counter. "Tall macchiato."

Madison found an available chair in the back corner near the hallway to the washrooms. She could see the front door when afforded the glimpse between bodies of lined-up patrons. A mass of people seemed to filter in and then dwindle out—men and women of all ages, nationalities, and statures. Then she saw one she recognized: Terry.

She rose to her feet and flagged him down. Maybe he'd brought a car.

Terry came over and stood across from her. His facial expression was serious.

"What is it?" she asked.

"We've got to go." He looked over a shoulder toward the front of the Starbucks, but dropped into the chair across from her, and then he let out a deep breath.

"We've got to go, but you sit down? Now I'm confused."

"Oh, forget it. Forget I said anything." He fiddled with the zipper on his coat. "How was your walk? It must have been a cold one." He moved his chair around the table, obstructing pretty much her entire view of the front door.

"Why are you moving closer to me? What's your problem?" She shifted her chair so she could see the front door, and the minute she did, Terry's strange behavior had an explanation. Madison knew the man coming through the door, just not the woman on his arm.

Who was she and why was she on Blake's arm?

"I'm sorry," Terry said gingerly, his eyes full of concern.

She swallowed roughly, blinking back tears. Her stomach sank as feelings of betrayal surged through her. How dare he propose that they be exclusive yet turn around so quickly and be out with someone else? Thank God she hadn't fallen for his words. She cleared her throat. "Why are you sorry?"

"This must be awkward…and I know that you've been dating for a while."

She couldn't allow herself to give into her emotions. She was stronger than this. She notched her chin. "Why would it be awkward?" It hurt so badly inside as jealously entwined itself around her heart and squeezed. "We aren't exclusive," she added while trying hard to take her eyes off Blake and the brunette dangling on his arm. But she was failing miserably. The woman was laughing like an airhead at everything that came out of his mouth. The man wasn't *that* funny. "Before you sat down, you said that we had to go. Was that just because of him?"

"No. He's why I sat down."

"Listen, Terry, it's all right. We have an open relationship. We're free to date other people." She almost sounded convincing to her own ears.

"And you? You're okay with that?"

Madison hated how Terry's pressing the matter was threatening to expose her sensitive and vulnerable side. Maybe Darren Taylor had been right about love. It was simply an excuse for being vulnerable, weak. "It's not really your concern," she responded.

"Heck, Maddy, sorry for caring."

She bobbed her head and took a deep breath. An emotional breakdown had been avoided, but sadly, it meant pushing her partner away.

"Let's go, then." He slid his chair out from the table, the steel legs noisily scrapping along the floor, and then he got up.

"Fine." Her voice was barely audible. Coming to her feet, she felt like she had rubber legs, unyielding and uncooperative, as if she was a baby giraffe struggling to find its footing.

Walking to the door, she looked everywhere but at Blake despite being aware of exactly where he was. And feet away from him, wafts of the woman's perfume saturated the air, muting the smells inherent with Starbucks.

The floral overtures thrust a dagger of jealousy into her chest.

She had to get herself together. She didn't need him. She was fine on her own.

"Maddy?"

Shit. It was Blake.

She casually looked over at him, avoiding the urge to glance at the woman. But maybe she should. It would show she didn't care. She forced a smile at Blake and the brunette pressed into his side, bouncing up and down as if warming herself by the movement. "Oh, hi," she said to Blake, nonchalantly, indifferent.

"It's so cold out there," the woman responded, her voice sickly sweet.

Like a bimbo.

The woman let out an insincere chuckle and pulled herself in tighter to Blake.

Madison made sure that he noticed her eyes go from the woman to him. "Good day, Blake." She walked out the door before he could say a word.

"You really are cold as ice, aren't you?" Terry followed her.

Outside the door, she stopped walking, her soul grounding her steps. She sensed eyes on her, but stubbornly refused to satisfy her curiosity by turning around to see if it was Blake.

Terry caught up to her and concern swept over his face. "So you said an open relationship?"

Madison nodded.

"How's that going for you?"

"Just fine." She tossed in a shoulder shrug.

"But the question is, are you fine?"

She narrowed her eyes to slits.

"Oh no, what did I do? I don't like it when you look at me like that." He pretended to wince, and protectively and preemptively put a hand over his shoulder.

Ironically, the movement brought back another matter to her mind—the fact that he'd been ripping her off for the last five years every time he went to Starbucks. But maybe she wouldn't bring that up just yet. After all, payback was a bitch. Now that thought brought a smile to her face.

Chapter 26

Madison gestured for Terry to move away from the driver's door and reached for the handle. "Hand me the keys."

Terry flailed his hands. "I never get to drive."

"Now you got it." She winked at him and he gave her scowl but placed the keys in her hand.

He walked around to the passenger side and they both got into the car.

She looked over at him. "So why did we have to leave Starbucks?"

"I got a call from the cleaning service—"

"We released Claire's house?" Normally they were notified when a crime scene was released, meaning that everything deemed evidence had been collected.

"They got the clearance. It would have had to come from Cynthia Baxter and the sarge."

"And he says I don't communicate," she mumbled. A few seconds passed, and apparently, Terry needed encouragement to continue. "All right, you got a call from the cleaning service and…what?"

"They found Claire's missing underwear."

"So the killer obviously didn't eat them, then?" She put the car into gear.

"Ha-ha."

She smirked and glanced over at him, but he was facing out the passenger window.

"Officer Ranson will let us know once Taylor's lawyer gets there," he said without looking at her.

"Good job."

He turned to her now. "See, I can handle things without you

holding my leash."

"Oh sh—" She had been in such a hurry to leave that morning that she had this sinking feeling that she had forgotten to put Hershey in the kennel—again. "I've got to stop by the apartment for a minute."

At first, Madison didn't smell anything. Maybe Hershey had behaved himself while she wasn't there. At least she could hope.

"Hershey," she called out as she moved around the apartment. "Hershey." She had insisted it would only take a moment and made Terry stay in the car. It wasn't easy as he kept insisting on a visit with his *old friend*.

"Hershey."

Where could he be? She had been through the living area already. Then she saw him. He was so tiny, and his brown fur blended him into the shadows. He was at the end of the coffee table and his head lowered when he saw her.

"What are you doing over there?" When she got closer, she got her answer and had to muster the strength not to strangle him. There were teeth marks in the corner of the table that her grandmother had left her.

Hershey sank to the floor, sensing he'd done something wrong.

"Bad dog!" Her roar frightened him to a pause, and he looked up at her. His eyes were large and his ears drooped. "In your kennel. Now!"

He trembled but otherwise his paws were planted to the floor. She picked him up and put him in the kennel, latching the door behind him. She wagged a finger at him. "Bad dog!" The anger brought tears, and she let them fall.

That coffee table was one of the few tangible things she had left of her grandmother. She quaked with rage as she ran her fingers over the damaged wood, trying to see some way of rescuing or reversing what had been done. But the table had been destroyed by the gnawing teeth of a canine. How could Hershey do this to her?

She glared over at him and in that instant, she wanted to tote the entire kennel with the encased animal down the elevator and place it in her partner's lap. After all, he was responsible for her having this four-legged chewing contraption in the first place.

"Bad dog!" Her scream contained a few more tears. She couldn't muster more than the two words.

Her home phone rang, and she wiped her cheeks and answered.

"You coming back?" It was Terry.

"Why are you calling my home phone?"

"Because I'm in the lobby. You coming back down or what? We've got to get to Claire's house."

"I'm coming." She slammed the phone down and her eyes drifted to the demon dog. As much as she'd like to just ignore him right now, she had to take him out before she left him again.

OUTSIDE CLAIRE'S HOUSE, Terry said, "I had the cleaning crew stop all work as soon as they called."

"Sorry, I'm out of gold stars," Madison replied sarcastically.

He snapped his fingers, letting the action say the word. *Snappy.*

He should be happy that all she was doing was spewing sardonic comebacks, because what she wanted to do, well, it could mean life imprisonment. Terry was to blame for the coffee-table-eating varmint she had in her apartment.

They didn't need to knock; the door was opened by an Asian man in his late sixties. "Detective Grant?"

"Yes, and this is Detective Knight."

Madison hesitated to take a breath, the smell of blood permanently etched into her memory from their first visit here.

"I just knew it might mean something. Come in." He stepped back to let them inside and closed the door behind them. "It was just a little out of place. And there's more than the underwear."

"What's that?" Terry asked.

The man brushed him off with a wave of the hand. "We'll get to that. I assume you have your evidence collection kit?" His eyes traveled down their arms to their hands, settling on the kit in Terry's hand. The man smiled. "Wife's favorite show, *CSI.*" His clipped English became more apparent as he continued to speak. He stopped next to the couch and extended a hand to Madison.

"Where are my manners? I'm Ramesh Huang." He smiled, flashing a mouth full of chipped and yellowed teeth. It made Madison cringe, and by contrast she thought about Cole Richards's perfectly white smile.

A woman walked in from the kitchen, and Madison allowed herself a full breath. Thankfully the smell of blood and decomp wasn't as strong as it had been when they got called to the crime scene days ago.

"This is Lucia," Ramesh said. "My wife."

The woman nodded but avoided eye contact.

A pair of underwear sat on top of a couch cushion. Madison pointed to them. "Where did you find the underwear?"

"The couch. My wife and I were in the room, same time. I was working on the couch—" Ramesh lifted another cushion and pointed to the crack between the arm and pillow "—found here."

"So just right there?" Madison was furious. How could the investigators be so careless as to miss finding them? Had they not searched there? Maybe the murder weapon was lodged in there somewhere, too. She glowered at Terry, although her disappointment wasn't directed at him. Her cheeks flared, no doubt to a brilliant red, and the lobes of her ears were on fire. "This isn't acceptable," she said primarily to her partner, not really caring about the Huangs' presence. "If this pair of underwear ends up factoring into the case, they will be inadmissible. The chain of custody has been broken!"

Terry looked at the couple. "Excuse us for a minute."

The Huangs left them and slipped into the kitchen.

"It was an oversight," Terry began. "The investigators are only human."

"Human? That's what you're going with here?" Madison shifted her stance. "I just hope that this pair of underwear doesn't end up being a pertinent part of this investigation." Her gaze shot to the couch. "Can we be sure the murder weapon isn't in there? And maybe they found it and are keeping it as some sort of novelty?"

Terry glanced toward the kitchen, then back to her and cocked his head. "Yeah, I can see that happening," he said sarcastically.

Madison knew the probability was zilch. And the couple had called them regarding the underwear... She pulled the cell phone off her hip and hit the quick key for Cynthia.

"What are you doing?" Terry asked.

"I'm going to give Cynthia a piece of my mind," she fired back.

"Can't let you do that." Terry grabbed her phone and ended the call.

"Everything's been compromised," she said through clenched teeth, tapping a foot. Anger surging through her made it impossible to stay still.

"You've got to let it go." He put a reassuring hand on her shoulder but removed it not long after making contact. He must have sensed her silent message to get his hand off her.

"I don't understand why you're staying so calm." She held eye contact with him for a few seconds but he wasn't going to amuse her with a response. She turned in the direction of the kitchen. "Ramesh Huang?"

The man came out of the kitchen with his wife behind him.

"You were both in this room when you found the underwear?" Madison asked, clarifying what he'd said before.

"Yes."

"Your wife saw you find them there? She was looking at you when you pulled them out?"

"Yes."

"We'll need you to go on record to that effect." Madison knew they would never be accepted in as evidence, but the underwear still might provide them with some direction for the investigation.

"Certainly."

"Perfect." Madison directed Terry to retrieve the underwear, which he lifted with tweezers and placed into a paper bag. Clothing always went into paper to preserve trace evidence. "Now you said that there was something else?" Madison asked.

"Yes," Ramesh began. "Over here."

Madison motioned for Terry to do a quick search of the couch while she followed the older man toward the front window.

"Right here." He pointed out a smudge on the window.

Tilting her head to alter the way the light refracted off the glass, Madison realized the smear was on the outside and that it was a palm print. She felt another surge of rage course through her. She would have remembered that being cataloged in the evidence file. Had they missed the entire living room?

Terry came up behind her, and she turned to him.

"Nothing else in the couch," he said.

She pointed to the window. "Mr. Huang, the *cleaner*, found a print on the outside of the glass." How a cleaner had found all this when the trained experts hadn't was beyond her comprehension. Maybe Ramesh should become an investigator.

Terry acknowledged the find but didn't say anything.

Madison continued. "Our killer could have been watching Claire from this window, and when he saw the opportune moment let him- or herself in."

"I help solve murder." Ramesh's voice held excitement.

God, the couple is still standing here.

"Scene was released," Ramesh said, obviously having sensed her irritated energy. "Have authorization to be here. I can get paperwork."

Terry held up his hand. "It's okay. We are aware the scene was released."

"Who hired your services?" Madison blurted out. Crime scene cleanup wasn't paid for by the city but covered by family or friends.

"One minute." Ramesh turned to his wife and spoke to her in another language. She went into the kitchen and returned with a clipboard.

Lucia ran her finger down the page. "The name is Darcy Simms."

Chapter 27

Madison stormed into the lab and dropped the paper bag containing Claire's underwear and the card with the lifted palm print on the table. "What the hell were your people thinking or were they?"

Cynthia pulled her head back from the microscope she had been looking through. "Excuse me?"

Madison bobbed her head to what she'd set down. "That was collected from Claire Reeves's house."

Cynthia stared at her blankly but there was a lick of agitation in her eyes. "That scene was released."

"So you realize that?"

"Yes."

"Maybe a little too prematurely given the fact that it wasn't thoroughly examined." Madison waved toward the articles on the table. "I mean obviously."

Cynthia's face fell and went pale.

"A *cleaner* found these, Cynthia. The underwear was in the living room couch. And that's a palm print lifted from the front window. Someone—maybe the killer—was watching Claire. Not that the print will do us any good now. It's virtually useless."

Cynthia stood there, her mouth gaped open. "Maybe the cleaner put it there to make them look good? Are they aspiring for a lab job?"

"Come on, Cyn, that's your response to this?"

Cynthia looked away from her.

Madison continued. "The underwear matches the lingerie Claire was wearing at the time of her death. The killer could go free because your lab screwed up."

Terry stepped next to Madison. Until then, Madison had forgotten he was in the room.

Cynthia braced her hands on the table and stretched forward, extending her back. "You said the couch?"

"Who was responsible for processing the living room?" Madison held eye contact with her friend and colleague.

She shook her head. "Doesn't matter. I'm responsible for the lab. I will assume full responsibility."

"So it was Mark," Madison stated matter-of-factly.

"What part of this don't you understand? It comes back to me." Cynthia's eyes begged to be relieved of the finger-pointing exercise. "I will speak with the investigator—" She stopped abruptly and held up a hand to keep Madison from cutting in. "And here I thought you were going to love me today. Guess you never know, do you?"

"You have something for us?" Madison's eyes diverted to the microscope.

Cynthia followed the direction of Madison's gaze. "It's nothing to do with that, but I have some results in from a swab of Claire's neck slash. It contained two DNA profiles."

"Claire's and another?"

"What one might expect, but actually the two I referred to were in addition to Claire's."

Madison moved in closer and Terry with her.

"In addition?" Madison asked.

"Uh-huh. When Richards prepared for autopsy, he recovered a single hair from the wound tract."

"He never mentioned that to us."

"I'm mentioning it to you now," Cynthia ground out.

"Fine. Go ahead." Madison was still sour. "Tell us about the hair."

"It belongs to a *Rangifer tarandus* caribou."

"Okay, I understood caribou."

"Boreal woodland caribou, to be precise. They are hunted primarily in Newfoundland and the Mackenzie Mountains during the months of August and September. It seems like Newfoundland is the most popular area based on a Google search."

"Newfoundland?" Terry said. "That's a little journey from here."

"Just a little," Cynthia agreed.

"So it's probably safe to assume that our killer was an avid hunter," Madison began. "Otherwise, what else would Newfoundland have to offer?"

"Whale watching," Terry snapped back and had both women looking at him.

"Anyway…," Cynthia said through a smile of amusement, "I found a popular outfitter there by the name of Natural Adventure Outfitters. They offer guided hikes, professional hunters to answer their guests' questions, and accommodations. The place looks quite nice, actually. Dare I even say modern? Given this information, a Bowie knife would make complete sense because caribou have a thick hide, almost like a moose. It would make easy work of tearing through the flesh."

Bluck! Madison's gut turned. All the blood that would result from that… It brought back the vivid memory of Claire lying on the floor in the puddle of deep crimson.

Cynthia went on. "The Bowie knife, if wielded the right way, could have actually decapitated Claire."

"Okay, enough." Madison looked around the room in search of something else to focus on so she could divert her mind from this unpleasant conversation.

Cynthia had a huge smile on her face and addressed Terry. "So she's a major crimes detective, but start talking blood and decapitation and she gets queasy."

"Enough about me," Madison retorted. "Back to the case. We're looking for a hunter who travels to Newfoundland and hunts caribou. That should help narrow things down."

"We'll have to ask your new boyfriend if he's a hunter," Terry said.

Cynthia glanced between the two of them. "New boyfriend?"

"Terry thinks he's funny—" she shot him a glare and jabbed his shoulder "—but he's not."

"Hey!" Terry barked.

Cynthia looked from Madison to Terry and back to Madison.

Madison rolled her eyes. "His name is Darren Taylor, and he's in the drunk tank right now. You said you found two DNA profiles in addition to Claire's. What did the other profile belong to? A dog? A moose?"

"Try a human," Cynthia said. "Male to be specific."

"It could belong to the killer. He could have cut himself when he slashed Claire's neck."

"Possibly. Of course, we can't pinpoint with any certainty whether the killer cut himself at the time or if the blood was on the knife beforehand. Claire obviously didn't have a caribou in her kitchen, so that transfer got onto the knife from another time."

"Either way, the DNA could lead us to the owner of the knife."

"It could, but—"

"I take it no hits in CODIS," Madison surmised.

"On the caribou?" Cynthia teased her, but her smile fell short of touching her eyes when she seemed to notice Madison wasn't amused. "I'll let you know if there is. It's still running."

Chapter 28

Madison and terry were back at their desks when her cell phone rang. "Knight." She paused and listened to the person on the other end of the line. "He's going to be happy about that." Another pause. "Okay, thanks for letting me know."

Terry looked up from his side of the desk. "And why do I sense sarcasm?"

"Because you're astute. Taylor's going to have to spend the night. His lawyer won't be here until tomorrow morning. We'll meet with them at nine."

"We might as well get some shut-eye then," Terry said.

She looked at the clock on the wall. *7:06*.

"Yeah, I don't think so," she began. "There's lot of work to be done, and I could use your help."

"What could you possibly need done right now?"

"You have heard of the phrase 'there's no time like the present'? I need you to check into Taylor's story. Confirm with the airline that he really did leave for Tahiti in the wee hours of Wednesday morning. And—"

"And?"

"*And,*" she added further punch to the word, "when you're finished that, I'd like you to look up the largest trade industries in Tahiti."

"What for?"

"Just more or less for my curiosity. That way when I press Taylor more about this job he had there, we'll know if it makes sense right away."

"Fine." He sighed. "But if I'm doing all this, what are you going to do?"

"Don't worry yourself over that." She started typing.

"You're probably shopping for shoes online."

She looked around the monitor at him and searched the top of her desk for the perfect weapon. At first, she eyed some scrap paper, which she could ball up and toss at him, but the impact wouldn't be hard enough. Then she spotted the perfect instrument, a mailman's elastic—blue, tight, and holding fantastic snapping quality. She pinged it at him.

"What the—" He rubbed the point of impact, which was the meaty flesh near the armpit. "What was that for? It's going to leave a dang bruise."

"And you say it like it's my fault that you bruise easily," she teased.

"It would be your fault if I got a bruise." He glared at her.

Maybe she should feel bad, and maybe she did a little, but given his comment about searching for shoes online, hitting him brought some sick sort of satisfaction. Besides it wasn't like she was obsessed with footwear. If she was going to look into anything personal online, it would be researching a behavioral place to take Hershey.

Her desk phone rang and she answered.

"It's Officer Foster," her caller said. "I'm covering the front desk tonight. I've got a caller on the line who claims to be the girlfriend of Simon Angle."

Madison sat up straighter. "Okay, put her through."

Terry held a phone to his ear, but his attention was on Madison.

The line clicked. "Hello? This is Detective Knight. You have news about Simon Angle?"

Terry slowly lowered his receiver back to the cradle.

Madison spoke into the phone. "Okay. So he's been staying with you? ... It's all right. Slow down. Where are you? ... We'll be right there." She hung up and Terry was rubbing where the elastic had impacted. "I didn't mean to hurt you."

"Uh-huh."

All right, now the guilt was snaking its way in, but she didn't have time to wallow in it. "Grab your coat. We've got to go."

Terry mumbled something incoherently, but she wasn't about to ask him to repeat himself. She sensed it had to do with the fact that he just wanted to call it a day.

He followed her out to the car in silence.

Madison turned to him. "Are you're going to be like this all night?"

"*All* night? Just great."

"What is your problem?"

"My problem is you and your ability to ride me 'til it chafes."

"Excuse me." She stopped with her hand on the car's door handle.

"You're a slave driver, Maddy. Always have been. Suppose you always will be."

"Fine. You want to leave, go for it. Just don't expect me to cover your ass to the sarge when he asks where you were in this investigation."

Terry got into the car, closing the door heavily behind him.

She got behind the wheel.

"What about Taylor in holding?" he asked.

"While it's good to have a suspect, two are even better."

He didn't respond.

She looked over at him and hoped he wasn't still upset about the elastic. "Terry, what's your problem?"

"My problem is you. You effing pinged me with an elastic, Knight! I still feel where it hit. Hurts like a son of a gun."

"I didn't realize you were so sensitive. You've got to grow a thicker skin or you're going to die young."

"Easy for you to say. You've got no connections, no life outside of this."

His snap back stung more than any elastic would have. Tears misted her eyes.

"You go home and have a dog waiting on you. No one else," he stamped out. "You live and breathe this job, and that's fine. Maybe that's enough for you, but it's not enough for me."

The words impacted her like blows to the chest, and they rendered her speechless. She couldn't deny it. She was married to the job and always would be, but since when was that considered a crime or an existence of lesser importance?

She put the car into gear and headed to the house of Simon Angle's most recent girlfriend before she said or did something else she'd regret.

MADISON PARKED THE CAR IN front of the address she was given by Simon's girlfriend, Candice Sable, and got out without saying anything to Terry. The implication of his comment still hurt: that by her putting the job first she was somehow less.

The house was older but in a decent neighborhood and had been converted to accommodate four apartments. She led the way around the back as she'd been instructed to do. Apparently, there be would a "never-ending staircase" and a door at the top. Looking up, the woman hadn't exaggerated about how long the flight of steps were.

"We need to go up there?" Terry asked.

Madison didn't respond but headed up.

"Come on, you've got to speak to me at some point."

No, she didn't. At least not any time soon.

Just over halfway up, Madison was wishing she made use of the gym at the station.

Terry, for his earlier whining, didn't seem to be having an issue at all. He wasn't even out of breath. Guess that was the benefit of running on a treadmill every morning.

"Please talk to me." His voice held an apology.

It didn't matter, though. The words still hurt more than she wished to admit, and even if she wanted to respond to him, it would be physically impossible right now. She needed oxygen.

She looked up. Three more steps.

Reaching the landing, all she wanted to do was lean on the railing and take in a few deep breaths, but her pride wouldn't allow this demonstration of her poor cardio health. Instead, she had to settle for shallow breaths and standing on her own strength while hoping Terry didn't pick up on the fact that it was a show.

She moved past what resembled the shape of a barbecue, patio table, and a few plastic lawn chairs, all of them heaped with snow.

Madison had her hand poised to knock when the door opened.

"Thought I heard someone coming up the stairs." A woman with damp, frizzy hair stepped back to let them in.

"Thank you." Madison brushed the blowing snow off her coat and stomped her boots on the carpet inside the door.

"Cold one out there." The woman smiled.

"Candice Sable?" Madison asked.

The woman nodded.

Madison introduced herself and Terry, and asked, "Is Simon here?"

"Not right now." Candice headed toward an old dining set and pulled down on an oversized sweater she was wearing as she walked. This action drew Madison's attention to the olive-green cords she wore, which we also too big for her. As she took a seat at the end of the table, she pulled down on her sweater again.

Madison couldn't help but think how fake this world was, and how much emphasis was placed on physical appearance. Candice wasn't overweight in Madison's opinion at all, but the woman had obviously allowed herself to be inundated by the media as to what size she should be. At best guess, Candice was *maybe* carrying an extra twenty pounds.

"So what makes you think that Simon Angle murdered Claire Reeves?" Madison didn't see a point in delaying the question. When Candice had called, she had shared her suspicion.

Candice put a hand on a folded newspaper and let her gaze drift to the paper. Madison caught the headline—not that she needed that to know what it was. It was a small article on Claire's murder, and Madison had it stored to memory. Maybe it wasn't healthy, but she collected newspaper clippings for cases she worked.

Candice's eyes glazed over.

Maybe it would be best to go about getting answers another way. "How long has Simon been staying with you?"

"We met last week, Tuesday. He came over and we—" She stopped talking and glanced at Terry, seeming shy to admit to having sex in front of him.

"I'm sure anything you're about to tell us we've heard before,"

Madison assured her.

Candice nodded. "Yeah, I guess you probably have. Anyway, we met last Tuesday, as I said. We really hit it off and ended up back here."

"Was he here all night?"

"I guess? I'm not really sure." She let out a self-conscious laugh. "This is where it gets more embarrassing. See, I'm not normally the type of woman to hook up the first time she meets a guy, but we drank a lot. And I mean *a lot*. We pretty much passed out. I'm sure I did."

"So you can't really say for certain that Simon was here all night?" Terry asked.

Candice shook her head. "I can't. Am I in trouble here?"

"At this point, I don't see why you would be."

"All I know is on Wednesday morning when I came to, he was already up, sitting right there." She motioned toward the chair Terry was in. "He had brewed coffee and was sipping on a cup. I had such a headache and was chained to the toilet most of the morning. I don't know how he was doing okay."

Either he bounced back quickly or the drunkenness was a show. "Was that the last time you saw him?" Candice had said Simon Angle was staying with her. Was she referring to that brief interlude or a more substantial period?

"No, like I said, he was staying with me. We hit it off. He's been here since that night."

"Do you know where he is now?"

Candice shook her head. "I haven't seen him since yesterday morning."

Madison took a deep breath to conjure patience and returned to one of her initial questions. "Why do you think he killed Claire Reeves?"

"He has a temper." Candice met Madison's eyes.

Simon's roommate had said the same thing.

"He'd—" Candice swallowed roughly and her lashes soaked with tears. "He'd mumble sometimes."

"Mumble?" Madison sure wished this wasn't a wasted trip.

"About what?"

"About her." She pressed a fingertip to the article. "It started when he heard about her murder on the radio." Candice gathered her damp hair in her hands, twisted it, and swept it upward. She took a pen from the table and slid it into her hair to hold it in place.

"What did he say about her?" Madison asked.

"He said life was a lot better before she came into it. And that's saying a lot." She met eyes with them. "We haven't known each other long, but Simon wears his heart on his sleeve. He told me about his mother." She looked at them as if they should know what she was talking about.

Madison leaned on the table toward Candice. "What about his mother?"

"Oh, no. You don't know? I'm not telling you."

Claire had been a successful woman and maybe she had reminded Simon of his mother somehow and it wasn't a good thing. "Was his mother a powerful woman?"

"I'm sorry," Candice began. "He told me in private. He'd probably be mad at me for telling you this much." She continued in a low voice. "The murder… It happened last Wednesday?"

Madison could have slammed a fist on the table from frustration. The date of the murder was in the article under Candice's hand. And hadn't they just touched on how strange Simon was that day? "Yes," Madison said. "Between two and four in the morning."

"Well, like I said he was up on Wednesday morning like he didn't have a drop to drink the night before. He was kind of different with me than he was the night before. I don't know how exactly, just different."

It wasn't uncommon for a man to lose interest in a woman he had a one-night stand with, but that didn't really apply in this situation. Simon had returned to Candice, or more correctly stayed with her. But why? Was it just to avoid his ex-wife? Then the many possibilities hit.

Simon could have been establishing an alibi. If Simon had gotten up in the wee hours, gone over, killed Claire, and then just disappeared, it might seem suspicious to Candice. But that didn't make sense. Candice wouldn't necessarily be able to connect Simon with Claire. There were other good reasons for Simon to stay, though. One, he could use Candice as an alibi. He'd know she would have been too drunk to know he'd left the bed during the night. Two, to avoid his ex. And three, he could hide out here from law enforcement. He'd have to know that he would be a murder suspect given his background with the victim.

All their heads turned toward the door. They had all heard it—the steady thump of feet.

"Someone's coming up the stairs," Candice whispered.

Madison stood, bracing an arm in front of Candice while her other hand went to her holster.

Terry rose in rhythm with Madison.

"Candice, it might be best if you go into the other room," Terry suggested, and Candice complied.

Madison's heartbeat sounded in her ears. The thumping outside stopped. Whoever it was stood outside the door. The motion sensor light had turned on, revealing the silhouette of a man through a frosted sidelight.

She motioned for Terry to step to the side of her. The knob turned and the door opened.

"Stiles PD! Put your hands up!" Terry shouted.

"Fuck!" The man turned on his heels and started down the stairs in a run.

Terry bolted out the door first. Madison took her steps gingerly, taking note of the blowing snow, and appreciating that the staircase would be more slippery than when they had arrived.

"Stop right there," Terry called out.

The man's footing slipped out from under him, and he slid down the last few steps on his rear end. He sat there moaning in pain, his arms flailing to reveal the helplessness he must have been feeling. He was caught.

"Put your hands above your head." Terry came up behind him and had him cuffed in a matter of seconds.

"I didn't do it, I swear!" The man was speaking through sobs of pain.

Madison squeezed by Terry and got her first good look at the man who had been forced to his feet. "How nice of you to come out of hiding, Simon Angle."

Chapter 29

"I didn't do it." Simon Angle held to his original story as he sat across from Madison and Terry in the interrogation room.

"Then why run? Only the guilty run," Madison said.

"I think I need to see a doctor." He winced and clenched his teeth. "Fuck, this hurts. Can I stand up?"

"No, you can stay seated right there."

"This is abuse. I'll report you."

"If you're smarter than you look, you'll sit there and be thankful that we haven't booked you yet," she said, stretching things.

"I know why you're looking for me. I knew from the moment I heard about her murder that you'd be coming after me. That's why I had to disappear."

Madison cocked her head. "So you admit to hiding from law enforcement?"

"Ah, yeah." Simon might as well have added *duh*. "I've never been a lucky man. Thought I was when Claire came along but you obviously know how that turned out."

"The truth of the matter is, you do look guilty." Madison flipped open a file. "Here's how I see it. You planned Claire's murder and manipulated your way into staying at Candice's house. She had no prior connection to you, so why would the police or your wife or anyone know where to look for you? You never even updated your friend Jim Sears on where you were."

"It's not how it looks."

"You disconnected your cell phone," Madison stamped out.

"That's 'cause all every person wants from me is a buck. And I'm fucking tired of supporting everyone! And I'm fucking tired of sitting in this wooden-assed chair!" He rose to his feet.

Madison allowed it, but she sensed her partner's anger rising because of Simon's foul mouth. "Tell us this. Why would you think we'd come after you for Claire's murder?"

"Hmm, I wonder." He pressed a finger to his chin. "Because I'd have a very good reason! I hated that woman, what she did to me, to the life I had before she came into it. She took it and turned it to shit."

"From what I hear, your life wasn't that great before." Madison was referring to his mother and a childhood that seemed to hold some mystery.

Simon rolled his eyes theatrically. "You're really reaching."

"Why react so strongly to a simple statement? Obviously the past still affects your present."

"You're twisting things."

Madison remained calm. "Don't really think I am. You were heard saying you'd kill Claire the next time you—"

"My wife told you that, didn't she? I don't know why I even allowed myself to get involved with that trash in the first place."

"So you'd like us to believe you went into hiding to avoid bill collectors?"

"For that. Among other things." He braced a hand on the small of his back. "I am just sick and tired of supporting everyone. And my day job sucked. I said, 'screw it,' and gave my notice a couple Mondays ago. I'm tired of my life being sucked out of me. Working for the man… Might as well be called day prison. Anyway, there's more to me than one might think. I have…dreams…and…aspirations." The latter statement was fragmented through clipped breaths, seemingly due to back pain the way he was gritting his teeth.

Madison remembered what his roommate had said about Simon helping that stray cat and hunting women, but she had to ask a question nonetheless. "You ever hunt animals, Mr. Angle?"

His face scrunched up. "What? Do I hunt?"

"That's what I asked." Now it was her turn to add the inferred *duh*. "What about woodland caribou?"

Simon's face paled. "I would never hurt one of God's little creatures."

"Have you ever been to Newfoundland?" She would keep going until she felt satisfied.

"No. Is that where those caribous are hunted? Detective, I would never hurt an animal or a person for that matter. Even Claire. Even after all she did to me. And just so you know, I'm a vegetarian. I don't even want other people slaughtering animals for me to eat." His eyes held conviction.

Maybe he was telling the truth, but she couldn't afford to let her guard down when she was hunting a killer. "We'll need a sample of your DNA."

"If it gets me out of here, let's do it."

MADISON LEFT THE INTERROGATION ROOM and headed for her desk.

"Do you think he did it?" Terry followed her.

She didn't respond.

"You're still not talking to me," he said skeptically.

Madison stopped walking and turned to face him. "We can talk about it all we want, but until we get the results—"

Terry was shaking his head. "Since when don't you speculate?" He flailed his hands in the air and walked off in the opposite direction from their desks.

She watched him leave, but she was still mad and hurt, even if she didn't care to admit to the latter. Just because Terry was married and she wasn't didn't make his life more valuable.

Madison dropped into her chair, opened the drawer, and pulled out a Hershey's bar. She peeled back the wrapper and took a large bite, savoring it with her eyes shut.

Maybe if she poured herself into her cold case for a bit…

She pulled out the folder for Bryan Lexan from her drawer. Her mind instantly started to work through the investigation. At the time, they had done everything they could. They'd conducted searches of the residences for both Dimitre Petrov's men, along with the main Russian mafia business front. But everything had led to a dead end.

She shuffled through the crime scene photographs and stopped on one of a torn piece of envelope. It was part of the flap, but they hadn't been able to lift any prints or DNA.

She pinched the photo between two fingers and held it at an angle; her gaze drifted to the report that documented the envelope into evidence. There was another photo in the file that was zoomed in on the stationery. It showed the fibers that weaved and repeatedly formed the…

Infinity symbol?

She dropped the photograph. For some reason, it took until now for this to come together. She rifled through another desk drawer and found what she was looking for. It was an envelope addressed to her from Dimitre Petrov. And just as she'd thought, it was the same stationery.

She dialed the lab. "Cyn, I need you to do something for me."

"WE HAVE THE REPORT BACK on Simon Angle's DNA." Terry was coming toward Madison and she quickly worked to stuff everything back into the folder.

Too slow… He pointed at it. "Please don't tell me that's the file on Lexan."

"I won't tell you." She tucked the file back into the drawer. "What were the results on Simon?"

"You've got to let that case go." He was referring to Bryan Lexan's.

"Are you going to hand me that report?" She rose to her feet and scooped a folder from his hand.

Terry let it go and held up both his hands in mock surrender.

She read the results and looked up at her partner. "It's not Simon."

"Nope."

"You know, I had a feeling. The guy's a vegetarian, and I believed him when he said he's not a hunter."

"Oh, so now you're talking to me? Before when I'd asked if you thought he was guilty, you shut me out." Terry's eyes were cold and he looked utterly exhausted.

She was feeling tired herself, and flashbacks to Hershey and what he did to her grandmother's coffee table were stinging reminders of what she would be going home to. She wasn't even allowing herself to think of Blake's betrayal, the brunette on his arm. "Can we just let it go?"

"Yeah, whatever you'd like," he stated drily and headed for the door.

"You want me to speak my mind?"

Why didn't I just let him go?

He turned around. "By all means."

With his eyes on her, she found it hard to formulate her words. She wanted to vent to him, tell him how stupid it was that he got her a dog, how her life had been fine before that. But what would be the point? Then the words he had spoken earlier came back to her with renewed impact. "Just so you know, my life is good, Terry. I have no regrets. I put one hundred percent of myself into this job, and why is that a bad thing?" She held up a hand. Now that she'd started opening up, talking about Hershey would be easier. "Let me continue. It's Hershey—"

He let out a big moan, slightly exaggerated.

"We're not going to work out," she ground out.

"Not going to work out? You haven't even given him a chance. You had your hard head set against him from the beginning."

"Don't say that," she said. "That's not the truth."

"Who are you trying to fool? Damn right it's the truth, and your eyes testify to that. You've had him less than one week."

"Normally, I know what I want in that amount of time…or less."

"He's a dog, Maddy, not a goldfish. It will take adjustment, but trust me when I say it will be well worth it. Not long from now you'll be singing my praises—"

"Right now I wonder how that's possible." She tapped her fingers on her thigh. "You know what? Forget I said anything."

"Sure." He turned to leave.

"He gnawed on my grandmother's coffee table." Her voice fluctuated, bordering on cracking. "It's all I have left of her."

"I'm sorry, Maddy. I just thought you'd like having something with a heartbeat in your apartment who looks forward to your coming home and who loves you unconditionally."

He spoke that word—*love*—the one that had become taboo to her. No good came of it. What the hell was love anyway?

"I don't need you looking out for me." It came out more defensively than she had intended.

"'Night." He waved his hand in the air and left.

Madison wrapped her arms around herself and rubbed at them as if she were fending off a chill.

Sometimes—and even more lately—she felt so alone in this world. Maybe she should be thankful for the heartbeat in the chest of that four-legged animal. He did have such soft velvety ears, and when those eyes looked at her, they had a way of seeing through her. The warmth they contained, the love of life, like every day was a new adventure, every activity an event to be excited and thankful for. She could learn a lot from him and benefit from his company. But her grandmother's table… Had he not committed an unforgivable sin by chewing on it?

She wiped at a single tear that dripped unexpectedly down her cheek. Her grandmother had meant so much to her, but maybe it was foolishness letting herself become attached to a tangible item like it would bring her closer to a memory. If she thought about it, she could still smell her grandmother's fabric softener. She remembered staying with her on summer vacation, the aroma of homemade macaroni and cheese baking in the oven and the scent of her gas stove as the flame burned under a pot of chicken soup.

The memories were so vivid it was like she was still here… But she wasn't. That realization never got any easier. She could never talk to her or listen to her advice again. More tears fought to escape the corners of her eyes, but she stubbornly refused to release them. It probably didn't matter that the table had been marked. If her grandmother were here, she'd likely say, *It adds character, dear*. Leave it to her grandmother to roll with whatever life sent her way.

Maybe Madison could be like that. At least this time. Terry could have been right and maybe she wasn't giving Hershey a fair shot. He was just a puppy, and he couldn't be trained overnight.

A yawn encompassed her face, and she drew her eyes to the

clock on the wall. *10:32.*

She still had work to do, and in less than eleven hours, she would face Darren Taylor and his lawyer.

Chapter 30

A COUPLE OF BUSINESS CARDS slid across the printout Madison was reading. "What the—" She glanced up to see Terry standing there and went back to the cards, shuffling through them and reading off the sales pitches as she went along.

"Man's best friend, behavioral training for your canine. Ben's boot camp for dogs, obedience training. Make your dog your best friend. Teach your dog to only chew on what you want him to." She looked at Terry, and he placed a Starbucks cup on her desk. She inhaled and took a small draw on the drink.

Yum, caramel cappuccino.

"What is all this?" She held up a card at an angle between her index and middle finger.

Terry smiled at her and took a seat at his desk across from her. "Just let me know what you're going to do with him, and Annabelle and I will pay for half of it."

"I can't accept that."

"Hey, we got you into this."

He did have a point. Besides, he probably had quite the savings built up from ripping her off for all the cappuccinos in the past. But she'd wait for the most opportune time to broach that subject.

"You've just got to promise me that you'll give him an honest try," Terry added.

"I will." With the thought of Hershey being trained, hanging in seemed easier to imagine. But maybe it also had something to do with Terry's talk before he left last night about Hershey being given to her out of kindness. She opened her mind toward Hershey a little more. She'd even taken him for a walk before crawling into bed. And he could be kind of adorable when he chose to be.

"So are we ready to nail this guy's ass to the wall?" Terry asked, steering the conversation to work. "I really think that he did it."

"That would make two of us." She filled him in on what her research had turned up last night—or this morning, depending on how one looked at it.

"Can't believe you found out all that after I left. Okay, maybe I can. Oh, and just for the record, I couldn't sleep, so I made calls and did some research at home."

"Thanks." She reached for her cappuccino and took another sip of it, savoring the flavor, appreciating the full body of the beverage and the smoothness. Never a bitter edge with a Starbucks. She wished she could sit there and enjoy it until it was finished, but no such luck. Her desk phone rang.

She didn't pick it up but looked toward the front desk where Officer Ranson was facing her. Ranson hung up.

Madison didn't need to hear Ranson's message, she saw the man at the front counter. "Looks like the suit's here."

"Yeah, only he's not wearing a suit."

Suit or no suit, he still radiated defense attorney. Clean-cut, angular-jawed, trim, and reeking of money from a distance. He wore navy-blue Dockers with a gabardine wool sweater.

"Good morning." He held out a hand toward Madison. "I'm Randal Irving. I assume you're Detective Knight."

He held her hand firmly, as any professional lawyer does, with forced eagerness and an added flavor that indicated you could confide in him yet at the same time not fully trust him. "Yes, I am." She wondered how he knew she was Knight and figured Darren Taylor must have told him she was a woman.

"Detective Grant." The lawyer shook Terry's hand. "All right. Now that we have the pleasantries out the way, please lead me to my client. I'd like to consult with him before you bombard us with your questions." Randal had a face that warranted mistrust, with busy eyes that seemed to take in everything all at once.

Madison and Terry led Randal to interrogation room one.

"Go on in and we'll have Mr. Taylor brought up from the cells shortly," Madison said.

"Well, Darren was right about one thing, Detective." Randal moved around a piece of gum in his mouth that he must have kept concealed until now. "You're one fine-looking woman."

Had he seriously just said that?

"I suggest you align your focus to your client. Or don't." Madison hitched her shoulders. "Your choice."

Twenty minutes later, Madison and Terry sat across from the lawyer and Darren Taylor. Darren's stubble, which had given him an allure yesterday, had become scraggly overnight.

Madison didn't say anything as she opened a thick beige file folder. Inside were pages of evidence reports and crime scene photographs. She took her time finding and pulling out the two pictures she was after—the one of Claire in the morgue that Darren had seen the day before and one of a log cabin surrounded by woods. She placed them on the table.

Darren's gaze first went to the photo of Claire. His expression was similar to his initial reaction from yesterday. There was no real shock either time.

"I've seen this before." He looked at his lawyer. "Make her get rid of it."

Randal gestured with a sweep of his hand for Madison to put it out of sight.

"No, this stays," Madison began. "It's there to remind us of what happened to Claire."

"Do we really need a photo?" Darren moaned, but he didn't show any emotion.

Maybe he doesn't need the picture because he can vividly remember how she looked after he slaughtered her.

She pointed to the photo of the cabin. "Does this place look familiar to you?" She tried to lock eyes with him, but he was looking at Randal.

"I don't see what this place has to do with the case, Detective." Randal Irving sat back in his chair, crossing his arms in front of his chest, and then he pushed his pointed index finger on the picture.

"Was the victim not killed in her own home?"

"She was, but he likes to vacation here." She slid her gaze to Darren, but he was avoiding eye contact.

"What does that have to do with anything?" Randal steamrolled. "You're holding my client in regards to questioning for murder, not where he decides to vacation."

"It's ironic how your client chooses to vacation where woodland caribou are hunted."

Randal sighed. "I'm failing to see the relevance."

"Mr. Taylor stayed in one of these cabins back in—" she consulted her file for dramatics, not for a forgetful moment "—September."

"Point, Detective." Randal pressed his brows.

"Point, Mr. Irving, is that Claire was murdered with a Bowie knife. A Bowie knife, in case you don't know, is used for hunting."

Randal's teeth clenched. "So because Mr. Taylor stayed at this cabin sometime in September, you're trying to pin a murder from last week on him? The connection?"

"It's coming. Don't worry."

Randal clasped his hands impatiently in his lap.

"As I mentioned, woodland caribou are indigenous to the Newfoundland region, where these cabins are, where your client stayed. But this is where it matters to me." Madison leaned across the table. "Forensic evidence suggests that the blade used to kill Claire had DNA trace from a woodland caribou."

"Suggests?" Randal mocked. "Surely, you have something better than *suggests*." He smirked at Darren, who returned the expression. "And how does a caribou being tied to the murder weapon pull in my client?"

"There was also male DNA."

"From the murder weapon?" Randal waved a finger over the table. "So you recovered the knife that killed her?"

"Not exactly."

Randal chuckled. "What's that mean?"

"This trace, the caribou, and the male DNA were taken from Claire's wound. It's obvious caribou DNA didn't just magically get there. It makes logical sense the trace would have been on the knife."

Randal chose to remain quiet.

Madison turned to Darren. "Why were you at that cabin?"

Darren looked at Randal, who nodded his consent for Darren to answer, but he didn't say anything.

"Is there something you're hiding from us?"

Now Randal spoke. "You're implying that my client is withholding information."

"It sure seems like it." Madison held a stare with Randal that communicated maybe if he kept his mouth quiet for a moment they could make some progress. She then looked back at Darren, who just sat there staring into space beyond their heads with no real focus but in obvious concentration. He rubbed at the growth on his face.

"Why were you at the cabin?" she prodded.

A few seconds passed…

"Oh God." Darren pinched his nose with one hand and waved the other in the air, silently requesting a tissue. There wasn't any on the table, but Randall pulled one from a pocket and handed it to him. Darren dabbed his nose. A nosebleed again. "I wasn't hunting," he said.

"What were you doing there then? They cater to hunters," Madison stated with an air of indifference.

Darren's face took on hard lines. His mouth set into a scowl, and his eyes were licked with the heat of anger and betrayal.

"Give us your DNA to rule you out. It would be that easy." *If you're not guilty.*

"My client is not going to do that."

"Guess we keep talking, then." If she got enough out of him, they could obtain a warrant for his DNA. Her gaze went to Darren, and he seemed to be looking everywhere but at her. "What are you thinking about, Mr. Taylor?"

"I'm thinking that I'm an idiot, a naive bastard who bends to the power of the female, who allows himself to be manipulated and played with like a pawn in a chess game." He moved a hand over the table as if moving an imaginary piece on a board.

Randal was subtly shaking his head and passing looks at Darren.

"Because Claire took your program?" Madison kept pushing. He'd previously acted like it was no big deal that Claire had stolen it, but now he seemed to be letting his guard down and showing his true feelings. The question was, was he upset enough about it after all these years to kill over it?

"Yes," he hissed, "it's because she *stole* my program." He flailed a hand toward the file folder and turned the photo of Claire over in the process, but his gaze settled on the cabin.

When Madison had called Natural Adventure Outfitters and asked about Darren Taylor, the owner had remembered him right off because Darren had left the cabin a mess. He'd also said that Darren wasn't alone, but that he'd been there with two women. Madison had an idea who one of them might be. "Did you go there with Claire?"

"Darcy Simms."

I hadn't expected that.

"Why were you there together?"

"What does this have to do with Claire's murder?" Randal asked.

Madison looked the lawyer in the eye and said, "Both Darcy Simms and your client stood to inherit money from Claire's will. Maybe they were planning the murder?"

Darren dabbed the tissue to his nose and balled it in his hand. "If that's what you think, then why isn't she in here being interrogated?"

Huh, no reaction to the mention of an inheritance.

"She doesn't fit the physicality of the killer," Madison said. "But you do."

Chapter 31

"Physicality of the killer," Randal repeated Madison's words and leaned across the table.

Madison mirrored his action, indicating by her body language that she wasn't backing off. "Your client is the perfect height. Add this to other evidence."

"*Circumstantial* evidence," Randal interjected.

Madison continued. "He stayed at a cabin where woodland caribou are hunted with Darcy Simms. Both of these people had reason to be upset with Claire Reeves, and they were beneficiaries of Claire's will… That equals motive."

"Listen, it wasn't just me and Darcy at that cabin," Darren said.

This was the second time that Darren hadn't given any reaction the mention of being a beneficiary in Claire's will. He must have known, and then it would seem that he was going out of his way not to give them any indication that he did. But by not responding to it at all, he was tipping his hand. If he hadn't known, in the very least it wasn't a surprise to him. But she'd get back to this. Right now, she wanted to keep Darren talking. "Who else was at the cabin?"

His eyes dived to the table.

"I know there were two women," she said, revealing the hand she'd been holding back.

Darren shrugged. "She was a great piece of ass. Had red hair, shoulder length." He rubbed his knuckles against his chest. *"Caliente."*

Madison snapped her fingers. "Why were all of you there if it wasn't for hunting?"

He stared at her blankly, a twisted smirk spreading to the corners of his mouth. "Ever hear of a ménage à trois, Detective? Let me know when you want a go sometime. I could arrange it." He winked at her.

Terry stepped up beside Madison. "Shut your mouth. That is no way to speak to a law enforcement officer." Terry glared at Darren until Darren broke eye contact, then Terry continued. "I'd suggest you start talking. We know you and Darcy had a reason to want Claire dead. Maybe this other woman did, too? By not telling us her name, you're interfering with a police investigation."

Randal squared his shoulders. "That's quite the specul—"

"How did you know they both wanted her dead?" Darren interrupted his lawyer.

"Oh Lord." Randal flailed his arms in the air.

Terry leaned over, bracing both hands on the table. "What was the other woman's name?"

No response.

Terry looked at Madison. "They all did go up there to scheme a murder."

"I think so," she responded to her partner.

Terry turned his attention back to Darren. "I just don't think you thought your plan all the way through. I'm having a hard time seeing how you're getting off, Mr. Taylor."

Madison sat back, letting Terry take a run at the interrogation.

"Where did you go when you left Claire's Wednesday morning?" Terry asked.

"I told you yesterday. I caught a flight to Tahiti. You can check it out."

"Don't worry about that, Mr. Taylor. We will."

Madison looked at her partner. She'd asked him to look into the flight records, but he obviously hadn't gotten around to that.

Darren was sniffling and squirming in his chair. "I left on a flight at five in the morning."

"I thought you said that you left Claire's at three in the morning."

"You have to be there…beforehand." He seemed to struggle for a fast response.

Terry played the power for silence for a few beats, then said, "Are you sure you don't want to rethink the time you left?" Terry slipped his hands into his pockets and jingled change he had there. "Keep in mind, you've already confessed to being in Claire's home within the actual window of time of death. Sounds suspicious enough to me right there. Not to mention your motives."

"You're referring to the will?" Randal asked.

"That and the fact Claire had stolen a valuable program from your client," Madison said. "She made a lot of money because of it. Add to this that Claire set your client up and pretended to marry him, but she knew it was all a sham."

"How much money did she leave me?" Darren asked, and it warranted a sideway glance from Randal and a shake of the man's head.

"One million," Madison punched out.

"Wow." Darren was grinning. "Claire did like me."

"Obviously, my client had no prior knowledge of this, thereby eliminating a motive."

"Maybe he was surprised by the amount, but he said nothing when I first mentioned he was a beneficiary."

Darren motioned for Randal to move in closer to him.

Randal held up a finger to Madison and Terry, asking for a moment.

Madison glanced at Terry and tried to suppress a grin. They were getting somewhere with this case now.

Darren and Randal broke their huddle, and Darren said, "Okay, maybe I got confused about my days."

"Seriously?" Madison asked skeptically.

"Those wee morning hours always confuse me, whether it's to be considered Tuesday night or Wednesday morning." Darren's mouth curved slightly upward but a smile wasn't given full birth. "It was actually Thursday morning that I caught a plane to Tahiti."

"For a job? That part's still true?"

"Yes."

"All right, well, that still leaves Wednesday morning unaccounted for, Mr. Taylor. You said you were at Claire's Tuesday until the wee hours of Wednesday. Or are you confused there, too?"

"Yes... No. I'm not confused. I was there."

Madison felt a surge of excitement. He'd kept to his original story that placed him at Claire's during the time-of-death window. "But originally you lied to us? About leaving to catch a flight? Wasn't that the reason you provided for leaving Claire's in a hurry?"

"I was in a hurry. I had to work." Darren remained adamant.

Terry let out a moan. "If you lied about when you flew to Tahiti, why should we assume you're telling the truth about anything else?" Terry paced behind Madison. "Why should we believe that you left before Claire was murdered? Why should we believe that you didn't do it?"

Darren dabbed at his nose with the tissue.

"And where did you go when you left Claire's? We know it wasn't the airport now," Madison said.

Darren glanced at Randal, who splayed an open hand suggesting he answer her. "I went someplace."

"We figured that," Terry said sharply. "Where?"

Her partner could really be a hard-ass when he wanted to be.

"Can't believe I'm involved in this mess," Darren moaned.

Terry smacked his hand on the table as he had earlier; the loud thump awakening the urgency of a response.

Darren was avoiding eye contact again. "I went to another woman's house."

What was this, a daytime drama? Everyone sleeping with everyone, everyone having multiple partners?

"Her name, Mr. Taylor. Now." Terry glared at him.

Darren held up his hands in surrender. "Fine. Allison Minard."

Madison's heart fluttered for two reasons. Allison was the one who had found Claire, and now she knew why Darren's voice had sounded familiar when they were introduced.

"Darren was there...at Allison's on Christmas day." Madison stood outside the room with Terry.

His face scrunched up.

"Remember the man who was upstairs calling down to her?

That voice was Darren Taylor's. I'm pretty much positive."

"Pretty much?" Terry smirked at her and she rolled her eyes. He added, "You could be right."

"Don't say it like I'm rarely right about things—"

"Well…"

Madison was tempted to hit him, but after the elastic incident and what followed, it wasn't worth it. "So he leaves Claire's, assuming he's telling the truth about how early, of course, and goes over to Allison's."

"I can't help but wonder if Allison is the other woman from the cabin. Nah, that woman was a redhead," he said, dismissing his own suggestion.

"Women change their hair all the time, Terry. Look at Officer Ranson. Her hair's a different color every week."

"Fair enough. And then when I pressed him about his flight…"

"He had no option but to blow his timeline," she finished his sentence. "He'd know we'd find out the minute we looked into flight logs, which I take you haven't done yet?"

Terry shook his head. "I didn't get to it."

"We have to find out who the redhead is and why he's protecting her. It could have been a type of conspiracy with Darren committing the murder and the women being accessories. Either way, we need his DNA. I'll give him one more chance to volunteer it. If he doesn't, I'll get started on the warrant." She took a breath. "And we need to round up Allison and Darcy and bring them in. I'll go between the two women."

Terry's eyes lit with boyish mischievousness, and she knew immediately that his mind had went to the gutter.

"If you say one word about ménage à—"

"Ménage à trois?"

So much for hitting him not being worth it. She jabbed him in the shoulder. "I tried to warn you."

Chapter 32

"I don't understand why I had to come down here. This is ridiculous." Allison Minard sat in the interrogation room with her legs crossed. Her dark hair was down and flowed over her shoulders with volume and soft curls. Her makeup was applied with a light brush, disclosing her as a natural beauty.

"I'm going to get to the point. We have Darren Taylor." Madison watched for a reaction and got one. Allison's crossed-over leg started swaying. "He's in the other room," Madison added.

"I don't see what that has to do with me."

"This is what it has to do with you, Ms. Minard. He named you as his alibi."

"His alibi?" She nearly choked on the word.

"What time of day did he come to your place on Wednesday morning?"

"This is crazy. He must have hit his head on something." The swaying leg picked up speed, but came to a standstill when Allison's eyes met Madison's. "We aren't involved."

"You don't have to be involved to have sex." Madison looked at her like a woman who knew what she was talking about. And if she gave it any more thought, she'd lose focus. She was in that type of relationship right now or at least had been up until a few days ago.

What is the status of my whatever-it-is with Blake anyhow?

Madison dismissed her musing and put her mind back on Allison and Darren. "Let's go back to my question. What time did he get to your place?"

"I don't know. Early."

"We have Miss Minard in the other room." Terry had opted to remain standing.

Darren sniffled and it drew Terry's attention to the collection of used tissues that sat all scrunched up on the table in front of him. "You ask her and she'll tell you I was with her that day," Darren began. "Around that time. She will." His tone didn't hold conviction in his words. His gaze kept flicking to the back of the closed door of the interrogation room. "Can I see her?"

Terry shook his head. "Not going to happen. You two would just corroborate each other's stories. Although, you probably did that when you all went on your little getaway to Natural Adventure Outfitters together."

"Again, implications based on nothing more than speculation," Randal said. "Either you're going to charge my client or let him go. Why are you dragging him through this? You have his DNA now, that, may I add, he willingly provided."

After some manipulation.

It had taken Terry and Madison quite a bit to convince Darren to cooperate without forcing them to obtain a warrant for his DNA. Darren eventually consented and this was taken care of by the time Allison and Darcy got to the station.

"Can I go?" Darren had obviously latched onto the false hope created by his attorney's words.

"Until forensics have confirmed for a fact that you were not involved in Claire's murder, you will be sitting right there." Terry added as a second thought, "Unless you'd like to go back to holding."

"Thank you for coming in." Madison said to Darcy Simms, nearly choking on her words. She could go the rest of her lifetime not seeing the woman and be quite happy about it.

"Whatever. What's the point of this? Haven't you harassed me enough? I've lost my best friend." Darcy sat in the chair, her legs crossed like Allison. And while Darcy spoke of loss, her facial expression and body language didn't indicate grief, just agitation.

Madison slipped into a chair across from her. "You must be looking forward to that payday coming your way."

"Please, you insult me. One million is not—" Darcy's eyes met Madison's.

"Please, continue. I'm curious what you were going to say after that. Not *enough*? Maybe not enough repayment for what Claire had done to you?"

Darcy's eyes narrowed to slits.

Madison tossed a photo of the cabin onto the table. Darcy flinched.

"What about it?" she asked, trying to recover from her physical reaction.

"The cabin? I assume you recognize it."

"Maybe, maybe not." Darcy's legs bounced.

Madison read the same body language from both women. Either they were both involved in the conspiracy or both had seriously considered taking revenge and thereby projected guilt.

"Is that a yes or a no?"

Darcy licked her top lip and then spoke through clenched teeth. "Yes."

"Why don't you tell me why you went to Tahiti?"

"You don't have to tell him anything, Darren," Randal spat.

"I have nothing to hide there."

"There?" Terry was quick to jump on the inconsistency, as if it implied he was hiding something otherwise.

"Poor choice of words. I have nothing to hide—period," Darren corrected himself.

"So tell me. Just curious." Terry rose on his toes and then back down again, standing at the edge of the table, hands back in his pockets playing with change. He found that it could be an effective distraction for those being interrogated. It had the opposite effect on him, though. It helped him focus.

"I had a job there, like I told you."

"So that part was true?" It warranted Terry a corrective glare from Randal. Terry shrugged it off. "What line of work are you in now? The same as when you met Claire or something different?"

"What's the point of this?" Randal asked impatiently.

Terry ignored the lawyer. "I'm just curious." He let the change in his pocket filter through his fingers, each coin making a jingling sound as it landed on the ones below it.

Randal let out a deep exhale.

"Not very good under pressure, Mr. Irving? Not a very good quality in a lawyer."

"You're just wasting our time here."

Darren looked over at his lawyer. "Quiet, Randy."

Terry picked up on the fact he addressed the lawyer informally.

"So, YOU NEVER DID SAY what time it was when Mr. Taylor made it over to your house." Madison was back in the room with Allison Minard. This time she remained standing.

"Early," Allison began. "I don't know. About two, say."

"Two?" Madison repeated it because Darren had been adamant about leaving Claire's at three in the morning. "You're certain of that?"

"Quite. Actually, it was closer to two forty-five now that I'm thinking about it. I was wondering what was taking him so long. He was supposed to be to my place about midnight."

Madison wondered if Allison knew the reason for the delay was that Darren had been in bed with Claire. "Do you know where he was before he went to your place?"

"Yes, Detective—" Allison crossed her arms "—and I know he was sleeping with that bitch."

"I don't understand why you're trying to protect him."

"Excuse me?"

"He said he left Claire's house at three o'clock."

Allison's eyelashes fell slowly. "Claire's? No, that can't be right."

"One of you is lying, and we will find out who and why."

Chapter 33

"Glad to hear that you're not denying knowledge of the cabin, Ms. Simms." Madison pulled the photo of the structure back to her side of the table. "From what I hear, woman to woman, it was a good time."

Looks like the hint of a smile on her lips.

Madison picked up on the fact that Darcy never asked where she had heard about the cabin or the "good time." And she hadn't disclosed that Darren was in the other room to Darcy. "Why were you there?"

"For a good time." Darcy forced a laugh. "Just like you said."

Madison leaned against the wall and crossed her legs at the ankles. "I'll tell you what I think."

Darcy waved her hand. "Sure. I like story time."

"I think you were up there scheming a way to knock off Claire."

"Well, you do have quite the imagination, Detective. I could tell that from our first meeting." Darcy leaned back in her chair. "Now I'm going to ask you a question."

"By all means," Madison said drily.

"Who told you it was a good time? Darren Taylor?" She looked quite pleased with the fact she had put it together.

Madison was surprised Darcy admitted to it, but spoke her next words with a tone of indifference, and it melted the smug look from Darcy's face. "Now that seems quite obvious, doesn't it?"

Terry's goal was to keep Darren talking. The more that he said, the greater the likelihood that inconsistencies would surface. "What job did you have in Tahiti?"

"I was doing the same thing I did before I met Claire, after I met Claire."

"Her stealing your program didn't really affect your business, then?"

"It set me back. I had to start over."

"What industry were you helping out down there?"

"Industry? Or do you mean company?"

"Industry."

Darren shifted in his chair and looked over at his lawyer. "I'm going to take my counsel's advice now: sit here and shut up."

"Suit yourself. I'm going to talk, though." Terry jingled his change. "I just find it odd how what you offered would benefit them over there." He studied Darren's eyes and could tell he debated whether to speak. Terry poked just a little more. "Maybe I'm wrong, but I can't see your service being useful there."

"My techniques can be used anywhere," Darren spat. "For any business, for any industry."

Terry smiled. "I highly doubt that. The largest industries in Tahiti…do you know what they are?" Darren shrugged his shoulders. "I'm surprised a businessman like you, who was working down there, wouldn't know." Terry let his statement stay out there for a moment before continuing. "I looked it up online. It's fascinating what you can find with a Google search these days. The largest industries in Tahiti, besides tourism, are coconut products, cultured pearls, fishing, and vanilla. I'm thinking that the farmer harvesting vanilla or the men toiling in the heat to catch fish wouldn't be at all interested in your modern take on things."

"What is the point to all this?" Randal asked.

"Credibility. And Mr. Taylor doesn't have it. He didn't go to Tahiti for business. Another lie."

Darren avoided eye contact and plucked another tissue from the box and pressed it to his nose.

"So you knew Darren was sleeping with Claire?" Madison found it hard to believe Allison was fine with that.

"I'd have to have been an idiot not to know. I cleaned for her, remember?"

There was something else Madison remembered, too… Allison had called Claire a conniving bitch.

Allison continued. "It's not like I ever walked in on them…you know…doing it. And don't look at me like I'm some cheap whore. Our relationship was open. I knew he was banging her, and it didn't bother me. When he was with me, he was with *me*. He wasn't doing me and thinking of—"

"How do you know that?" The question came out but Madison hadn't expected the personal repercussion. How did she know that when Blake was having sex with her, he wasn't thinking about the young brunette that had been on his arm at Starbucks?

"I just know," Allison stated coolly. "I have answered your questions and cooperated. I'd like to leave now." Allison scooped her purse from the table.

"Soon."

Allison flopped against the back of her chair.

Madison took out the photograph of the cabin. It was worth a shot if Darren had been initially trying to protect her from being identified as the third woman. "Look familiar to you?"

She held it in her hand and shook her head.

"So the name Natural Adventure Outfitters up in Newfoundland doesn't ring any bells for you?" The cliché came off her lips, and she wanted to talk sternly to her mother for the corruption.

"No. Should it?"

"Truth of the matter is, it's not looking good for you. You found Claire. You had reason to want her dead."

"Really? We've come around to that? I didn't kill her." Allison crossed her arms.

"Maybe, maybe not. How tall are you?"

"Why?"

"How tall?"

"Five eight, five nine. Why?"

"That's in the range of the killer's height," Madison said, exaggerating slightly. "Maybe you staged the discovery?"

"I vomited at the sight of her or don't you recall?"

"That's your story. Maybe you forced yourself to? Stuck a finger down your throat to force it out? Some people do that every day."

"I didn't fake it."

Chapter 34

"Did you find out about Claire sleeping with Darren, and it made you jealous?" Madison searched Darcy's eyes.

"You insult me with your questions." Darcy picked up her purse from the table and motioned to leave.

"Not sure why that simple question insults you."

"Because I know what you're getting at. You're accusing me of something I didn't do. Again."

"Actually, I know you didn't commit the murder. You're not the right height. Too short." Madison let her words hang for a bit. "Unless you wore heeled shoes, but then there's no evidence of heels in the snow. And I can't imagine a woman like you wearing wedged heels."

One penciled brow arched. "Then what am I doing here?"

"I believe you were involved. I think you and Darren and Allison—"

"Allison?" Darcy laughed. "Yeah, I don't think so."

"What elicited that response?"

"For one, I don't speak to Allison. And two, what went on in that cabin…the thought of it involving Allison? Gross, all right? Not into that."

"Then who was the other woman?"

Darcy went white and stuttered her words. "I-I don't remember her name."

"Don't remember or you're choosing not to tell me?"

Darcy shot to her feet. "I'm out of here."

"Don't leave town—"

"Yeah, yeah, I get it." Darcy left the room and slammed the door behind her.

Madison had to let her go. She didn't have enough to hold her, but at least this meeting had established a couple things: she had verified Darren's story. Darcy had been with him at Natural Adventure Outfitters. If Darren was found guilty of the murder, by a stretch, it might be possible to prove she was an accessory.

"Why would I kill Claire?" Allison asked Madison outright.

"You had motive, like I said. She slept with the man you loved."

"Hold it there. Who said anything about love?" Allison shook her head. "I don't believe in love."

"Glad to hear that, because that's how Darren feels about it, too." Madison gauged her reaction.

Allison fought to keep her composure, but little inconsistencies belied it. The weight with which her eyelashes fell and the soft biting down on her bottom lip said she had true feelings for Darren.

Madison added, "Not to mention what she did to you."

"You don't know what she did to me."

Madison smiled with satisfaction. "No, but now you just confirmed she did *something*."

"You tricked me."

"Part of the job."

"Listen, I'm talking to you without a lawyer present. Believe me when I say that I didn't kill her."

"I'd love to believe you, but you have to give me more than that. We hear that line a lot here."

Allison's face softened a bit, but it was apparent from her eyes that she was hurt and embittered. "My husband had a company named Westmount Technologies. When he met Claire, he was so excited. He went on about how it would turn the business around. We'd be rolling in money."

"You're married?"

"Not anymore. Divorced."

Madison nodded, suspecting what was coming next. Claire had factored into another marriage going up in flames. "What was his name?"

"Adrian Unger."

He was the third on Claire's list of former business partners.

"Anyway, things were looking good, profits were turning around," Allison began. "We were happy. At least I thought we were. But I came home to find him in bed with that…that slut." Her voice fractured from emotion. She took a few breaths and said, "She ruined my marriage. She took my husband, my best friend, from me." A tear ran down a cheek, which she was quick to wipe away. "Now, I did love him. He was the last man I ever will." She looked in Madison's eyes. "I thought that if I took up with Claire's husband, Darren—this was after my divorce went through—it would hurt her like she had hurt me." Allison sobbed and held the back of a hand to her nose. "And this is where life took another shitty turn. They weren't actually married!" She glanced at Madison. "I take it that part isn't news to you."

Madison shook her head.

Allison lowered her hand. "Anyway, when I told Claire about me and Darren sleeping together, she laughed at me. Laughed. I'll never forget that."

"Why did you keep working for her? Why not get as far away from her as you could?"

"I just figured one day I'd find a way to get even." Her eyes matched with Madison. "I never murdered her. But I thought if I could somehow touch her where it would hurt, I'd feel better. I thought it would be Darren, but then I was enlightened. It was her pocketbook. Money. That was the only way to hurt her. So while I made a buck cleaning for her, I tried to come up with something."

"How many years did you—"

"Too many. I could never contrive something that would get to her, hurt her enough."

There was a knock on the door.

"Just one minute." Madison walked to the door and opened it to Cynthia.

She handed a folder to Madison. "Your results."

"Thanks."

As Cynthia walked away, Madison peeked at the report. She

had to let Terry know, but she was close to getting something out of Allison. She went back into the room. "Sorry about the interruption."

"It's okay. I was pretty much finished anyway."

"So you never came up with anything to hurt her financially," Madison said, hoping to get Allison to pick up where she'd left off.

"Unfortunately, no. I just thought of something, though." She looked straight at Madison. "I can't believe I'm doing this… I might be able to help you find her killer. That bitch deserves to go without justice. She didn't know of it…"

"I'm not defending in any way what happened to you, Claire, and your husband. But it was him that made the commitment to you, not Claire. Your husband was the one who broke a promise." Madison wasn't sure why she had been motivated to say all this.

"I know." Fresh tears fell down Allison's cheeks. "There's something you might not know. She was in business with someone at the time she died and sleeping with him, too. That seemed to be her MO. She never said his name around me, but I do know that she keeps her current business agreements in a safe-deposit box. Maybe if she was getting ready to screw him over…"

"He could have preemptively killed Claire over it."

"She's probably got all the originals there, too, for the older businesses, for that matter. I know she kept most of it electronically." She noticed the question in Madison's eyes. "Don't ask me how, I won't tell you. Anyway, she keeps the key to the deposit box behind a ceiling tile in her office. Three in from the doorway, four to the right, as you walk in."

"Thank you."

Allison nodded.

"Which bank was the box at?"

"I don't know."

Madison peered into Allison's eyes and she was telling the truth. "Okay, you're free to go. Just don't leave town until this is all over in case we have more questions."

"Of course." Allison dried her cheeks and went to get up. "Oh, and I almost forgot. I had heard her on the phone one day, and she was going by a different name. You might find that the safe-deposit box is in the name of Angie Carter."

"Angie Carter?"

"Yeah, don't ask me where she got the name." Allison left the room.

Randal tapped the face of his wristwatch. "How much time does it take for your lab to get results?"

"You have somewhere more important to be?" Terry asked.

Someone knocked on the door. Terry answered it to Madison and slipped out into the hall with her.

"It's about damn time. I've been singing and dancing in there," he began. "But I must say, he's looking pretty guilty, Maddy. He's a chronic liar about everything. It wouldn't even surprise me if he's a hunter and that he hunted caribou in Newfoundland."

"He didn't do it."

"What? Everything adds up."

Madison handed him the file she'd gotten from Cynthia. "Unfortunately, his DNA doesn't. He matched the condoms but not the trace from the slash or the vaginal swab. We have to let him go."

"Crap."

"Yeah… *Shit*."

"Well it's been nice getting to know you, Detective." Darren waved good-bye to Madison with a smile of redemption on his face. "Anytime, though, you want to try out a ménage à trois call me, and I'll arrange it."

"Angie Carter," she blurted out. Darren and Claire went back a long way and maybe the name would mean something to him.

"What did you say?" Darren walked back to her.

"Angie Carter. Does that name sound familiar to you?"

Terry was watching her profile, likely wondering who this woman was, as she hadn't filled him in on the name or the safe-deposit box yet.

"That's my mother's maiden name." Darren pressed his brows.

"Why are you asking about her?"

So Claire took his mother's name as her assumed identity. Why? Maybe she and Terry would figure it out and maybe they wouldn't. Madison smiled at Darren. "You might want to go home for a shave. Good day, Mr. Taylor." She turned her back on him and walked away.

Terry caught up with her. "What was that all about? Who is Angie Carter?"

Chapter 35

"So why would Claire use Darren's mother's name?" That was Terry's response when Madison enlightened him on how she happened upon Angie Carter in the first place.

Madison and Terry were on the way to Claire's house, but traffic wasn't moving quickly. Another snow squall warning was in effect and falling snow was already making a mess of the roads. Too much coming down in too short a time, and the city couldn't keep up no matter how "prepared" they were for it.

"We might never know why. Let's just hope we find the key where Allison said it would be." Madison tapped her hand on the steering wheel. "What is it with the freakin' traffic today?"

"All I know is people see a flake and they all panic and drive like old women."

"Yeah, and this isn't one flake or a light dusting of snow. Lucky us." She had thought about stopping in at the apartment to check on Hershey, but at this rate, it wasn't feasible. She needed to get that key in her hand. The one thing she dwelled on was the fact that she didn't know what bank in the city housed the box. Hopefully, the key would have the bank's name or an identifying mark on it.

Terry looked over at her. "I still think they're all connected somehow."

"But *all* you mean Darren, Darcy, and Allison?"

"Yeah, I think so. Everything just seems too…" He stopped, and the way his face was contorting, he was searching for the right word.

"Connected?" Madison laughed. "If so, I agree. It's almost as if everyone in Claire's world knew each other and were involved.

Like a daytime drama."

"Pretty much. Everyone sleeping with everyone—"

"And is it just me or is everyone beautiful, too?"

Terry looked at her with disbelief. "Beautiful? I'm not sure how Darren Taylor would like that description."

"I'm sure he'd take it. Besides his ego's large enough for a few people." If she wasn't in a department car, she'd blare the horn at the slow-moving driver in front of her, but she wasn't completely out of options. She glanced at Terry and smirked when she saw the reflection in his eyes. He knew what was coming… She turned on the lights and sirens. "That's right, dumbass. Outta the way."

SHE SAID IT WAS THREE IN, three to the right? There's a vent there. Doesn't make much sense." Terry was looking up at the ceiling in Claire's home office.

"No, three in and *four* to the right. Calm down, Casanova."

He looked at her. "Thank God you don't call me that often."

"Well I wouldn't want to wear it out."

"Yet you have no problem when it comes to my shoulder?"

She grinned at him. "Nope, no problem at all."

Terry went up the ladder and shifted the tile aside. "Strange to have ceiling tiles on the main level of a house. Normally people put them in basements."

"Maybe the original ceiling wasn't that pretty so she had a drop one put in."

"Or more likely the place was electrical heat at one time, and then when it was converted to forced air room was needed for ductwork. Dropped ceilings are cheaper. Not that she really needed to worry about money."

"Now who's the smarty?"

"Me. Always."

"You do realize all I'd have to do is shake this ladder," she teased and looked at him menacingly.

"Don't you dare!" Terry's voice was riddled with panic.

"Afraid of heights, *Casanova*?" Madison was laughing.

"We'll see who will be laughing at the next bloody murder scene."

Her expression fell into a flat line. "Why would that bother me?"

"You must think I'm really dumb—" he put a hand up into the opening "—I think I feel something."

She was happy he had continued searching for the key without becoming fixated on her fear. "Did you find it?"

Terry pulled his hand down from the ceiling tile and held a key pressed between his thumb and index finger. "We got it." He smiled at her.

"Does it say which bank on it?"

He gave her a dirty look. "Seeing as I've had all this time to look at it, examine it in depth…"

"Stop being sarcastic. Give it here." She put out her hand, palm up, and wriggled her fingers.

He stepped down the ladder. "I risk my life by climbing the ladder and you're going to claim the find now?" He held the key out for her and pulled back just before she reached it. "I don't think so."

"Come on, Terry. We need that box."

"And we'll get there." He turned the key over, likely searching for any identifying markers. "No name, but we have a number and a logo. It looks somewhat familiar… Here, take a look." He handed the key off to her now.

Madison turned over the key as Terry had and was hoping she could conjure answers.

"And Allison knew about all this but not which bank the box was at?" Terry sounded skeptical.

"That's right."

"Huh. Didn't know or didn't want to tell you?"

"Why would she tell me everything else and hold that back?" Madison cocked her head to the side.

"Are you two good friends now or something?"

"Don't be ridiculous." That was Madison's first reaction to the thought, and technically they weren't good friends or anywhere close, but she had connected with Allison on a level.

She could sympathize with Allison's situation, that of having feelings for someone who was incapable of reciprocating. The last few days that had passed in silence from Blake only cemented the fact that love was a fabrication invented to make one feel better, or worse. And he hadn't even reached out to her after she'd run into him at Starbucks with another woman. She really had to let him go.

Madison focused on the key. "I'm sure Cynthia can help us narrow down the bank. Maybe she has some sort of database she could go on or something."

"A DATABASE FOR KEYS?" CYNTHIA looked at Madison as if she was out of her mind.

"So there's nothing you can do for us?" Madison hovered over Cynthia's shoulder as she worked at analyzing evidence of some sort. None of it looked familiar, though, and it must have been for another case.

"I didn't say that. Let me see the key." Cynthia held her hand out and Madison placed it in her palm. Cynthia took a look at it. "Okay, just like I thought. See that number?" She pointed at it.

"Yes, we saw that. Is that the box number?" Madison asked.

Cynthia shook her head. "That would be the serial number or model of key. If I type this number in online, we *might* get back the manufacturer of the key."

"I'm not sure how that will help us."

Cynthia looked at Terry. "She really has no patience at all, does she?"

Terry said, "Nope."

"Come on, guys. We need what's in that box now."

Cynthia glanced at Terry again, the meaning behind which Madison couldn't quite decipher. Cynthia then headed to her computer and keyed in the number. A few seconds later she was pointing at the screen. "There. Look, I'm brilliant. This key was manufactured by Birmingham Safes for their Platinum series."

"Okay, so now we just have to find out which bank ordered those keys in Stiles." Madison paced a few steps.

"Assuming the box is in the city," Terry said.

Madison turned to him. "You always have to point out the

negative, don't you?"

"I'm the negative one?"

Madison disregarded Terry's remark. "Unfortunately, calling the banks again may be the only choice we have."

"No one had a safe-deposit box under Claire," Terry fired at her.

Madison waited for it to sink in.

"Oh, right..."

She held his gaze. "Right. So?"

"Are you serious? You want me to call all of them again asking about Angie Carter?"

"You might not have a choice."

"*I* might not have a choice," he mumbled. "And what are you going to do?"

"While you're working on that, Cynthia will be calling the manufacturer—"

Cynthia looked from Madison to Terry and back to Madison. "How did I get involved with this? Besides, I can't do that right now." She gestured back toward the table and the waiting evidence.

"You're kidding, right?" Madison asked. "That's not even evidence from our case, Cyn."

"There are other cases out there besides yours. You do know that."

"Fine. I'll do your job again." It was one of those moments where, in her mind, Madison slapped a hand over her own mouth.

"Excuse me?" Cynthia snapped and put both hands on her hips.

Terry slinked toward the door and made a quiet exit.

Madison hadn't meant for those words to come out and especially not in the harsh tone in which they had. But now that they were out there, she realized the fact that a cleaning crew had found evidence that Cynthia's team had missed still bothered her. "Your team let us down, Cynthia. The evidence Terry and I had to go back—"

"Stop there. I can't believe you're bringing that up again. We've been over this. The person who missed it has been spoken to—"

"But you're the one in charge out there. You should have double-checked to make sure your team did their jobs."

"So you'd prefer that I go around behind my employees scrutinizing everything they do in minute detail? That's not even logical. And I don't work that way."

"You don't work that way?" Madison's voice raised a few octaves. "Someone could get off with murder because—"

"The evidence that will put the killer away is in your hands, Knight, not mine. You have the murder weapon, you have the blood, you have the DNA, and you have the suspects. I doubt a single pair of underwear and a palm print will prove who put the knife to her throat—"

"I know that a Bowie knife was used, but I don't *have* the murder weapon. What if it was missed? What if it is still in the house somewhere? You released the scene. Even if it is found in Claire's house now, it will be inadmissible." Once Madison got started, she found it hard to stop. She'd always had such faith in Cynthia's abilities and her attention to detail and thoroughness.

Cynthia's face was red and her teeth clenched. She walked back to the table and to the evidence she'd been working on when they came in. Madison followed her.

"Just disappointed, that's all."

Her friend looked up at her. "Maybe you should get used to it, Knight."

My last name? She's never called me by that before.

Cynthia added, "People are prone to disappoint you at some point."

Sadly, that was one lesson Madison was learning all too much lately.

HOURS LATER, MADISON WAS STILL agitated by her confrontation with Cynthia. How could Cynthia even begin to defend herself and her team when they had been so incompetent? And Cynthia's last words—*"People are prone to disappoint you at some point"*— seemed to imply that she'd also disappointed Cynthia somehow.

She was at her desk and Terry was at his. He looked over at her.

"I've called all the main banks in the city. No Angie Carter." Terry seemed to be studying her. "What's up with you?"

She hated that she was never any good at concealing her moods. "Did you try the smaller ones, the independent banks?"

"You're kidding, right?"

"I wasn't."

"What about you? Have you gotten ahold of the key manufacturer?" Terry asked her.

"I have a message in to them. Mentioned it was in regards to a murder investigation and asked that they return my call immediately." She glanced at the clock. "That was a couple hours ago."

"So much for urgency."

"Tell me about it. And short of chasing after every possible suspect that would have wanted Claire dead, we need that box. Maybe we'll find the contract Claire had with Aaron."

"So Aaron might be a lead, after all."

"He might be." She hitched her shoulders. "Besides, we have to keep our minds open."

"What you're telling me is you've changed your mind about him?"

"Sure."

"Guess you are a woman." Terry laughed.

She glared at him. "And what's that supposed to mean?"

"Oh, I think you know." He was smirking.

"You know I'm going to let this go, this once." Truth was, she didn't have the energy to defend herself and women everywhere right now. She desperately wanted to shake her earlier confrontation with Cynthia, the stress of it, and get on with the investigation, but she was finding it difficult. Cynthia's friendship meant a lot to her. "It's been a long day," she added.

"Yeah, that's for sure. Maybe we should call it a day."

"Really? You're wanting to bail on me again? We have a case to solve, not to mention twenty-some people let go from the embroidery company we could question and the other business owners from the USB drives."

"We can't question everyone, Maddy. It's just not humanly possible. You had said so yourself."

She glanced at the clock. *7:03.*

"Guess I'm not getting a call back from the key manufacturer to—" Her phone rang.

Could that be them now?

She answered without consulting caller ID.

"Hey, Maddy." It was Cynthia, not Birmingham Safes.

Hearing Cynthia's voice delivered mixed emotions. Was she just supposed to forgive her friend, forget about the missed evidence and move on, be fine with the fact that her friend was okay with the oversight?

"I got a hold of the key manufacturer," Cynthia said.

"Thought you were too busy for that." *Shit*. She had just blurted that out.

"Let's not start." There was a long pause. "I don't want to fight with you."

"Fine."

Madison heard Cynthia take a deep breath.

Cynthia waited a few beats and continued. "I got a hold of the president of the company who told me that key line was sold in large quantity to Stiles Investments and Savings."

How was she able to get through to someone?

"He said the keys were sold back when they opened their doors in 2001. I looked up the address for you. They're located at three fifty-four Bloor Street."

"I don't know what to say."

Cynthia laughed. "You could start with, 'Cynthia, you're the best!' I wouldn't have as much success without you. Or just a simple thank-you would suffice."

"Well thank you, and all that other stuff you mentioned, too." Madison found herself smiling.

"Yep, and I also wanted to let you know there was a match to the male DNA pulled from the wound."

"And?"

"*And* it was a match to Claire's vaginal swab."

"So the man Claire had unprotected sex with was her killer?"

"Seems likely."

Poor Claire. She'd slept with the man who'd killed her. Of course Madison had considered this possibility before, but to have the forensic evidence pointing that way drove home how badly Claire had been betrayed. "Okay, well, I better get going."

"We haven't got together in a while," Cynthia said in a rushed manner, probably trying to make sure she caught Madison before she ended the call.

"We got together a few weeks ago." Madison was referring to the night they'd met up and exchanged gifts.

"I suppose." Cynthia laughed. "It seems longer ago than that, though."

"Tell me about it." Madison tried to think forward to her weekend plans: dinner with her parents at Chelsea's house. "I'd say let's get together on Sunday, but it would be for selfish reasons."

"Your mom's coming to town?"

"You're one good investigator." Her friend knew her well, maybe sometimes too well.

"It comes with the job. Okay, I'll let you go."

Madison hung up and caught Terry watching her.

"Everything good in paradise again?" he asked.

"Shut up, Terry." Madison balled up a piece of paper and threw it at him as she was laughing.

"I'm just happy it's not another elastic."

"Crybaby."

Chapter 36

THE NEXT MORNING MADISON AND Terry were at Stiles Investments and Savings. They'd already explained their purpose for being there and requested access to the safe-deposit box and were sitting with the bank manager in his office.

"I can't let you into her box." Oscar Moniz, the manager, seemed mortified by their request. He viewed them through his oversized glasses, and he had a head of black hair and bushy brows to match. "If I let you into her box then it would get out, business would suffer. You see, we are entrusted with people's most valuable possessions."

"As we've explained, Claire Reeves—or Angie Carter as you knew her—was murdered," Madison began. "We have probable cause to believe that information in her box may lead to her killer."

He leaned across the desk toward them. "I'm sorry, but there's nothing I can do without a death certificate."

Madison took a deep breath. "There won't be one."

"You just said she's dead, no?"

"Angie Carter was an assumed name, as we told you," Terry interjected.

"I cannot believe that. We require full identification from those who rent our boxes."

"So much for privacy." The words slipped out of Madison's mouth.

Both men looked at her, but then settled their gazes on each other.

Oscar said, "I would need…" He rolled his hand as if trying to conjure up the proper wording. "I think you call it a warrant, at the minimum, if what you say is true."

"What if we could prove that Claire Reeves is dead and that she was also Angie Carter?" Terry asked.

"And how would you do that?"

Terry went on. "What social security number do you have on file for Angie Carter?"

"We can't disclose that information. Surely you should understand that." Oscar's brow pressed.

"All right, we'll tell you Claire's and you tell us if it matches your system. Fair enough?"

Madison looked at her partner.

Oscar seemed to mentally chew apart his proposal syllable by syllable. "Fine. I will do that for you." He logged on to his computer terminal and then looked up at Terry. "But I'm not agreeing to let you into the box, just so we're clear." He placed his hands over the keyboard. "The number?"

Terry rattled it off, causing Madison to look at him. He wasn't consulting any notepad, cell phone, or other method of data collection. He had the figure stored in his head.

Oscar typed the number in and then looked up at them. "How is that possible?"

"I take it it's a match?" Madison said. It had been a reach to think that Claire might have used her social security number despite the fake name, but it had panned out.

"Yes."

Instead of just taking the victory, though, she didn't quite understand how Claire had gotten away with using her own number, especially considering that Oscar said they took identification. "When she set up the account, why wasn't the discrepancy between her name and social security number noticed?"

"We take ID, Detective, but we do not conduct background and credit checks."

"Interesting." Madison ruminated on that for a while. She remembered a news story that took place in England involving organized crime and Scotland Yard. They had seized millions of dollars in drugs, guns, and stolen jewelry from multiple safe-deposit boxes that had been set up to store them. One would think a background check could prevent such a thing from reoccurring.

Oscar seemed embarrassed. "No personal check. Not here anyway."

"So since we have her social security number, and we're obviously officers of the law—" Terry held up his badge "—and we have the key to her box. How about you let us have access?"

Oscar seemed to consider the proposal but shook his head before giving a verbal answer. "I am willing to strike a compromise. Bring me a death certificate for this Claire woman, and then I will allow you in." The intent in his eyes revealed no further room for negotiation.

"Not a problem." Madison stood. "We will get your confidential fax number from the girl up front and have that forwarded to your attention immediately."

Oscar consulted his wristwatch. "I have a meeting I must go to."

"All right, when should that be wrapped up?" Madison asked.

"One hour at the most."

Madison stepped out onto the sidewalk in front of the bank and held her coat tight at the zipper. Her breath came out in wisps of white in the cold air.

Terry was finishing up with his call to Richards for a copy of Claire's death certificate. He hung up.

"So we've got an hour to kill," she said.

"Imagine an entire hour of downtime. Oh, what are we going to do?"

They'd been working this case so hard it was beginning to take its toll, and who knew how much longer they'd have to go before they had their killer. *Case closed* would be such welcome words.

She looked at the buildings surrounding the bank, and she spotted the perfect place to spend an hour. "I suppose we could take a break." She glanced at her partner and put her hands in her pockets in search of her gloves but remembered she'd left them in the car.

"A break? Unprecedented."

"That's a big word for you."

"Hardy har."

"How about we go over there?" She pointed to the Starbucks.

Terry followed the direction of her finger. "Sounds good to me."

The place wasn't busy, and they had their choice of where to sit.

Madison gestured toward two armchairs near a fireplace. "Why don't you save those seats, and I'll get our drinks. You want a venti hazelnut cap, right?"

Terry didn't move. "Normally, I order for us."

"Oh no, I insist." She wondered how long it would take him to piece together the fact that she'd caught on to the little scam he had going.

"All right." He took his coat off and headed for the chairs.

"Wait. Terry, aren't you forgetting something?" She held out her hand.

He turned. "What?" His eyes went to her open palm. "Oh, right. Money." He pulled out a handful of change from a pocket and fingered through it. Madison sensed this little charade he had going was killing him. "I only have a buck seventy-three. Can I pay you back?"

Madison fought off a grimace. She had to wait things out and let him hang himself. "I guess."

"Thanks, I'll owe you." He smiled and then headed off to the table.

She wondered why he was even letting her go through with getting their drinks. The minute she reached the counter the gimmick he had going would be over.

A hand landed on her shoulder. It was Terry. "No, you go sit. I'll get it—"

"But you don't have money."

"They take debit. Or I could pay you back."

Madison shrugged her shoulders. "Sure." She handed him fifteen dollars. "Venti caramel cap for me. Bring back my change."

A couple minutes later, Terry had returned and was setting her cappuccino down on the small table beside her. He dropped some change next to it.

Madison moved the coins around with the tip of an index finger. *A buck fifty-three.* "This place is really becoming expensive." She knew he'd just pocketed the fifteen dollars and gave her some of the change that had been in his pocket.

"Tell me about it." Terry looked out the window and back at her. "Partially why I have no money."

Was he really stupid enough to believe that he was still getting away with this?

He sipped on his drink but quickly put it down and was fanning his mouth. "Hot, hot…oh-oh."

Madison laughed.

"I burned my tongue and you're laughing at me?"

"Yes, yes I am."

"Nice." He let out a rush of air trying to cool his mouth.

She drank some of her cappuccino careful not to burn her tongue. "You're not poor because of Starbucks."

"Sorry?"

"I just don't see how you could be."

"What do you mean?" He fidgeted in his armchair.

She let some time pass and decided to switch the direction of their conversation. "It was pretty impressive how you knew Claire's social security number right off."

His mouth twitched like he was going to smile but he didn't. He was obviously uneasy by her sudden change in subject matter. "I'm just good with numbers."

"Never knew that about you before." She took another drink and watched the flames dance in the fireplace for a few seconds and then turned to meet his gaze. "Does that include math?"

"I'm okay."

"You're probably being modest."

He smiled sheepishly. "I'm pretty good."

"That's probably a good thing."

"Why's that?"

"Seriously, Terry? You're going to play stupid?"

"What are you talking about?"

"You've been stealing from me for the last five years."

"I have—"

She held up a hand. "Since you're so good with numbers—and

math—maybe you could calculate exactly how much you owe me from the last five years. You can start with the fifteen you just took from me."

"What are you talking about?" He rubbed the back of his neck, a mannerism that displayed itself when he didn't have the answers or felt under attack.

She remained silent for a few seconds and solidified eye contact. "You really have no idea? If you actually paid for the drinks with the cash I gave you there would be more change." She pointed to the menu board. "Five twenty-eight each. I can do basic math, too."

"You know about the free drinks to law enforcement."

She remained silent.

"I-I," he stammered, "didn't know right away."

"I don't want to hear it. I just want my money back—with interest."

"With interest? Are you crazy? You would have just thrown that money away after something else."

"It was *my* money." She scoffed. "You're such an ass. I can't believe you did that to me."

He laughed, a nervous uneven tone. "I just wanted to see how long I could pull it off. You know until the great Knight figured it out. Can't believe it took this long."

"So now this is my fault?"

"Not what I meant," he said, backpedaling with his words.

"But don't worry, I have your money in a safe place."

"You better. I want all of it back starting with my fifteen." She flexed her hand and he dropped the bills into it. "Why, thank you." She was quick to pull her hand back. "Now where's the rest of it?"

"Back at the station."

"The minute we get back there—"

"I know. I'll get you your mo—" Terry's phone rang and he answered. "Detective Grant. ... Thanks." He hung up. "That was Richards. Our banker friend should have the copy of the death certificate now."

"And look at that—" Madison pointed to a clock on the wall "—it's almost been an hour."

Chapter 37

The woman at the bank's customer service desk nodded at Madison and Terry as they approached. "Mr. Moniz is expecting you." She picked up her phone and Oscar was coming toward them within a few minutes.

"Follow me," he said and led them into the basement of the building. Security guards were stationed next to a desk where a man sat perched with his feet on the desk, a newspaper in one hand, and a half-eaten sandwich in the other. "What are you doing?" Oscar's tone contained a stern reprimand.

The man hurried to pull his legs down and set his sandwich on the desk. "Mr. Moniz." He forced a smile.

The two guards were struggling not to laugh at their colleague's predicament.

"These are Detectives Grant and Knight. They will need access to box S-one-eight-one-two."

"Yes, sir." The man was moving but not efficiently. His newspaper fell to the floor and he nearly upset the container that held his lunch.

"Hurry. Please," Oscar said drily to his employee and then turned to Madison and Terry with the trace of a smile on his lips. "We number our boxes like the grid on a map. The first two digits represent latitude and the second two longitude. We have four sections. The box you need is in the S section, the south section. It will be twelve in from the left and eighteen up." He flashed them a proud smile. "Anyway, he"—Oscar gestured to the man at the desk—"will help you." Oscar turned to leave.

"Sir?" The employee called out to Oscar, who turned around.

"Yesssss?"

Madison could only imagine how he would have treated this man if it hadn't been for her and Terry's presence.

"I'll need your code—" the employee pointed to a small machine with a number pad that was affixed to the counter "—for overriding the one established by the box owner and for assumption of legal responsibility."

Oscar hurried over and punched some keys.

"Thank you, Mr. Moniz." The pitch in the man's voice disclosed his nerves from the need to address his superior.

Oscar turned his attention to Madison and Terry. "If you need a good place to keep your valuables or decide to change your banking arrangements, come and see me."

Once the manager was out of earshot, the man behind the counter called out to one of the guards. "Retrieve box S-one-eight-one-two." He handed him a slip of paper.

Madison was watching everything they were doing. She didn't have a safe-deposit box and wasn't too familiar with the process, but she had a feeling Stiles Investments and Savings took more precautions than did other establishments.

"Normally, the person taking out the box would sign that sheet." The man must have caught her eyes and the inquisitive nature behind them. "Since the manager signed out the box for you, you don't have to. Assume you have the other key?"

"Other key?" They had the one…

"You don't have the key to the box? You won't get in without it."

Terry sidestepped closer to Madison. "By 'other key' he means Claire's key. There are two required for most boxes, the bank's and the box owner's."

"Oh." She addressed the man. "Yes, we have the key."

"If you get comfortable in room one—" he pointed toward a door numbered accordingly "—the box will be brought to you."

"Okay," Terry said.

"It has Internet access—no password needed—and faxing capabilities, scanning. You name it," he said, walking along with them to the room.

Opening the door revealed a space of about eight feet square. Squeezed in the room were two chairs and a table with a multifunction machine.

The bank employee headed back to his post.

"This kind of reminds me of a movie I've seen," Madison said, taking a seat in one of the chairs.

"It could be a lot of them. Banks make popular settings and safe-deposit vaults even more so. Adds some mysterious overtures. Not many people are familiar with them or how they operate. They figure it's only for the rich."

"You seem to know a lot about them."

"Nah, not really. My dad had one for a while, though, and took me with him a few times. I don't remember all the guards and security but his unlocked on a two-key system."

"Well, at least you know a bit about all this because I'm oblivious."

"Finally something the Great Grant knows and the Great Knight doesn't."

"Ha-ha."

There was a knock on the door.

"Box S-one-eight-one-two." The guard held a box approximately five inches deep, ten wide and twenty-five long.

"Yes." Terry directed him to the table.

"Put your key in first," the guard directed them.

Terry did as he'd said and twisted, and then the guard did the same with his key.

The guard lifted the lid on the box and said, "There you go." He left the room then and closed the door behind him.

Terry locked it.

"Why are you locking it?"

"Are you scared to be in such close quarters with me?"

"Not quite. But after you ripped me off with the whole Starbucks thing you should be afraid of being in such close quarters with *me*."

His hands were headed inside the box. He paused and looked at her. "Yeah, you've got a point."

"Don't worry, I won't forget."

"Why do I believe that?"

"'Cause you're a smart man." She got up and patted his back. "Now, get in that thing." She leaned over the table, anxious to see its contents.

He pulled out a bunch of papers. "Partnership agreements." He stopped talking as he read the names. "These are the same as the ones on the USB sticks."

"Don't tell me—" Madison took them from him and set them on the table. "So we went through all this for paperwork we already had. Now what?" Her gaze fell on the agreement at the top of the pile. "Elizabeth Windsor. Claire's first victim," she mused aloud. She went to put it back into the box and noticed there was a small manila envelope at the bottom. It was only about three inches by five. She picked up the envelope and could feel the impression of its contents. "It's another key." She held slid it out. "I'll be damned."

"What is it?"

"This key has the same logo on it. Wonder what secrets it's holding."

There was a rap of knuckles on the room's door and Madison answered. It was the guard, and he was back with another box.

"S-one-five-one-zero."

"Set it over here by the other one," Terry directed him.

Terry and the guard repeated the process they'd gone through the first time.

With the box open, the guard asked, "Would you like me to take the other one away?"

"Not right now." Terry pretty much pushed the guard out the door. "Thank you."

"This one is about the same size." Madison stated her observation as she dove right in. She pulled out more paperwork and spotted the name almost immediately. She held up the contract it was on. "Looks like we found Aaron."

Chapter 38

"Hunting at Its Best. Interesting name for a business," Terry stated as he and Madison walked out of the bank to the department car. "Coincidental that our girl was killed with a hunting knife?"

"I don't believe in coincidences," she said, reaching for the driver's-side door handle. She was about to get in the car when her phone rang. "It's probably the sarge wanting an update."

"I'll leave ya to it." Terry had a smirk on his face.

"But you're so good at teamwork."

"Nope." Terry got in the car and closed the door.

She stood on the sidewalk, shivering, before realizing how crazy it was to take her call outside… But she had to stop the constant ringing. "Detective Knight."

"Maddy?" It was Blake.

"Why are you calling me?"

"I thought we were dating."

"Are we? I haven't heard from you in days," she fired back harshly, but why should he expect anything different? He hadn't talked to her in days and then there was the matter of a brunette…

"We need to talk." His voice was solemn.

"There's nothing we need to talk about." She tried to sound callous even though pain chewed on her insides.

"I can come over tonight."

She wanted to end things with him, tell him that she needed space, but her heart ached. She hated being so vulnerable, but she couldn't quite get herself to end things right now. "I can't tonight. Work—"

"Tomorrow night, then. It's Friday. Maybe we could go—"

"Can't tomorrow night, either." Maybe she'd just keep the excuses coming.

The line went silent.

She added, "I'm in the middle of an investigation."

"Fine. You let me know when it's good for you, then." He hung up on her.

"Argh." She snapped her phone shut. Why the hell did he call if he had nothing meaningful to say? Why was it so hard to just confront the issue head-on? He wasn't in love with her, and he never would be. No, instead he plays this psychological mind game. *We need to talk.*

She paced in a circle on the sidewalk. With her heart and mind battling for dominance, the cold air lost its bite.

"You coming?" Terry had gotten out of the car and walked toward her.

She looked at him with more determination than ever. Maybe if she poured herself deep into this case, the voices in her mind would go silent. "Yeah, I'm coming."

"WE'RE DETECTIVES WITH STILES PD. We'd like to speak with Aaron Best." Madison addressed the man at the front counter of Hunting at Its Best. No sign of a woman in sight. Although one would assume that the hunting world would cater primarily to men.

The man's hazel eyes fell to the badge Madison had on, clipped to the waistband of her pants. "Of course." The man picked up the phone, and Madison turned to Terry.

"I'm feeling a little outnumbered in here," she said to her partner.

"You shouldn't—" he leaned in closer to her "—you have bigger balls than some men I know."

Maybe she should take offense to his comment, but she didn't. If anything, she was flattered by it. She'd rather be seen as tough as opposed to the weak and vulnerable individual she felt on the inside some days.

She looked around the reception area. Wood-paneled walls, an old couch, a coffee table, and a magazine holder that was overflowing with newspapers and magazines. A large painting over the couch depicted a peaceful setting of two deer grazing on long grass beside a river. All in all, the place had a masculine feel to it. There wasn't a retail storefront, which Madison found odd.

The man behind the counter hung up the phone and said, "Aaron will be out in a minute."

"Sure," Madison said. "I'm curious. You don't have a storefront, so who is your target market?"

"We—"

"Detectives." An attractive man about six feet tall wearing a collared shirt and pressed pants stepped into the room. He was lean and muscular, but not to the point where bulging muscles strained against his shirt. His eyes were a deep brown, his jawline sharp and angular like Darren's. He extended a hand first toward Madison.

"Mr. Best?" Madison asked.

"Please call me Aaron." He flashed a smile, which exposed crease lines and two deep-set dimples.

After formal introductions, Madison said, "We'd like to speak with you in regards to your business partner, Claire Reeves."

Aaron glanced at the man behind the counter and cracked his knuckles. "Could we talk in private?"

"Yes, of course." Madison was still struck by the look he gave the other man. Were they hiding something? Possibly Claire's murder? Was the knuckle-cracking threatening? It didn't seem so, but she'd need to talk with him before she jumped to any conclusions.

Aaron led them into an office to the immediate right, but before they entered he called out, "Bring us a couple chairs." He went inside and turned to them. He clasped his hands, unclasped them, clasped them.

Why is he so nervous?

"Sorry about this. Don't get too many visitors." He slipped his hands into his pockets, as if becoming aware of his fidgeting.

"Here you go." The assistant handled two chairs by their backs, dangling them on an angle as he moved them into the small office.

The chairs, just like everything else, were outdated. Claire's money hadn't evidenced itself in plain sight as of yet, and they'd entered their contract about a year ago.

The walls in Aaron's office were wood paneling, but they'd been painted a rich toffee. More paintings of wildlife adorned the walls. On a filing cabinet, a frame showcased Aaron beside a caribou. When the assistant left and closed the door behind him, a ski jacket swayed on a hook.

Aaron took a seat at his desk and leaned toward them. Based on that body language alone, he showed interest in what they were going to say.

"We'd like to start by saying that we're sorry about the loss of your business partner, Claire Reeves," Terry said.

Aaron shifted in his seat at the mention of her name. His eyes softened with seeming grief. Madison attempted to read them further. Was there any sign of guilt or regret?

"Thank you." Aaron tightened his jaw and swallowed hard.

"What does your company do here exactly?" Terry relaxed back into his chair. "I mean, obviously it has something to do with hunting," he tossed out with a smile.

Aaron pinched the tip of his nose and sniffled. He was visibly affected by Claire's death. His hand came down to rest on his mouse, where it sat a moment before he clasped his hands, his thumbs circling around each other in slow motion and then stopping. "We manufacture all types of hunting knives."

Did he just open with hunting knives?

"What kinds?" Madison asked.

Aaron tugged on his collar and ended up undoing the top button of his shirt. "Sometimes it can get hot in here with the door closed." They kept their eyes on him as he rambled. "In an old building like this, there's no balance with the heating and cooling system. Poor insulation."

Madison bobbed her head. "What kind of knives, Mr. Best?" she pressed.

"Like I said, we make all types here. Skinning, gut hook, drop point, Bowie, caping. They're all assembled by hand. That's what sets us apart from the competition. If you want a standard knife, go to a mainline hunting store or order it online. But what we offer is special, unique, one of a kind. The blades are forged using only the finest stainless steel and the handles are burl wood."

Terry pressed his lips, seemingly impressed. "Fine materials."

Aaron's eyes lit with pride. "Only the best quality here."

"So how did Claire Reeves figure in?" Terry straightened out in the chair, leaning forward a bit. Madison noticed that as he moved forward Aaron moved back. His hands remained clasped on the desk, though, his thumbs continuing to twirl around each other.

"I don't understand the question."

"Well, it seems like you've got a pretty good thing going here. You have a high-end quality product. Why bring in a woman?" Terry let out a small laugh, trying to act as if he were chauvinistic. Madison played along and shot him a glare.

Aaron looked between the two of them but settled his gaze on Madison. "Women have a lot to offer." The tone of his voice carried offense to Terry's attitude. "I shouldn't have to point this out to you. Look at your partner." Aaron unclasped his hands and waved one in her direction. "She's a beautiful woman, but she's intelligent. I could tell that right off. I'm pretty good at reading people, always have been. Your partner is strong, she's determined, and she gets whatever she wants. She's not one to be messed with and neither was Claire." His hands clasped again, the thumbs spinning quickly around each other again. "Claire—" His voice choked up. "She was a terrific asset to this company. She brought in a solid business perspective. As you can tell, she wasn't here to pretty things up," he said, referring to the business front as a whole, not just his office. He looked at Madison. "I'm sure you picked up on that right away, and most women have an eye for that sort of thing, but Claire didn't. Not that she didn't like things to be nice, to be pretty, but when it came to business, that's what it was. Business, nothing more. The dollars she could make."

"Then you can understand why someone wanted her dead," Madison fired back.

Aaron's thumbs stopped moving. "No." His voice was gravelly and his eyes were unfocused, exposing the fact he wasn't convinced of his verbal response. "Can you excuse me for a moment?" He rose to his feet.

"Sure," Terry said.

Aaron left and Madison turned to Terry. "Easy access to hunting knives. And did you notice the coat on the back of the door? Expensive ski jacket. Maybe the down found under Claire came from that coat."

"I don't know," Terry began. "Something tells me he cared about her more than—"

"Sorry about that." Aaron entered the room again. His white shirt showed wet spots that hadn't been there before. He must have sensed Madison's eyes on them, and he ran a hand down the front of his chest.

Madison envisioned him splashing his face with cool water, resulting in the pattern. People did that to calm their nerves.

So what is Aaron nervous about?

"What are you suspicious of? Me? I see the way you're looking at me. You don't believe me when I say no one wanted her dead?"

"Mr. Best, it's obvious that Claire's killer was fueled by a lot of anger and emotion. They wanted her to die. They didn't just want to nick her, make her bleed a little. They wanted her dead." Her statements carried such weight that they sank in the air.

"What Detective Knight is trying to say," Terry said, warranting a glare from Madison, "is we know that she wronged a lot of people along the way. Like you were saying, she was very business orientated, money driven."

Aaron's thumbs moved slowly. "It wasn't that way with me. You hear rumors, everyone does, but I couldn't believe them about her. Just couldn't. But she was starting to benefit this company. I wasn't really on board when she first approached me."

Madison noted that she had approached him, just as she had approached Darren Taylor. Claire seemed to have a way of sniffing out either opportunities or struggling companies and sweeping in to their quote, unquote rescue.

"The company wasn't turning the profits it used to. Everyone wants something for nothing these days. With the economy the way it is, the customer wants everything and a cheap price tag to go with it. Well, something has to be sacrificed." He unclasped his hands long enough to press a fingertip into his desk. "And here it's not going to be quality." His resolute stance weakened as his straightened finger bent and then lifted. "But Claire helped me to see the bigger picture. You don't have to sacrifice all quality for price. If I streamlined in some areas, used her negotiation skills to get good deals on the raw product. Then with the cost of goods down, I could lower my selling price. Be even more competitive. She also started putting a marketing plan into place. She suggested that we expand our line and approach large gaming corporations to boost sales, offer specialty touches such as engraving on handles. She had a beautiful vision." Seemingly caught up in a memory, he half laughed. "I do admit that I was blinded by the sales figures she had projected."

Madison looked at Terry, wondering if he had any doubts about the man. Aaron talked affectionately about Claire and seemed to respect her. But maybe he wasn't completely honest when he said he'd paid no attention to the rumors about Claire's business dealings.

Chapter 39

Madison couldn't shake the feeling that Claire's past business dealings affected Aaron more than he was letting on. "So you really don't believe anyone had a reason to want her dead? Or at least anyone you know."

Aaron remained silent and still enough that she could barely see his chest rising as he breathed.

There was something underlying that he wasn't telling them, something substantial. "If you have something to say, now would be the time."

He shook his head, his gaze falling to the desk before rising back up to meet her eyes.

"You said you heard the rumors. What rumors exactly?" She was trying to feel him out. Did he know what Claire had done to so many before him? Did he know that she likely planned to do the same to him?

"I know she had prior business partners."

"Then you know that she used those people to get what she wanted," Madison countered.

"What I *know*, Detective, is she was a smart business woman." His voice rose, exposing an underlying rage.

Was she so blind that she hadn't noticed any earlier projection of it? Or had he been good at concealing it until now? Her thoughts went back to Darcy Simms and the two-faced person she was, how she pretended to be Claire's best friend, and how she had presented herself as right-handed instead of left. Madison's gut tightened and she turned to Terry. "Can I talk to you for a moment? In the hall?"

"We'll be just a moment," Terry said to Aaron. In the hallway, he turned to Madison. "What is it? Couldn't this have waited?"

"Darcy's involved."

"We've been over that. She's not the right height, she had an alibi."

"But how did she know about the killer being left-handed?"

"Huh?" He was agitated. "Why are we discussing this again? You *thought* she picked up her pen with her left hand."

She gestured toward Aaron's office door. "He's hiding something. Darcy is hiding something. Both of them pretend to be who they're not."

"I don't see it."

"Okay. Aaron acts like he's concerned, affected by Claire's death. Maybe his fidgeting, his twirling thumbs, has more to do with guilty energy and him being uncomfortable." Terry's mouth opened and Madison held a hand up. "He has rage under the surface. I really think that Aaron knew what Claire was going to do to him."

"Fine. What about Darcy, though? How does she fit into this?"

"She's the same way. She pretends to be what she isn't starting with being Claire's best friend and ending with being right-handed." Madison attributed finger quotes to *right-handed*. "And why do that if she wasn't involved in some way? She had to have known that the killer was left-handed."

The door opened beside them and Aaron stood in the doorway. "Are you going to be much longer? I should be heading home."

At that moment, the man from the front popped his head around the corner and said good night.

She pulled out her phone to look at the time. *5:10.* Through the windows, Madison could see that it was already dark outside. You had to love winter.

"We won't be much longer." Madison stepped toward Aaron, hoping that he'd go back into his office.

Aaron did, but remained standing near the door and put his hands in his pockets.

"Do you know a woman named Darcy Simms?" Madison asked.

"Of course I do. She was Claire's best friend." Saying her name caught in his throat.

"Your relationship with Claire, it was more than just business, wasn't it?"

Now Aaron walked to his desk and took a seat. "I'm a married man."

Madison slipped back into the chair she had been in before. Terry sat beside her. "That doesn't stop a lot of people. It's quite common for a partner to be unfaithful these days."

"I would never do that to my wife."

Madison's eyes went to his wedding finger. No ring but there was an indication that one belonged there. "You're tanned, Mr. Best. Where have you been?"

He pulled his hand in and tucked it out of view.

"It seems you wore your ring while you were away."

"Listen, this has nothing to do with Claire—"

"I believe it does."

Aaron crossed his arms in front of his chest and took a deep breath. "I was away on business two weekends ago now."

That would make it just days before Claire was murdered. Assuming Aaron took her with him, maybe something happened while they were away. "Where did you go?"

"Tahiti."

Madison resisted the urge to give Terry an I-told-you-so look. Tahiti had been Darcy's alibi and had also come up with Darren.

"Nice place to go for business," Madison began. "Did you go with Claire or someone else?"

"With Claire," he answered eventually. "It would make sense seeing as we are, *were*, partners in business."

"So you weren't attracted to her at all?"

"She was a beautiful woman. I think I mentioned that."

"You never thought of her *that* way, then? Strictly business? Even though she was going to turn your world around and make you rich?"

"Even though," Aaron said coolly.

"I wonder if she didn't tell you she wanted out when you were in Tahiti. The contract you signed gave her the right to opt out at any time. You would have been forced to buy her share."

"I didn't kill her." He rose to his feet. "I think it's time for you to go."

"Maybe we should go talk to Mrs. Best."

"I don't know what you want from me."

"We want the truth. Were you having an affair with Claire Reeves?"

Aaron flung his arms in the air. "Yes. Is that what you want to hear? Oh—" he wiped a hand down his face "—my wife can't find out about this."

"You don't think she's aware of the affair already?"

"I'm certain."

"Women can be pretty astute when it comes to things like this," Madison pressed.

"I don't know for sure. I suppose. Maybe she does." He ran a hand along the back of his neck.

"Where were you on December twenty-fourth between two and four in the morning?"

"Are you being serious?"

Madison's lips settled into a flat line, communicating her seriousness without a word.

"I would never raise a hand to her, let alone kill her." His cheeks got a shot of color.

Terry leaned forward. "Then you shouldn't have a problem telling us where you were."

Aaron closed his eyes briefly and said, "I was there."

Madison looked at Terry then back to Aaron. "Where is *there*?"

"At Claire's house."

"What were you doing there?"

"I have to spell that out for you?" he spat.

Madison disregarded his temper. Darren hadn't matched the DNA from the vaginal swab; it likely belonged to Aaron. "So you had sex, then you killed—"

"Crazy. No way."

"Which hand do you write with, Mr. Best?"

He contorted his face; his brow forming a vee. "What does this have to do—"

"Answer the question," Terry said.

"Left. Why?"

"We'll need you to come downtown."

"What? Why? There was someone else there."

"You're going to need to come up with something better than that." Madison went up to him on the right and Terry on the left.

"You don't even want to hear me out on this." Aaron slammed his hands on the desk.

"We know there was someone else there, but we're glad you did, too." Madison paused a moment. "Just gives you more motive."

Chapter 40

Aaron Best slouched in his chair, and Madison was seated across from him while Terry stood behind her. They were in interrogation room one back at the station, and so far, Aaron hadn't requested a lawyer.

"You believe that I killed Claire simply because I knew someone else was there?" Aaron asked.

"Sure. Why not?" Madison asked.

"Why would I kill her if I knew someone was there? They'd find out, stop me, call the cops, something."

"Assuming they were still there when you committed the murder. Maybe you came back once they had left." Madison tossed a photo of Claire's lifeless body across the table. "You realized she had someone else there, got jealous. That was all it took after she told you her intentions while vacationing in Tahiti. You snapped." She drew out the last word.

Aaron turned away from the photo. "I'm going to need to call my—" His cell phone rang, interrupting him. "Probably my wife now. She's going to kill me."

Nice choice of words. And speaking of killing, Aaron was in the right height range for the murderer.

Aaron looked at his phone. "It is her. Can I get it?" The ring kept on, getting increasingly louder.

"Go ahead. Answer it," Madison said.

"It's okay?"

She nodded. She wanted to keep him talking and sometimes that involved extending niceties.

"I'll be home soon," Aaron said. "Yes…I know. I'm sorry. … Go ahead without me. ... Not long, see you—" Aaron pulled the phone from his ear, a rapid pulse tapping in his cheek. "She hung up on me. She can't find out about me and Claire. She'd never forgive me, probably kill me."

Madison couldn't care less about his relationship with his wife. He had betrayed her trust and failed to honor his commitment to her. He deserved what was coming his way. Of course, not to be literally murdered.

"Describe the other person that was at Claire's that night," Terry said, his pen poised over a notepad.

He looked at them sheepishly. "I didn't see him."

"You didn't see him?" Madison stated incredulously.

"You sound like you don't believe me." Aaron put his hands on the table, clasped them and twirled his thumbs. "I guess maybe I wouldn't, either. But Claire told me someone was there."

"Claire told you?"

"Uh-huh."

Madison recalled the palm print on the front living room window. "So you didn't watch Claire having sex on the couch with this other person before coming in?" Of course she was stretching things here; she didn't know Claire had sex with anyone on the couch that night.

The thumbs stopped. "No. Like I said, I didn't see this other person. She told me about him," he repeated.

Building on her fabrication, she said, "It was you and Claire on the couch."

Aaron crossed his arms and then uncrossed them, resuming his annoying habit with the twirling thumbs.

Madison took his response as admission and pointed at his hands. "My uncle used to always do that, twiddle his thumbs. Every time he had to concentrate or display patience."

Aaron put his hands under the table.

"What are you concentrating on, Mr. Best? A good defense?"

"Why must I defend myself? I'm innocent." He raised his voice.

"Well, answer this question, how involved was the affair?"

"I don't want to discuss this."

"Because of your wife?"

"She can't find out."

"She might not have to, but we need your full cooperation." If he killed Claire, that would be a different story; then his secret life with Claire would be exposed.

"You know I've been speaking with you guys for the better part of—" he looked at his watch "—two hours. I have cooperated. You have nothing on me. Nothing but your speculations and theories. Just tell me what makes you think I did it." Madison was going to speak, but he continued. "Based on reality."

If he wanted to play things this way, it was fine with her. She preferred the direct route. "The murder weapon was a Bowie knife. They are used for hunting, although I don't need to point that out to you."

He swallowed deeply and his face paled.

"Do you have one of those?" she asked, fully aware of what his answer would be.

"You know I do."

"You have access to the type of murder weapon, and you had good motives, whether it be jealousy or Claire wanting out of her partnership agreement. Either way life as you knew it would be over."

"Claire would never do that…to me." He splayed a hand over his chest for dramatic effect but dropped it quickly.

"You don't seem convinced of that, Mr. Best."

There were a few seconds of tangible silence. "She never would have gone through with it."

"She was planning to get out?"

"I never said that—"

"You pretty much did." She kept her eyes on him, but his gaze fell to his hands. "Don't take it personally, Mr. Best. That's how she made her living. She destroyed a lot of marriages along the way, too. You were nothing special to her."

"What the hell would you know about that?" Spittle flew from his mouth. "She wouldn't have done that to me. We loved each other."

Madison remembered Darren's words. "Claire didn't believe in love," she said.

"Well, she did with me."

"She was sleeping with other people. That makes it conceivable that you killed out of jealousy and to prevent her from bankrupting your company, possibly yourself personally."

"I was still having sex with my wife, Detective. Just because you love someone, it doesn't mean you must be with them all the time, exclusively, and with no one else." More spittle managed to come through clenched teeth. "I asked her to marry me."

"Marry you? You're already married."

"Of course I'd divorce my current wife. Claire was worth it to me. She was smart, savvy."

"All right, let me get this straight. You don't want your wife to know about the affair but were going to divorce her? She'd find out why."

Aaron exhaled loudly. "You still don't get it. Claire gave me an ultimatum. Leave my wife and keep the business or lose the business, her, and she'd expose the affair. That's why I was at her house that night. I was trying to talk her out of it, trying to make her see things clearly. I care for my wife, but Claire…" His words dissipated.

"So for the sake of your business and your penis, you were willing to sacrifice your wife?" Madison sensed Terry's eyes on her, but sometimes she had to speak her mind.

"You make it sound cold and calculated. It wasn't how I planned it. I didn't see this beautiful woman and think, 'Geez, I wanna fuck up my life.' She improved my life and made it worth living."

"So now you don't have any purpose in living? That's what you want us to believe? You want us to dismiss the motives you would have just because you wouldn't want our investigation into you to expose the affair to your wife? Now that Claire's gone, you don't have her to fall back on. Your concern isn't over your wife and never was. It's only about what suits Mr. Best. And to us—" she gestured toward Terry "—that speaks to a man who only looks out for himself. It looks like a man who would be willing to do anything to ensure that things work according to his plan. This soft spot Claire had for you could all be a lie. Maybe she was going to go through with forcing you to buy her share and expose the affair."

Aaron crossed his arms. "I want a lawyer."

Chapter 41

It was eight o'clock at night and Aaron Best's lawyer wouldn't be making it in until morning. Madison and Terry were back at their desks.

"No one could blame him for requesting a lawyer. You went down his throat and out his—" Terry stopped speaking when her eyes narrowed.

"We're getting close on this one. He's not going to willingly hand over his DNA and calling for a lawyer was just a matter of time. Everything seems to line up with him: means, motive, and opportunity."

"I have to agree. Claire would have opened the door to him and thought nothing of doing so."

Madison nodded. "She wouldn't have thought twice about him wrapping an arm around her from behind."

"Tomorrow's going to be an interesting day." Terry pulled his keys out of his pocket. "See you in the morning."

"Hum, wait a minute, aren't you forgetting something?" Madison held out her hand flexing it opened and closed.

"Don't think so."

"Hand it over."

"Oh, your money?"

"Yeah. Oh." She smiled at him as he opened a drawer in his desk and pulled out a thick envelope. Her eyes bulged. "How much—"

"Probably just shy of…" He winced, handed her the envelope and backed away. "Probably a few grand."

"A few grand? That's a felony." She thumbed through the wad of cash, and when she looked up, Terry's back was to her and he was a good twenty feet away. "You'll have to come back sometime." The words came out even though he wouldn't have heard them. *What a little shit!*

With Terry gone and nothing more that needed doing tonight, she decided to head home, too. Stepping outside, the cold air felt like spikes and daggers to her lungs; her car couldn't warm up fast enough. As she drove home she thought about Hershey and all those business cards Terry had given her for canine training. Maybe she'd research them online when she got home.

One thing was certain: most days she missed the times when she could just crash on the couch at the end of the day, watch a bit of mindless TV, and go to sleep. Tonight, the thought of doing that brought on feelings of sadness and loneliness.

And she'd be going home to face the damaged coffee table from her grandmother. But it wasn't just the brooding over Hershey and days gone by, loved ones who had passed…she missed Blake.

Her chest heaved when she dwelled on his name. She was reminded of his calling and then hanging up on her. Whether it hurt or not, she didn't have time to deal with all the drama. She had to cut him loose. Her job demanded her focus. Then she thought of Terry, of Richards, of Cynthia. Even though her friend wasn't married, she had a life outside of the lab.

Aren't I entitled to one, too?

She parked her car in her apartment building's lot and headed for the front of the building. There was a man sitting on the bench near the sidewalk. The area was illuminated by the streetlights, but it wasn't possible to make out his appearance right away, although the size and mannerism seemed familiar. As she got closer, his identity was confirmed. Blake. Her stomach tossed. "What are you doing here?"

"We need to talk." Blake reached out for her, but she kept moving.

"I told you that tonight wasn't good." She was determined to keep walking but stalled when she realized he was following her. She turned to face him.

"I've been here for hours. Standing in the cold—" His voice held a defensive anger.

"I didn't ask you to," she fired back.

His face fell, the shadows of light and darkness changing his expression.

In the silence that passed between them, her feelings of loneliness forced her to speak. They didn't make a commitment to each other, so what right did she really have to be angry?

"Come on," she said. "I'll make you a hot drink."

He dipped his head and followed her inside the building. When she opened her apartment door, Blake went straight for Hershey's kennel. "Hey, buddy…hey."

Hershey scampered, barking and whimpering. Blake unlatched the cage and the dog jumped around his feet.

Blake turned back to Madison. "He remembers me. I'll take him out."

You're hard to forget. Pride made her hold back.

"Sure," she said. "I'll get the kettle on." Maybe if she kept her hands busy, her mind and heart would get on the same damn page. "Oh, this will help." She handed him the key to the building and her apartment.

Blake took them from her and left with Hershey. With them gone, the place felt so empty. It would have been quiet except for her thoughts felt thunderous.

What does he want to talk about?

Minutes later, the door opened again. "Brrr. It's stinking freezing out there." Blake undid Hershey and hung the leash on a hook.

"What are you doing here?" Her words were sharp, but she had to protect herself, and her heart was getting carried away.

He walked toward her. "You smell good."

Why did he ignore what I said?

She'd been on the job for hours and she didn't wear perfume to work. "Do you tell her that, too?"

Blake's eyes were full of emotion, warmth and coolness blending together. "It was agreed that we could see other people."

She couldn't breathe. *Did he just say that?* Her worst fears were coming to reality. But she refused to allow him to see her true feelings. "It was." She turned her back on him, pulled down a couple mugs from the cupboard, and dropped a tea bag in each. "Assume orange pekoe is ok?"

He didn't say anything but leaned against the counter. Hershey stood at the door and pranced in front of it, then put his nose to the floor.

"Is he asking to go out again?" Blake asked.

"I guess." She couldn't have been more clueless when it came to animals, but she took it as an opportunity to step out. "Did he not go?"

"Number one."

"Oh, he should have the other on board. I'll take him this time."

She was in no hurry to get back upstairs, even though it was cold enough to freeze to the sidewalk. Snow fell in tiny flakes. The air was even too cold for them.

She let Hershey sniff whatever he felt like. Maybe if she stalled long enough, she'd know how to get her emotions under control. She had feelings for Blake—she begrudgingly had to admit that— but it was up to her where it went from here. Would she allow herself to continue being vulnerable? She didn't think she could handle having her heart broken again. If she called an end to this, she would be the one in control and the pain would subside faster. She tried to convince herself of that.

Hershey sat at her feet, looking up at her and sniffing the air. Guess he wasn't going to go, and she couldn't put off going back inside any longer.

"Where have you been?" Blake walked toward her with a steaming cup. "He must have had quite the load on board." He attempted a smile. "I put two sweeteners in with a splash of milk. I believe that's how you like it." He handed it to her.

It was exactly how she liked it. How did he know her so well in some ways but in other areas be so oblivious? She took the tea from him and sat at the kitchen table. She waited for him to take a seat and then said, "We do need to talk."

"We do." He blew on his tea and took a sip. "That woman—"

"You don't have to tell me who she is."

"I know that, but I want—"

"I'm thinking it doesn't really matter." She had to cut him loose before he killed her. "Maybe we should…" Her words stalled but her message got through.

He got up from the table. "Maybe we should."

Chapter 42

THE NEXT MORNING, Madison was at her desk at the station by six thirty. It had been a long night of tossing and turning and seeing most hours on the clock. At least she had Hershey. It was almost like he knew that he'd never see Blake again and sensed her pain. His fur was extra soft, smooth as velvet. She'd held him close to her chest, sniffing in the smell of his fur and absorbing his love.

She had been wrong to think it would hurt less to be the one to decide to end things. It didn't really matter which way it went, but maybe the fact that Blake was so readily in agreement hadn't helped her feel like she'd made the decision, that she'd been in control. Maybe he'd come there to break up with her. But why wait for hours in the cold to break it off? She should have listened to him when he tried to tell her about the brunette, but there was no turning back now.

"Hey," Terry said as he draped his coat over the back of his chair.

"Hey back. I've done a little research this morning on Aaron Best. His driver license puts him at a height of five eleven."

"That's spot on for the estimated height of our killer."

"Yep." Madison closed the folder in front of her. "And his lawyer should be here any time now."

She looked at the clock. *8:40.*

Where had the time gone?

Her gaze drifted to the front desk and Adrian Lambert was standing there. This attorney had graced their interrogation rooms before. Fresh to his law firm, his vigor and determination to advance his career manifested itself in strong determination and negotiation skills. He had a confrontational energy that exceeded his rivals.

Madison nodded her head toward Adrian to direct Terry's gaze there. "I think he's here now."

She walked up with Terry.

"You spoke with Mr. Best without my presence." Adrian's silver eyes possessed the wild nature of a wolf. Apparently, he didn't believe in wasting time with greetings.

"We didn't question him after he requested a lawyer," Madison said.

"He was under the impression he was being questioned in regards to the murder, not suspected of the actual crime. He was under the impression he was cooperating to help find a killer."

Obviously, Aaron had shared quite a bit on his phone call to Adrian. "Mr. Best is a grown man. And no doubt you are familiar with the law, Mr. Lambert. We are entitled to question someone as long as they have agreed to talk. And we also have the right, by law, to hold a suspect in custody for twenty-four hours without a formal charge—"

"Don't discredit me by rehashing the law. What proof do you have against Mr. Best?"

"Why don't we get settled in an interview room?" Madison presented it as a question, but it was really a statement.

"Don't you mean *interrogation* room?" Adrian responded dourly.

"Follow me."

Madison had Terry arrange to have Aaron Best brought up from cells. Once everyone was in the room, she sat across from Adrian and Aaron.

"Let's get to the evidence, shall we?" Adrian began. "What proof do you have against my client?"

Madison leaned back in her chair. "Your client had the means, motive, and opportunity to kill Claire Reeves. He admitted to being at her house the night of the murder. He was in love with her, but she threatened to leave him and reveal their affair to his wife—and destroy his business—if he didn't do as she wanted. And he had access to the murder weapon."

"I assume then that you have the murder weapon."

"A Bowie knife and your client makes these."

"But you don't have the actual weapon?" Adrian raised his brows. "How can you connect it with my client? Surely there are hundreds of thousands of knives in this world."

Madison continued in another direction. "He's left-handed like the killer. He's five eleven and that fits the height of the killer."

The lawyer didn't say anything. Aaron shifted in his seat. His hands came together on the table, his thumbs twirled once but stopped when he must have noticed Madison looking at them.

"Do you like to hunt, Mr. Best?" Madison asked.

Aaron's face paled as if he was going to vomit. Adrian gestured for him to answer.

"Yes," Aaron punched out.

"Do you like to hunt woodland caribou?"

Aaron began to answer., "I—"

"What does this have to do with the case?" Adrian asked.

"Forensics found a hair from a woodland caribou in the victim's wound," Madison began and turned to Aaron. "Have you ever been to Newfoundland?"

The lawyer consented for Aaron to answer.

"Yes."

The one-worded answers were effective but aggravating. Madison wanted elaborations because they would make it easier to catch him if he was lying. "When were you last up there?"

"Sometime in early September."

Aaron was telling the truth. This morning one of her first calls had been to Natural Adventure Outfitters to see if they had any record of him staying there.

"Forensics also found male DNA." She locked eyes with Aaron. "Will it match yours?"

Silence.

"If you're innocent like you claim to be, you'll volunteer a DNA sampling, and you wouldn't mind us searching your property for the murder weapon."

Aaron's eyes got enlarged, and he looked at Adrian.

"If you honestly believe that you have enough to substantiate and obtain a warrant, detectives, then my client will comply. Until then—"

"Rest assured we have enough. Mr. Best can go back and wait it out in holding," Madison said.

Aaron let out a sigh, one hand briefly rubbing his left temple, and then he placed one on the Adrian's forearm. Adrian turned to his client, the fire in his eyes communicating that he didn't care for being touched.

Madison worked on Aaron. "If you cooperate, this will look better for you."

"I don't have anything to hide."

"So you will give us written consent to search your properties, your business, and your home and collect your DNA?"

"Mr. Best will require a warrant," Adrian interjected before Aaron could say anything.

"Fine with us." Madison rose to leave, but her eyes settled on Aaron's ski jacket, which was on the table. There was a small hole in the sleeve of the left arm, down feathered at its edges. She pointed at the puncture. "What happened to your coat?"

Aaron pulled his jacket to him.

"It's all right, you don't have to answer. I know what happened to it."

"His coat was right in front of us, in plain sight. We had every right to take it." Madison laughed. Aaron and his lawyer hadn't been too willing to part with it, but there was nothing they could do. Not when it could factor into solving a homicide.

"We've got a gift for you, Cyn." Madison chimed the statement off like a song as she and Terry walked into the lab. Madison set a large paper bag on the table.

Cynthia looked up from her microscope to the sack.

"This needs to take top priority," Madison began. "The suspect's already clocking well into his holding hours."

Cynthia was already wearing gloves, and she pulled out the contents of the bag. "*The* ski jacket?"

Madison smiled. "Guess we'll find out."

Chapter 43

"I STILL DON'T THINK THIS is a good idea, Maddy." Terry had repeatedly stated his concern on the ride over to the Bests' residence. Now they were headed up the front walkway.

"I strongly disagree." The search warrants hadn't come through but Madison wanted to speak to Mrs. Best and see what she had to say about her husband.

"It could hurt our case."

"We're just going to talk. Maybe she knew about her husband's affair and she has something to offer the investigation." Madison rang the doorbell, and seconds later, it opened to reveal a beautiful woman in her late thirties. For midmorning and being at home, she was made up like a model. Her red hair came to just above her shoulders, mostly straight but curled to frame her face. Her eyes were heavily yet tastefully colored with shadow and liner. Her eyelashes were long and no doubt had seen the pressing end of a lash curler. Her brows were thin and tweezed. She made Madison think *Desperate Housewives*. "Mrs. Best?"

"Yes. Beth." She passed a look between them as if to say, *Who are you and what the hell do you want?*

Madison made the formal introductions and said, "We'd like to talk to you about your husband."

Beth backed into the house and motioned them inside. "Would you like something to drink?" She smiled at them, but the speed with which it formed and faded said it was simply a veneer she had painted on.

With the expression, Madison suspected Beth used her looks to manipulate and get what she wanted out of life. And why was she being so accommodating? She must have known that her husband was being questioned by police in regards to a murder. Then again, maybe Aaron hadn't been honest with her.

"We won't take up too much of your time," Madison said.

"Let's sit in here, then." Beth directed them to a front sitting room. Framed photographs of the couple accented bookshelves. In all of them the couple's smiles and expressions were pretty much identical, and it made the presentation of a perfect marriage seem staged.

Beth crossed her legs, and as she did so, drew Madison's eyes. She was quite attractive and Madison wondered what would motivate Aaron to cheat on her. Of course, logic wasn't usually involved in the decision to be unfaithful. Madison also noticed that Beth was tall for a woman.

"Aaron couldn't do it." Beth's curt—and seemingly random—statement surprised Madison. "He wouldn't do it…kill her."

Okay, so Aaron had told her.

"I sense part of you wonders about it," Madison responded.

"Maybe I do, but we've been married sixteen years. You know a man after that long." She pulled a tissue from a box on a side table and dabbed her nose. Her crossed-over leg pulsed up and down. "We used to be close, but he's been distant for a while." Her eyes got wet and a few tears fell, but Beth pressed a clean tissue to her face to wipe her cheeks.

It struck Madison as odd. If she were sincerely hurting, why would she care about how she looked? Something about her reactions seemed on cue.

Beth continued. "I didn't even know he had a business partner until last night. I can tell you don't believe me." She waved a tissue in the air as if to imply she didn't care whether Madison was buying her words or not.

"Not even in passing? She was his business partner. Silent but she invested a lot into the business."

"He never told me."

"You never noticed the change in the business? More money coming home?"

"I didn't take care of the books or the budget for the business or for our household. Aaron handled all of that. I'd have no clue if there was a change." She paused and dabbed her nose. "But he did start talking more about vacations and where he wanted to take me. Italy, Australia."

"Not cheap getaways." Madison clearly recalled Aaron's weekend trip with Claire. "He just went away recently."

"He did? Oh, yes, for business. You made it sound like it had been for pleasure."

Something about this woman wasn't sitting well with Madison.

Beth continued. "I guess I never gave his talking about exotic trips much thought. He was always a dreamer and liked to talk as if we had more money than we did."

Madison decided to change the subject a bit. "Your husband take any more hunting trips than before?"

Beth's brows pressed downward for a second. "Not more than usual. Why?"

"Is there any way we could have a look around?" The question just came out, and Madison felt Terry's eyes on her, but she refused to look at her partner. He'd just want her to back off.

Beth dabbed her nose. "I...don't see why not."

Madison and Terry rose to their feet. Madison thought it was strange she never asked what they expected to find.

"I'd start in the garage," Beth said.

Madison's eyes shot to her.

"Well, I assume what you're looking for has something to do with hunting?" Beth shrugged her shoulders and then felt the need to explain herself. "You asked about hunting trips and the paper said she bled out. I think the paper said something about a knife slash."

Madison had memorized the article on Claire Reeves' murder and there had been no mention of a knife slash. She held eye contact with Beth, but the woman's eyes revealed nothing.

Beth led them to the garage and ran a hand over her hair and Madison noticed a gold hairpin. It had a small crest on it, like a university or college logo, and it looked familiar.

"You'll have to excuse the mess out here. It's Aaron's space."

Meanwhile, Madison thought the garage was better organized than some people's homes. Shelving lined two walls and labeled boxes filled them.

"Where were you on December twenty-fourth in the wee hours?" Madison asked.

"Me? You think I had something to do with the murder? I didn't even know her."

Madison didn't say anything for fear of risking Beth's permission to search the home. If she withdrew that, they'd be back to waiting on the warrant to go through.

"If you must know—" Beth crossed her arms "—I was out with a girlfriend for drinks. I didn't get in until about seven in the morning."

Madison nodded and pressed her lips into a smile. She would let it go at that for now.

Beth left the garage, leaving Madison and Terry to look around. As soon as the door closed, Madison looked straight at Terry.

"What? Why are you looking at me like that?" he asked.

Madison stood in front of her partner, her heart beating so fast it made her lightheaded. "She said the paper said something about a knife slash, but it didn't."

"She could have just remembered wrong."

Madison shook her head. "I don't know, Terry, but something is seriously messed up here."

Terry bobbed his head side to side. "She is rather tall."

"Uh-huh. I noticed that, too. Probably about as tall as her husband. If she found out about her husband's affair, her self-esteem would take a huge hit. Maybe enough to kill for."

Terry headed toward a shelving unit, and she walked over to a large tool chest decaled with racing and fuel stickers.

"There's just something we're missing," she mumbled as she opened drawers in the tool chest. "There has to be."

"Maddy, you're getting ahead of yourself again. Let's just look things over, go from there. Okay? We can only do one thing at a time."

"You maybe." Madison smiled at him and noticed the box he pulled down was labeled MEMORABILIA. She went back to looking in the drawer she'd just opened and added, "And with you being a guy, multitasking would be a little out of reach for you." A few seconds passed and he hadn't snapped back with some smart aleck remark. "Terry?" She looked over at him; he was bent around a sheet of drywall that was leaning against the wall.

"What is it?" She walked behind him.

He reached into the crevice between the sheetrock and the garage wall and came out with a bloody tea towel. He took time unfolding it to reveal its contents. "Is this what you were hoping to find?"

Chapter 44

Hours later, Madison and Terry were in the lab. She stood there with a hand on a hip wondering if the case had finally come to an end. One thing seemed certain, someone in the Best household was the killer. Now they just had to verify which one. Madison found it hard to believe that the affair and partnership were news to Beth. Maybe she knew about both and killed Claire Reeves because of it.

"Well, the tea towel matches some others Claire had, and the knife is a match to the murder weapon. I'll have to confirm it's Claire's blood," Cynthia said. "But I had a look at Mr. Best's ski jacket and there was blood inside the sleeve."

"Was it Claire's?" Madison asked.

"Unfortunately no usable DNA." Cynthia pressed her hands over the jacket, stopping near the hole. "But I can tell you that the down in this jacket was a match to the feather found at the scene."

"We have him," Terry said.

"Him. Or her?" Madison stated it and both her colleagues looked at her.

Cynthia looked confused. "It was male DNA in the wound."

As confirmed with those words, Madison knew that even if Mrs. Best had committed the murder, she'd walk away at this point.

Madison and Terry had Aaron brought up to an interrogation room and directed his lawyer there. Madison walked in to the room first.

"Do you have the warrant?" Adrian asked.

"Actually we won't be needing one. At least not for the murder weapon."

"So you found the real killer, then?" Adrian motioned like he was going to leave and placed a hand on Best's shoulder. "Told you, Aaron. Let's go."

"Not so quick," Madison began. "It turns out your wife was quite helpful."

"What's that supposed to mean?" Aaron asked.

The lawyer settled back into his chair.

Madison went on. "The truth has a way of coming out, don't you agree?"

Aaron swallowed audibly.

"The murder weapon was in your garage wrapped in a tea towel soaked in blo—"

"That's impossible."

"Reality, actually, seeing as that's what happened. Your Bowie knife is in the lab right now. How much do you want to bet we'll pull your prints and Claire's blood from it?"

Aaron's facial expression was a blend of mortification and rage. "It's...that's not possible."

"I assure you those are the facts." Madison pulled out a piece of paper. "And actually we do have a warrant." Both men's eyes were on her. "A warrant for your DNA."

MADISON AND TERRY CAME OUT of the interrogation room; he walked off in the opposite direction from where she was headed. She spun to face him. "Where are you going?"

"Thought I'd go home for a bit. Call me when the results are in."

"I don't think so."

Terry turned around and closed the distance between them. "And why is that?"

"It's just not sitting right with me. Why would his wife be so willing to direct us to the garage? On top of which, she knew exactly what we were looking for."

"Oh, here we go. The OCD trip has started early. Normally you wait until someone is formally charged. Although, I guess this way is better."

"Doesn't any of that stand out to you? What if she knew about the affair? Would that be enough reason for you to suspect that she might be the killer?" She sensed his impatient energy. His mind had already clocked out.

"I'm going home for a couple hours, Maddy." He turned around, waving a hand in the air.

His actions infuriated her. Why was he always in such a hurry to tend to his personal life? This case wasn't closed yet and it deserved their attention.

Her cell rang, and she answered. "Knight."

"Have charges been laid as of yet?" It was the sarge.

"I'll let you know when they—"

"Hasn't that man—what's his name? Aaron Best?—been in holding for hours already?"

"Yes..." Her words stopped there as she debated whether to give him more information. She decided it wouldn't hurt. "We're still waiting on some results from the lab. I thought you'd be happy that I'm waiting for all the details before making an arrest."

"Don't stall this, Knight. If you have enough, do it."

His directive angered her more than Terry's leaving. "Of course." She hung up on him. She knew she'd likely hear about it later, but it felt like the right thing to do at the time. Her cell rang again. *Maybe later had come...* "Knight."

"It's Darcy Simms." There was a small silence. She continued. "I heard you have a suspect."

"How would you know that?"

"I have my sources, Detective. It's not that large of a city. I know it's Aaron Best."

How are they all connected?

Madison's heart was thumping. "How? And why hadn't you said anything before now?"

"I didn't want to get involved."

"But you are now. Claire was your best friend. Why wouldn't you expose her killer if you knew who it was?"

Silence.

"What else do you know, Miss Simms?"

The line went dead, leaving her with an odd feeling. How was Darcy involved and what motivated her to call? There had to be a connection to all of them, somehow. Had Darcy found out about Aaron from Beth? Nothing had been put in the paper in regards to a suspect even being taken into custody. Then it hit her, Beth was short for Elizabeth. How could she have been so blind? She went to the file and ran her finger down the list of names from the flash drives, and there it was: number eight, Elizabeth Windsor.

Madison's fingers flew over the keyboard. She hit the wrong keys a few times and hurried to backspace. She couldn't log in to her computer fast enough to pull the background check. She tapped on the side of the keyboard as she waited for the result. "Come on." Then the information displayed on her screen. She scrolled down, looking for the first indication that Beth Best and Elizabeth Windsor were one and the same. She picked up her phone. "Terry, you have to get back here ASAP—"

"Cyn has the results already?"

She stared at the screen. "Something better. Get back here now." She hung up on him.

"What is it, Maddy? I was already in my living room drinking a beer."

"You probably didn't even make it to the parking lot. Oh my, I'm so sorry." Her words were full of sarcasm. "I thought your job here was to solve murders, and I may have done this one for you." She handed him the printout of the background check.

He took the paper but didn't look at it. "Excuse me, from what I remember when I left here we had a viable suspect in custody, and were one DNA test result away from a formal charge." He glanced at the printout. "My god, it's about the wife…" He let the arm drop that held the sheet and looked at her. She used the power of silence, and he picked up the report. This time he looked at it.

"Pay attention to what I highlighted in yellow," she said.

A few seconds later, he glanced up at her.

"That's right. Beth Best is Elizabeth Windsor from the partnership list. She'd have more than an affair to get even for."

"And you're just assuming she knows about the affair."

"Yes I am. At this point. However, most women know when their man is cheating."

"Did you know that about Blake?"

His quick comeback was like a strike to her air supply.

"Maybe that was inappropriate," he rescinded.

"Yeah...maybe." She redirected her comments to the case. "Did you get to the part about education?"

"She went to the University of Stiles? What bearing does that have on the case?"

"I did some digging. That's the same school Claire Reeves, Darcy Simms, Allison Minard, and Darren Taylor attended. I just knew something was off. Everything, everyone, was just too connected." She went on. "What tipped me off to look at education was two-fold. Remember the framed diploma on Darcy's office wall?" She paused and he shook his head. She waved it off. "There was one and it was issued from the University of Stiles. Then I noticed that Beth Best had a gold pin in her hair. It had a logo on it that looked familiar. The University of Stiles logo. We know they were all connected to Claire. How they met is still a mystery, though."

"How does Aaron fit in?"

"Besides being married to Beth, I'm not sure. Aaron doesn't have an education past high school. He was essentially an outsider to the group."

"Allison seems like a bit of an outsider, too. At least she didn't have nice things to say about Darcy."

"And Darcy especially didn't have nice things to say about her when I implied Allison was at the cabin in Newfoundland." Her words stalled, her thoughts mingled together. "What about Mrs. Best? She was part of that circle. Her hair is red, same color as the mystery woman from the cabin. Maybe she was the one there?"

"We'll need more. Like you said, women change the color of their hair all the time. Can't prove she was a redhead then." He paused and continued. "Maybe they did conspire to murder Claire, to get revenge for their fallen businesses—"

"And rescue their bruised egos." She was thinking specifically of

Darren Taylor, who not only lost the program he had developed but was conned into a false marriage.

"And pin it on the cheating husband," Terry said.

"Bingo."

Terry went quiet again, but she could tell by the determination in his eyes that his mind was fully on the case. "We better go talk to the missus again."

Chapter 45

Beth Best stood at her front door, arms tightly crossed. She was wearing a winter coat and obviously getting ready to leave. "Haven't I been through enough?" She went to take a step out her door, but Madison and Terry didn't move. "Fine. Come in." Beth opened the door wider for them to enter. "Another visit from you two. The second time today. To what do I owe the honor?" she asked sarcastically.

"You've probably heard that your husband has been charged with Claire Reeves's murder." Madison studied her reaction to the lie and could swear the woman's mouth fought from curving upward.

Beth didn't make any move to lead them to the living area but kept them in the entry. "It's been one hell of a couple of days. First I find out my husband cheated on me and then he killed his mistress."

"So you didn't know about the affair before now?"

"If I had known about that, I would have left him. In fact, I'm on my way to meet with a divorce lawyer now. If you'll excuse me." Beth made a motion toward the door. Madison's feet were grounded where she stood.

"That was a quick, rash decision."

"Rash? That man took everything and squandered it. Risked it all on a five-minute lay!" Her voice escalated in volume and her body shook from anger.

"Where were you December twenty-fourth between two and four in the morning?" Madison knew she had asked the question before. Beth's alibi had been drinks with a girlfriend, but Madison thought she'd reconfirm that. Maybe with the woman in a hurry to leave, her impatience would reveal a discrepancy.

"I was here." The three words spat out quickly. Her eyes went to the door.

"I thought you were out for drinks."

Beth's eyes widened and she made another move toward the door. "I've got to go."

Madison glanced at Terry and then addressed Beth. "You're in quite a hurry to get to the lawyer's."

Beth's eyes snapped to Madison's. "You're accusing me of murder. I can see it your eyes, hear it in your tone. I thought you said you charged my husband." She pulled down on her coat.

Madison remained silent and held steady eye contact.

"You ask my husband, and he'll tell you that I was in bed when he snuck out of the house to go see that little slut."

Madison looked at Terry, then back to Beth. "So you did know? You lied to us twice now."

Caught in another lie, she appeared somewhat uncomfortable. "Lied about what?"

"First your alibi and second you said you didn't know about the affair. Why lie unless you have something to hide?"

"I knew I'd appear guilty if I confessed to knowing about the affair. I watch cop shows. I know when a slut like Claire is murdered it's either the cheating husband or the jealous wife who gets looked at. Only thing is I wouldn't kill for that." She stopped short, leaving the question in Madison's mind: what would she kill for?

Madison let it go for now because she needed Beth to keep talking. "What time did he leave?"

"Around one."

"After he left, what did you do?"

"I followed him to *her* house." The disdain that coated her words was impossible to miss.

"So you were there at the time of Claire's murder?" Madison glanced at Terry.

"No." Beth crossed her arms, her focus turning to the other side of the room.

"Why so certain? Time of death was placed between two and four."

Beth let out a huff of air.

"How long did you know about the affair?"

"Let's just say long enough."

"So what did you do after you saw him at her house?"

"I struggled to get out of the car. I wanted to confront them right then and there, but I couldn't." She went extremely still, calm.

"So you never got out of the car?"

"Not for a while, but then I couldn't just sit there, either. I walked to the front window and that's when I saw my husband humping that bitch on the arm of the couch!"

That would explain the palm print on the glass and confirm why Aaron hadn't denied having sex with Claire on the couch.

"That must have made you pretty mad."

"Made me furious, but what was I supposed to do? Go in there while they were doing it? I should have, you know? If only I knew this is how it would turn out. Anyway, I watched them until they were finished. Made me sick, but I was still pulled to watch."

There was something perverse about watching your own spouse give it to someone else. "Did your husband know you were there?"

"I don't see how he would have. I made sure to be back in bed by the time he got home."

"So you just left your husband with his mistress?"

"What was I supposed to do?"

Madison raised her eyebrows. She found it hard to believe given her experience of finding her fiancé in bed with another woman. She had yelled and thrown things at him. She even raised her gun. For seconds, she thought she'd actually kill him until she realized he wasn't worth the repercussions.

Beth continued. "I guess now you know I was there, I should tell you something else. When they were finished, she yelled something at him and started flailing her arms. He reached for her, but she shrugged him off and gestured for him to get out of the house. He looked furious."

"So why mention this now?"

"Well, now that you know I was there, I figured I would. Didn't see any point earlier."

"So you suspected his involvement from the start but said nothing?"

"He is still my husband."

MADISON GOT BEHIND THE WHEEL of the department car. Beth locked up the house and then got into her car. Madison reversed out of the driveway and parked on the road.

"She has some loyalty toward her husband," Madison began. "Enough not to name him as a suspect but not enough to hold back from killing his lover."

"*If* she killed his lover," Terry said.

Beth pulled on the road and took off.

"There's no evidence to show she was inside Claire's house," Terry added.

"But she would have had access to Aaron's ski jacket and the knife," she countered.

"Aaron would have, as well. And he's admitted to being inside Claire's house. Now we have eyewitness testimony to that fact."

"There's got to be something we're missing here."

"Why? Because you want it to be the pretty housewife?"

We're were back to this again?

"I'm not even dignifying that with a response. You know there's more to it than that—"

"Then prove it to me." He leaned his head back on the shoulder rest and turned to face her. "Prove it to me as if I were the DA. Beyond doubt, what *proves* Elizabeth Best was in Claire's house and killed her?"

"She knew right where the murder weapon was—"

"She knew where her husband kept his hunting supplies," he countered.

"She knew it was a hunting knife that was used." She expected to be cut short again, but Terry remained silent.

"Okay...that part throws me a bit," Terry said. "But she could have just assumed that based on what was in the paper."

"Nope, not buying it. She said the paper mentioned a knife slash. And she withheld information from us, lied about her alibi, and had prior knowledge of the affair."

He was quiet a moment. "She knew it would look bad for her. She was protecting herself."

"The question is, protecting herself from what? Just murder charges or something else?"

"One would think life imprisonment would be enough." Terry looked back to the road. "Besides, like we said earlier, she wouldn't be able to get close enough to Claire."

Madison put the car into gear.

"What are you doing?"

"I'm going to follow her."

"The sarge wouldn't like this."

"Then we won't tell him." She was careful to stay far enough back so that Beth wouldn't spot them tailing her. "Let me just say, we can't solve a case unless we take a chance now and then, and let our intuition take us along the path of evidence."

"Huh, and I feel we should let *evidence* take us 'along the path of evidence.'" He mocked her terminology. "We still need the results from Aaron's DNA and the bloody towel."

Her cell phone rang and she answered. "Knight."

"You're going to love me." It was Cynthia.

"Whatcha got?" She needed the results more than she needed to make small talk.

"A couple things. First, what you asked me to look into." Madison sensed that Cynthia referred to Bryan Lexan and Cynthia's next words confirmed her suspicion. "The envelopes are a match."

Madison smacked the steering wheel, a smile engulfing her face. Terry turned and gave her a look that had his face scrunched up as if to say, *What the heck?*

"Not sure how much closer it brings you to solving that case, though. You might just have to let it go," Cynthia said.

"You know that I can't. What else have you got?" She hoped Cynthia would pick up on the fact she was inquiring about Claire's case now.

"The caller history came back on Claire's phone. Of course, we can't see what was sent, but Allison Minard definitely received a text message from Claire's phone."

"She was telling the truth."

"But here's the best part, Aaron Best's DNA matches Claire's vaginal swab and the male DNA from the wound. There were no usable prints on the knife. However, the blood from the tea towel came back a match to Claire Reeves and—"

"And Aaron Best?"

"Try again."

Chapter 46

Darren Taylor gripped the handle of his wheeled suitcase as tight as he would a stress ball. "Are you sure there's no way this can be traced back to me?" No need to say "murder" and take the chance of other people in the airport overhearing him.

"Calm down, you're fine." She squeezed his other hand. "Aaron's been charged and everything's going according to plan. We're free to be together now."

"Flight three-eight-three to Tahiti now boarding." The call came over the speakers.

"The money will be wired to your account." She smiled at him. "We're millionaires."

He kissed her forehead. "I love you."

"I know." She smiled and laughed, tugging on his arm, and pulled him in the direction of the gate.

He stopped moving. "I just have a bad feeling."

"How is that even possible? All the evidence led them to Aaron. We're free. We can finally be together again, like the old days."

"It will never be like then." For a moment, his thoughts traced back to a time when the two of them were all that mattered. They were in love and planned on a making a family together. But one fateful trip to Tahiti had changed everything.

"Isn't it me who decides that?" she said. "You proved your love to me. I'm so happy that you were man enough to go through with it. She was what destroyed us in the first place."

Years ago, she wouldn't go with him on that trip even though he begged her to. She had finals to attend to. He just needed some time to relax. His semester had squashed his energy and ambition. He had put all his waking hours into the development of his program and needed to unwind. But she had told him it would be good for him to get away.

Claire must have followed him to Tahiti and stalked him like prey. She knew he was there, knew where to find him. She sniffed out the opportunity and seized it. She didn't just steal a program. Claire destroyed his relationship with the only woman he had ever loved and ever would.

Darren felt his nose drip and could tell it was another nosebleed. He reached into his pocket for a tissue and dabbed at it. It was a very minor one.

"Oh not again." She rubbed his arm. "You get so worked up. Retribution is ours. We were justified, baby. She took everything from me, from us. Now let's go spend her money." She laughed.

He smiled at her. Her efforts to calm him were working. He returned the used tissue to his pocket, and could hear his name despite the crowds. He turned to see Allison running toward them.

"What are you doing?" Allison cast a look to the other woman, who raised a single brow. "You're leaving me for her?"

"Darren, why don't you go buy me a chocolate bar? You know the kind I love." His loved one's voice was sweet with a bitter edge. He kissed her cheek and walked away. "How did you find us, Allison?"

"I followed—"

"So you're his stalker now?"

"Is there anything you won't do for this woman? Darren, I'm talking to you," Allison said.

He'd gotten about five feet away and stopped walking.

"She manipulates you and toys with you like you're her puppet."

Now he turned around and looked between both women, settling his gaze on Allison. "You knew what our relationship was and what it wasn't."

"Please," Allison pleaded with him.

His loved one spoke pointedly to Allison. "You know that Darren and I are meant to be together."

"I don't understand why you're so upset, Allison," Darren said. "I thought we were all friends. You knew everything, and you wanted payback just as bad as us, so don't play an innocent in all of this."

"I don't even know who you are." Allison's voice faltered. "She doesn't know, does she?" She glanced at his loved one.

"What? Know what?" the woman asked.

"It doesn't matter—"

"What, Darren? Answer the question. What don't I know?"

Just the look in her eyes, the distrust, the past flashing back to him in vivid screenshots. "It doesn't matter." He moved closer to his loved one and wrapped an arm around her and glared at Allison. "We are together now."

"You were with *her*?" His loved one pulled back, and her eyes were full of hurt and betrayal. She must have finally picked up on the dynamics of his relationship with Allison. "You were with her without my knowledge, behind my back?"

"What bothers you more?" Allison began. "The fact that he fucked me repeatedly or that you don't control him as much as you thought you do?"

"Please leave, Allison," Darren said firmly. "You'll be compensated. We'll send you something from the island."

"For services rendered? Was I your whore?" Allison stared at him blankly. "You were the one who sent me the text message to clean that night, weren't you? And from Claire's phone? You set me up to find her."

He said nothing. To hear the pain in her voice struck in him some sympathy, but at the end of the day, she should have known where she stood with him. For years, he had been trying to get his loved one back. Allison had been entertainment for the course.

His loved one stepped away from him. "You've been sleeping with her. Claire was bad enough, but that couldn't be helped."

"You're such a hypocrite, and don't pretend not to know what I'm talking about," Allison said to his loved one.

"You wouldn't dare bring that up."

He looked at the woman who he idolized over all others. "What is it?"

She held eye contact with him but didn't speak. He looked to Allison.

"You slept around behind his back when he went to Tahiti all those years ago! Yet you pretend to be all hurt by his actions there—"

"Well, I didn't get married like he did."

"Is this true?" The nosebleed that had felt like it had subsided was starting up again. He dabbed his nose. "You were with someone else?"

"Don't get all righteous on me." The eyes that had held such beauty and allure before had turned steely blue, cold and unfeeling.

He scrunched up his face. "So all the guilt trips, the control tactics—"

"Only the weak allow themselves to be controlled."

"So now I'm the weak one?" He dabbed his nose again.

She laughed. "You tell me, Mr. Nosebleed."

"I—" He felt someone put a hand on his shoulder and both women stepped back.

"Darren Taylor, you have the right to remain silent…" Detective Knight came up behind him. "I am placing you under arrest for the murder of Claire Reeves. You have the right to an attorney…"

The male detective came up behind his loved one, and she struggled to keep her wrists free. "Wha-what are you doing?" she asked.

"Elizabeth Best, you have the right to remain silent." He snapped the cuffs on her. "I am placing you under arrest for conspiracy to commit murder and as an accessory."

Darren looked at Allison, who was watching them from a distance.

Knight continued. "If you lack funds, an attorney will be provided for you…"

"You arrested Aaron! This is ludicrous! I had nothing to do with any of this!" Beth was screaming. "It was him!" She stared at Darren.

His head snapped to look at her. She had given him the mandate that to prove his love he would kill the woman responsible for ruining their relationship years ago. It would also compensate for the financial burden she'd created for him and Beth. How could she turn on him now when he needed her the most? "What are you doing, Beth?" Darren's eyes searched hers.

"He used me," Beth spat.

"How could—"

"See, I told you." She flung her head around, attempting to have mercy extended.

"Mrs. Best, you framed your husband for murder. You gave your husband's ski jacket and knife to your lover. That makes you an accessory," the male detective said.

"Prove it."

Knight responded, "You had prior knowledge of the affair. You went to Claire's that night and watched your husband have sex on the couch with her. You admitted to that. What have you left out?"

A small pulse tapped in Beth's cheeks and they turned a bright red that made it through the layers of makeup.

"And you were stupid enough to lead us right to the knife." Knight leaned in toward Darren's ear. "And that's where you messed up."

His wrists were behind him and secured in cuffs, but his nose was bleeding. He had no way of wiping it.

"The murder weapon was found wrapped in a tea towel and your blood was on the towel. I'm going to guess another nosebleed?" Knight said.

He could have screamed at the top of his lungs. All of this to prove his love to a woman who obviously didn't have a clue what that even was. It really would have been best to let sleeping dogs lie.

Chapter 47

ANOTHER MURDER SOLVED AND JUST in time to enjoy her Saturday evening. They had no proof that Allison was involved in the murder besides possibly serving as an accessory after the fact. It was all speculation and hard to prove. And the same held true of Darcy Simms. If she was involved, she hid her trail well.

Madison was curled up on her couch, cuddling with Hershey and mindlessly watching something on television. Terry had given her a huge lecture last night about taking some time to just unwind, and Sergeant Winston had followed it up with a suggestion they both take a few days. She lifted her drink and was interrupted by a knock on her door. Hershey barked.

Maybe it was the pizza she had ordered. It was strange the phone never rang to have her let them up, but maybe someone was at the front door and had just let them in. A lockout apartment building wasn't really that secure.

"One minute." She grabbed a twenty off the counter and opened the door. It wasn't the delivery guy. She turned around, leaving the door open for him to come in and then turned to face him again. "What are you doing here, Blake?" She felt her heart sink and a burning sensation start in her earlobes.

"One heck of a greeting." He moved closer to her. "There's something I need to say to you—"

"Thought we said everything."

"Please don't interrupt." He shut the door behind them and put a hand on her forearm to make her stand still. Her eyes went to his hand, but she didn't shrug to free herself. "You know what the problem is with people like you and me?" He paused and she remained silent. "We're too proud, too stubborn, and too damned logical—"

"Nothing you can—"

"Some things don't require logic, Maddy. Your job, mine, they demand it, but with this—you, me, our relationship—we need to throw it out. We need to allow ourselves to acknowledge what we really feel, even if it doesn't factor into our logic-planned lives." He moved in closer, putting his hands on both of her shoulders. "We've got to say what we truly feel sometimes, even when it scares us." He put fingers in her hair, his eyes following the movement of his hand before looking straight into her eyes. "I love you, too."

It was too much to handle. Her heart and her mind were pulling her in conflicting directions. "I…" She couldn't get any more words out.

"And that woman at Starbucks."

Her eyes snapped to his.

"That was my daughter, Emily."

Had it gotten to the point that she was so jealous that she wouldn't afford him any benefit of the doubt? No, she had him tried and convicted as a cheating lover. "Your daughter?"

He smiled at her. "Yes. And I'd like you to meet her."

"Meet her?"

"Assuming that we're back together of course." He held her tight, and she sensed if she went to move backward he'd tighten his hold on her.

She looked up at him, finding comfort and security in the eyes of the man she had tried to make herself hate in the last few days. The excuses that had thundered in her mind fighting for attention had all been silenced. She remembered her sister's invite to dinner tomorrow: *Bring your boyfriend.*

"Are you doing anything tomorrow?"

Catch the next book in the Detective Madison Knight Series!

Sign up at the weblink listed below
to be notified when it's available for pre-order:

>> http://carolynarnold.net/mkupdates/ <<

You will also receive:

Any updates pertaining to upcoming releases in the series (cover art, book description, firm release date)

Access to sneak peeks

Behind-the-Tape™ insights giving you an inside look at Carolyn's research and creative process

Read on for an exciting preview of Carolyn Arnold's next thrilling novel featuring Madison Knight

SACRIFICE

Prologue

HE EQUATED HIS PAST DEEDS to shades of gray with no distinction between black and white, right and wrong, good and bad. He knew others would see things differently, but it didn't matter. Few people possessed the ability to intimidate and influence him. The man he was meeting had the power to do both.

He walked into the dimly lit Fairmont Club, and as he followed the maître d' to a back table, he inhaled the smells of grilled steak mingled with imported cigars. Appreciatively, he watched her hips sway as if she put extra effort into it.

"Patrick, how nice of you to join me." The man in the pressed Armani, with whom very few conversed with on a first name basis, sat at the table. A glass of Louis XIII Black Pearl, priced at fifteen hundred an ounce, was in front of him.

Patrick noticed the man's bodyguard sitting at a nearby table. He was Armani's prized stallion who instead of being stabled was toted about and showcased. The man went by Jonathan Wright, but Patrick doubted that was his real name. He was super intelligent and a former marine. Wright nodded his approval and went back to his steak and red wine.

Another young woman, a potential Asian model, stood at the edge of the table. "Your regular, sir?"

"French with a twist." Patrick smiled at the waitress remembering the feel of her skin and the smell of her musky dew. Although a married man for thirty years, he didn't think his wife had noticed him missing that night.

A few minutes later, the waitress came back with his Perrier water and lime in a rocks glass. The weight with which she set it on the table told him her memories were back, but she had to act like a civilized woman; after all she was working. She had to know, with a body like hers, she begged men to take advantage of her. He still believed he could have her again if he were at all inclined.

Armani held up his glass in a toasting gesture before swirling it lightly and taking a deep inhale. He followed with a small draw on the cognac. "When are you going to join me and have a real drink?"

"I'm on the job."

"Time for that new chair, my friend."

"Is that why you called me here?" Patrick smiled. Maybe the time had come to be repaid for past favors?

Armani let out a laugh. "Hardly. I need your help with something."

Patrick's heart palpitated with adrenaline as it did every time this man made that statement. It was too late in his life to change to one of innocence. Should his past deeds ever require an accounting, his only option would be a bullet to the brain. "You name it."

Armani played things smart, though. He always reminded him of the stakes involved first. "You help me with this and I'll ensure you make Mayor."

Chapter 1

The pungent odor hit Madison instantly upon opening the morgue doors. She pinched the tip of her nose, but it did little to save her from the smell of decomp becoming embedded in her lungs and sinus cavities.

"Whoa, he's a ripe one." Terry, her partner, stepped through the doorway behind her. He grabbed for a cloth mask from the dispenser mounted on the wall and handed her one.

Cole Richards, the ME, stood by the body as a tall, dark guardian. "It's the exposure to the air accelerating the putrefaction process. That is why the autopsy must be done tonight," Richards said.

Madison noted Richards talked with his eyes on the dead, an unusual thing for him. Maybe something about this death touched him on a personal level? She looked from Richards to the body.

The male victim, estimated in his early twenties, lay on the metal slab, a white sheet draped over his extended abdomen to his shoulders. His skin was almost black and appeared separated from the bone as if one could peel it off like the rind of an orange. His face, like the rest of him, was distorted and bloated beyond recognition. His eyes were open and vacant, clouded by death. His arms lay above the sheet to his sides. Some of his fingers were missing nails. The skin of one fingertip had been removed. Madison deduced Richards had taken it for identification purposes and forwarded it to the lab.

There was no wallet found on the body, nor any identifying marks to flag him in the missing persons database. The only things on him were a napkin with a woman's name and number, a wad of cash, and a prepaid, untraceable cell phone. He wore a gold chain with a pendant that had the letters CC engraved.

The body had washed up on the shore of the Bradshaw River, which ran through the city of Stiles and fed from a lake an hour away. The property belonged to a middle-aged couple, without children, by the last name of Walker. The wife had found the body when she went to get wood for their woodstove. She said he hadn't been there the day before. They had interviewed the couple at length and obtained their backgrounds, which came up with nothing noteworthy.

"How long do you estimate he was in the water?" Madison asked.

"As simply a deduction from what is before me, at least two to three weeks." Richards pulled his eyes from the body to look at Madison.

Was pain buried there? It was as if he read her thought. He returned his attention to the body.

"I'm basing this on when he surfaced," Richards continued. "In cooler water, bacteria causing decomp multiplies more sluggishly. If this was a warmer season, and it was three weeks later, we'd have a skeleton. Stomach contents will provide the approximate time of his last meal and what he ate. I'll also be consulting with a friend of mine, Wayne McDermott. He's a forensic climatologist. He can provide us with recent temperatures so we can get a closer estimate for TOD."

"So what are your thoughts? Dead when he went in or did he drown?"

"This is still to be determined. He is young and appears to have been in excellent shape."

Madison's eyes diverted to the body. The currents of the Bradshaw River had swept away any trace of a fit male adult. His bloated features made him appear more like a character from a sci-fi movie than a once living human being.

"Assuming he was alive when he hit the water, it is unlikely that he had a heart attack on entry. Quick results would show frothy liquid in the lungs, but because he was submerged for a considerable time, any trace of this would be gone. Tissue samples from his lungs, however, will be taken and sent to the lab for further analysis. We'll also extract bone marrow in search of diatoms." He must have noticed the expression on their faces. "These are microscopic organisms which are specific to a region. If it made it to his bone marrow, he was alive when he went into the water. We could also find evidence of this in his kidneys, should this be the case. This will prove whether he drowned in the Bradshaw or was dumped in the river." His eyes went to the body. "We're not going to get these answers just by looking at him."

"Anything else you can tell us?" Terry asked.

"His neck is broken but, it might simply be the trauma the body experienced as it went down the Bradshaw. I will require a full tox panel be run on him. We'll find out if he had any drugs or alcohol in his system. As you know, that will take at least a week."

Madison latched eyes with the ME. "Well, let's assume he did drown. How would we know it was homicide?"

A faint smile touched Richards's lips, exposing a slit of white teeth. "It is dubbed the perfect murder. But until we can establish his identity, concrete his background, and get the tox results back, I will not be finalizing COD on paper."

"He could have jumped in. Suicide?" Terry rubbed at the back of his neck.

"Possibly, but unlikely. The reason for this is the natural tendency to surface. Drowning suicides usually involve the use of a heavy object to counteract that instinct."

"Maybe he didn't think things through and acted on impulse. Most suicides are executed in the moment. He could have got caught in the current and pulled under the ice. His restraint could have broken free from the body."

"I prefer not to speculate." Richards's eye contact scolded Terry. "But at this point, I would treat this case as suspicious leaning toward homicide. Look at this." Richards lifted the left hand of the victim.

Madison noticed the circular impression on the backside of the hand. "Cigarette burn, or possibly something larger." She studied it, and a few seconds later glanced at Richards. "It's almost large enough to be a car lighter or a cigar."

Richards's eyes narrowed, pinching the dark skin around his eyes.

"So our vic was definitely in some sort of struggle before ending up in the river. But intention is going to be hard to prove."

Madison glanced at her skeptical partner. "Hard, but not impossible." She went back to Richards. "So, you don't have an ID and only a speculative conclusion as to the cause of death. Why did you call us down here?"

Richards pulled back the sheet and pointed to the victim's shoulders. "This."

There were darkened lines, a subtle contrast, two widths, a mirror image to each other, and one on each shoulder close to the neck.

"Bruising."

"Yes, contusions."

"From what? What would cause something like that?"

"That I'll leave for you to figure out." Richards placed the sheet back over the body. "But if our guy did drown due to forcible action, these marks could have come from our murder weapon."

Chapter 2

Stepping out of the morgue, Madison braced a hand on her hip above her holster. "So, we're left without an identity and only have a surmised cause of death."

"Richards seems pretty certain it was a drowning even though he didn't want to speculate," Terry mocked the ME.

Madison had noted that too. Richards was typically a person who ran based on facts, not assumptions. She had found it strange how he kept coming back to drowning as the COD without being certain.

"And here we are, another Sunday night spent on the job."

"Terry, what else would you be doing?"

"Hmm."

Her phone rang, but she said to Terry, "If he was drowned, we have to prove someone did this to him. It's not going to be an easy case."

"Even more fun." He plastered on a fake smile and passed a glance to her phone. "And figures we get the case, and not Sovereign."

"The only reason we got it is because he's got the flu."

"Think they're calling it a super bug."

Madison shrugged it off. Her phone kept ringing, bringing with it the reminder she had to take care of something. "Gotta go."

She headed for the elevator, pushed the button for it, and answered the call without consulting the caller ID. "Knight." She answered professionally, but she had a feeling she knew her caller.

"Don't worry about coming for me." It was Blake, a man she had been seeing for a few months.

She looked at her watch. *11:00.*

Hours had passed since they last talked. They had been at her sister's for a dinner and get together with her parents, who were up from Florida. Originally Madison had staged a fake call to get out of it, but then the real one came in. Blake, playing the good boyfriend, stayed behind.

"Sorry. I'm caught up now."

"You said that hours ago. Besides, I'm home now and you're on the hunt. I get it. Just don't get on me when a case loads me down."

She detected amusement in his voice. That was the one benefit of dating another professional. He understood what it was to forfeit all else to focus on what needed to be done. "Who drove you?"

"Chelsea. She even wrapped you up a take home platter. You'll have to come over here to get it."

Chelsea was her younger sister, the seemingly perfect one, at least in the eyes of her mother. A family woman, a mother of three, married to the perfect man, living in the perfect neighborhood. One thing that wasn't perfect about her though was her cooking. Now Blake would know this.

"Yum." Madison laughed and it cooled rather quickly, as thoughts of leaving him there slapped her.

He must have sensed the mood shift across the line. "Are you upset with me for some reason?"

She wanted to answer him outright but didn't have the energy required for the argument. She disregarded his question and came back with her own. "How did it go anyway?"

"Not too bad."

She sensed hesitation. "And Mom?" Madison didn't know why she asked the question because she really didn't want the answer. She was sure she already knew it.

Blake's end went silent.

"She's not happy. You can say it." She felt as though a stranger had invaded her world. He didn't need to see this side of her life, the side her mother tried to dominate. *What was I thinking inviting him?*

"Well—" he cleared his throat "—things came to an impasse. I defended you. Your father seemed to like that, with my being a defense attorney and all."

"I don't need you defending me."

"I was just—"

"Don't bother telling me. Mom told you how the service eats people alive, probably tried to talk you out of a relationship with me." Her voice rose with each word. She turned around to face Terry who diverted eye contact.

"She's just concerned."

"But she doesn't need to be."

"Maddy, may I see you tomorrow?"

The elevator chimed its arrival. It seemed to have taken forever to reach the basement today. Terry came on beside her.

"Can I get back to you?"

"I'm sensing a brush off, and after you took me home to meet the parents?"

"Night, Blake." She hung up without waiting for him to respond.

What did all this say about her as a person? Was she getting defensive because her mother had a point? Maybe it was selfish of her. Not when it came to her career but that she had pulled someone else in to her life. In some ways, things would be less complicated if she stayed completely unattached. What was she thinking allowing her heart a portion of an opportunity to welcome the security of a real relationship? As long as there were killers to catch, she didn't have time for one.

"So how's that going?" Terry gestured to the cell she held clenched in a hand.

There was only one floor. She should have taken the stairs and gotten some exercise.

"You took him to meet your parents, didn't you? How did that go?" Their eyes matched.

"How did you know?"

"I overheard you and Cynthia talking about it the other day."

"I'm not sure how that concerns you. Not even sure how it really concerns Cynthia."

Cynthia Baxter headed up the forensics lab and specialized in documents, fingerprints, and other patterned evidence. But she was more than a colleague; she was a close friend.

"You did take him." Terry's face beamed. "Your relationship must be progressing. Before you know it, there will be a wedding."

"Terry, shut up before I punch both of your shoulders hard enough you'll lose all feeling." She stared at him, daring him to say one more thing before she turned toward the lit floor number. She would never let the relationship get to the point of marriage. And to think she could have avoided this conversation. How long would it have taken to walk up one flight of stairs?

"Did they like him?"

The elevator chimed to notify them they had reached the ground floor.

"Night, Terry."

Chapter 3

Madison had been to Blake's condo before. With its fifty floors, valet service, a lobby atrium, and front door security, it was a showy display. Blake nestled himself into the forty-ninth floor, and she was certain the only reason for that was the penthouse was purchased by an old man who had refused to sell his spot on the fiftieth. She often wondered where Blake's money came from and assumed his affluent lifestyle required more than a successful defense attorney's salary could accommodate.

The uniformed doorman opened the front door. "Detective Knight."

She nodded in response, still not sure why she ended up here.

Inside, the bellhop stood to the side of the opened elevator doors. He was all of five-five, but carried a confident air, one no doubt required when dealing with the type of people living in such a building. Except for his height, Madison could picture this man guarding Buckingham Palace with those high hats and straight faces. It seemed nothing would faze him.

"The forty-ninth floor, Miss."

The journey up was a long one on which she continued to question herself as to why she had come. She was still upset with Blake, and he was likely in bed already. It was nearing midnight.

She had debated whether she should see him or not. In the end, there was a compulsion that originated from a few veiled sources. The main one, despite the urge to silence it; she was lonely. Everyone else had someone to go home to. Terry had his wife, Cynthia had her current man, and Cole Richards had a wife.

Madison had a dog; Hershey, the chocolate lab, who would do

his best to house break her into a responsible, domestic person. She would have to make this visit quick so she could get home to him. Her stomach rumbled and she found herself desperate enough for her sister's leftovers. Maybe this was a bad idea. She could just forget it, grab a burger on the way home, and settle in there. The elevator chimed their arrival.

The bellhop stood to the side. "Good evening, Miss."

Blake greeted her from the other side of the doors. "Quite a nice surprise." He extended a hand for hers and pulled her in to him.

The front desk must have called up to notify him he had a visitor. He owned half of the floor, the elevator being in the middle of it with doors that opened to either side, dependent on which the bellhop requested. If the other side was a mirror image to Blake's, a small foyer inlaid with marble tile greeted visitors. Ahead of this, a set of oak doors set a regal tone and separated private space from the lobby.

"I didn't expect to see you tonight." He swept back a stray hair from her forehead and kissed her.

The touch of his lips made her come alive, despite exhaustion. With all the death she saw on a continual basis, it came as a welcome release.

She cocked her head into the nape of his neck and walked with him into the condo. He smelled of expensive cologne. This mingled with his personal scent and drugged her thinking.

Did it mean something more substantial than simply that? She knew there were studies out there that concluded women picked their mate based on scent. Ridiculous. She was getting more analytical by the hour.

He cupped his hand behind her neck, pulled her in tighter, and took her mouth. His kiss, his taste, made her hungry but no longer for the food she had craved earlier. Rather, for him.

It felt so good, so humbling to experience the love he conveyed. But as they kissed, her defenses recalled the betrayal she felt earlier in the day. She pulled back from him.

"Why did you do that to me?"

"Do what?"

"Pick my mother over me."

"Do you even hear what you're saying?" A smile teased his lips.

She waved her hand. "It was a bad idea to come here."

"Actually, it was a smart one because now I can tell you to your face you're crazy."

"Excuse me."

"Come on, Maddy, a choice between you and your mother? I'm not into an older woman. Simple pick."

Madison crossed her arms. "I didn't mean it like that. I meant—"

He put a hand on her shoulder. "You think because I stayed with your family I somehow betrayed you and your need to leave."

She nodded.

"Do you want your family to like me?" he asked.

"Yes." The response was instant and said aloud so she couldn't reel it back.

"Well, I couldn't exactly just leave. You were called away; I wasn't." He ran fingers through her short hair. "Even if the first call was a fake. You're such a bad actress." He smiled.

"Oh shut—"

He put his mouth on hers. She didn't fight it, but let herself melt into him. She excused her weakness as a natural hunger that needed satisfying. He led her to his bedroom.

MADISON LOOKED OVER AT THE clock on his dresser. *1:15.*

It was time for her to leave, get some sleep in her own bed, and spend time with her new four-legged responsibility.

She leaned across the bed and kissed Blake's lips. "I've gotta go."

He rolled over and pulled her to him. "Not even time for a shower?"

It sounded wonderful. His shower had seven jets, which covered every part of the body in a massaging pulsation that rid the body of stress, but there wasn't time.

"Not tonight." She turned a bedside light on. "I've gotta go. I'm a momma now."

"A momma? I wish I had recorded that."

She narrowed her eyes, yet played along. "You've just got to know where you stand. You can't have all my free time." She was smiling. "Besides, he's not that bad."

Truth was, even though Hershey demanded much of her time, she was willing to extend it. It could have been Terry's brainwashing at every opportune moment. *One day he'll be a great friend. His love is unconditional.*

Maybe she put too much faith in her partner's words, but when her relationship with Blake went down, which they always had a way of doing, at least her chocolate lab would be there to lick her wounds. Right now, though, all the thinking was only further exhausting. She had to get home before she fell asleep in Blake's bed.

He must have sensed her hesitation to leave and poked her side. "Get going then."

She kissed him on the lips, wishing she had time to stay, time to savor him again. She pulled herself out of the bed.

"You know if you lived here, you wouldn't have to leave."

Did he just say what I thought I heard?

She couldn't formulate words to make a coherent response, even though she felt him waiting her out, hoping she'd break the silence. But she could be stubborn, and this would be one of those times she'd win.

"You said you loved me. I love you. Why throw your money to rent?"

Her first reaction was that she didn't need anyone to take care of her. The second thought went to what her share of a place like this would amount to.

"My portion here would be more than what I spend now. I couldn't afford it." She pulled a sweater over her head and pulled up her jeans, while doing her best to keep her eyes off him.

"We could work something out."

She detected the smile in his voice. "So you'd cover the monthly expenses, and I'd put out in exchange?" She found amusement in his proposal.

"Sounds good to me. Of course, I'd also expect some light domestic duties to be taken care of. The cleaning, the cook—"

The pillow she threw hit him directly in the face.

HER RINGING PHONE ON THE nightstand felt like part of a dream. Only, in a dream you could turn it off. This noise was insistent and through slit eyes, she could see the blue glow shrouding her bedroom. By the time she settled into bed after going out with Hershey, it was past two and she remembered seeing three thirty on the clock. Thoughts of Blake's proposal kept her mind going.

The ringing continued.

"Hello?" It hurt to speak. Just a few more hours… What time was it anyway? She lifted her head enough to read her alarm. *6:03.*

"Maddy?"

"Yes." She didn't have patience at the best of times, let alone when she was waking from a deep sleep, one that morphed her ringing phone into a distant church bell. Why a church bell? The implication gave her a headache.

"It's Cyn."

Madison sat up. "We have an ID?"

"Sort of."

"I don't get it."

"I've been here all night, and before you say anything about it, you know I hate loose ends."

Madison smiled into the receiver. That was just another aspect of Cynthia's personality that drew her in.

"The fingerprint came back with a match."

"Who is it?"

"The file number is eight-three-four-five-seven-nine-two-three."

"A file number?"

"Here's the thing. The file is locked. I don't have a name to give you. The vic was wearing a gold chain with a pendant. Initials CC."

"Okay, I knew about the pendant, but why would his file be locked?"

"Obviously, our kid has a record we're not supposed to know about."

"Crap." She knew the fastest way to get that file unsealed would be to go straight to the top. Maybe he could use his position to expedite legal proceedings. "Looks like I'm going to have to speak to McAlexandar."

Patrick McAlexandar was the chief of police, and they never saw eye to eye, but if she was going to get her answer he would be the best place to start.

Also available from
International Best-selling Author
Carolyn Arnold

SACRIFICE
Book 3 in the Detective Madison Knight series

Finding justice comes at a high price…

When a young man washes up on the shore of the Bradshaw River, Detective Madison Knight and her partner are called in to investigate. But the case takes a complicated turn when he's identified as the son of local business tycoon Marcus Randall. As one of the wealthiest and most influential men in the city, he has a lot of connections, and one of them just so happens to be the Stiles PD police chief.

Madison and Chief McAlexandar have butted heads before, but with this case, her drive and determination to find the truth just might cost her the job she worked so hard to get. She's got her eye on Randall, despite the chief's protests of the man's innocence, and she's not the only one. The Secret Service is after him for suspicion of fraud and counterfeiting, and they want Madison's full cooperation to aid their investigation.

Stuck between the chief and one of the most powerful men in Stiles isn't the ideal place to be, but if Madison's going to find justice, she has no choice but to risk it all.

**Available from popular book retailers or
at carolynarnold.net**

CAROLYN ARNOLD is an international best-selling and award-winning author, as well as a speaker, teacher, and inspirational mentor. She has four continuing fiction series—Detective Madison Knight, Brandon Fisher FBI, McKinley Mysteries, and Matthew Connor Adventures—and has written nearly thirty books. Her genre diversity offers her readers everything from cozy to hard-boiled mysteries, and thrillers to action adventures.

Both her female detective and FBI profiler series have been praised by those in law enforcement as being accurate and entertaining, leading her to adopt the trademark: POLICE PROCEDURALS RESPECTED BY LAW ENFORCEMENT™.

Carolyn was born in a small town and enjoys spending time outdoors, but she also loves the lights of a big city. Grounded by her roots and lifted by her dreams, her overactive imagination insists that she tell her stories. Her intention is to touch the hearts of millions with her books, to entertain, inspire, and empower.

She currently lives just west of Toronto with her husband and beagle and is a member of Crime Writers of Canada.

CONNECT ONLINE
carolynarnold.net
facebook.com/authorcarolynarnold
twitter.com/carolyn_arnold

And don't forget to sign up for her newsletter for up-to-date information on release and special offers at carolynarnold.net/newsletters.

Made in the USA
Middletown, DE
28 November 2019